Mark felt something new and strong possess him, and he increased the pressure on Essence's mouth, overwhelmed by the feeling yet wanting to shout when he felt her respond.

The instant she did, he drew back. She was breathing a little harder, and her eyes appeared glassy. *Victory looms on the horizon*, he thought. However, he knew he would need all of the patience he could muster for the challenge.

He hadn't intended to kiss her, however, his curiosity had taken over. He wondered if he kissed her again, if he would have the same gut-level reaction.

And he had.

"Expect me in your life, Essence," he warned in all seriousness. An intimate warmth had traveled up his arm and spread through his body, leaving him momentarily unsure of his chosen course.

# TIME IS OF THE ESSENCE

## ANGIE DANIELS

Genesis Press Inc.

# Indigo Love Stories

An imprint Genesis Press Publishing

Genesis Press, Inc.
P.O. Box 101
Columbus, MS 39703

ISBN: 1-58571-132-2
Manufactured in the United States of America

First Edition

Visit us at www.genesis-press.com
or call at 1-888-Indigo-1

# DEDICATION

This book is dedicated to Major Terraine Saunders and Captain Levi Butler both of the United States Army, two brave men who have dedicated their lives for the good of this country.

# ACKNOWLEDGEMENTS

To Willie Mae Rogers and Eleanor Daniels. Where would the world be without grandmothers?

To the gang back home in Columbia, Missouri for all of your continued support. To my closest and dearest friends Tonya Hill and Novia Mearidy for her unlimited and unconditional friendships. To my girls Norma Jean Rhodes and Kim Ashcraft for taking the time to listen to all of my long and crazy phone calls. To Dennis Daniels and Terrence Moore, it is an honor to be able to call you both my brothers. To my Aunt Liz, Aunt Cynthia and Aunt Sylvia for reading everything I have written and letting me know how proud they are to call me their niece. I love you all! To my stepmother Gail Moore, who threatened to do me bodily harm if I didn't acknowledge her in my next book. To my new friends in Delaware, Maureen Hunter and Pamila Robinson for loving everything I have written. To the hundred plus readers who have taken the time to write me and share their positive feedback about my books. Thank you so much!

To my teddy bear husband, Kenneth Darryl Hills for allowing me to pursue my dream and for keeping me focused when I seem to have steered away from my goal. I love you!

# CHAPTER ONE

The beginning of a smile tipped the corners of Captain Mark Saunders' lips as he pulled off the interstate.

*I'm almost home.*

For him the toughest part of being in the military was being without family, especially during the holidays. After spending the better part of two years stationed in Germany, this was one holiday he would spend on American soil. Mark chuckled. He had four weeks leave. That gave him plenty of time to reconnect with his family.

Amusement flickered in his eyes as he drove past the Christiana Mall and found the parking lot full of customers, as well as several police officers that directed traffic. Christmas was less than two weeks away, so it came as no surprise. He hoped to get his own shopping started within the next couple of days.

Mark's mouth quirked with pleasure as he neared an intersection. This would be his first Christmas in Delaware in over five years. He planned to enjoy every minute.

He pulled into the exclusive community of Blackshire Estates, nestled within the rolling hills of Wilmington. The winding streets were lined with houses that boasted more architectural character than in any other neighborhood in the city. The area was not only elegant, but also secluded and convenient. His parents' residence was surrounded by vintage mansions and cozy townhouses. The fifty-year-old brick structure was located on a prime corner lot at the very back of the development.

The trees leading into the subdivision were strung with lights that, at dusk, would brighten the path. In addition, several houses in the upper class neighborhood had either a wreath hanging on the front door, or a Christmas tree prominently displayed in a window.

Mark exhaled a long sigh of contentment. Just like his mother, Christmas had always been his favorite time of the year., ven before he had turned the corner, he knew her home would also be festive. Sure enough, as he pulled onto Westwood Drive, he found that three lighted reindeers had been strategically placed around the yard, and Santa Claus sat in a sleigh on the roof. Before injuring his back three years ago, outside decorations had always been his father's job. A curious expression overtook Mark's features as he wondered whom his mother had conned into climbing on top of the two-story structure this year.

After pulling his new black Navigator in the driveway behind his younger sister Kelly's Mustang, Mark climbed out the car and strolled toward the door. Before he reached the porch, he could hear his mother's rich laughter coming from inside the house.

*Won't they be surprised.*

He had debated calling his mother before he had left the airport, but in the end he had decided against it. Dorlinda Saunders wasn't expecting her son home for another four months. The expression on her face would be priceless.

Mark didn't have long to wait. Seconds after ringing the bell, Kelly came to the door. He proudly grinned down at his five-foot, three-inch little sister.

Kelly had inherited their mother's raven hair and slender body, while her dark mocha coloring came from their father. Already a beautiful woman, if possible, she had grown lovelier since he'd last seen her.

After a quick observation, he knew he would have to get used to the new look. Kelly had her naturally curly hair cut to frame her round face. She had worn a ponytail for over two decades, but after being mistaken as a teenager while student teaching, she switched to a style that exuded maturity and sophistication.

Staring down at her, deep cinnamon eyes confronted him. Instead of the warm welcome Mark had expected to receive, her lips twisted in a sour expression.

"Is that how you act when you haven't seen your big brother in two years?" he teased as his eyes sparkled mischievously.

Not the least bit amused, Kelly rolled her eyes. "Be glad you're even allowed to enter this house," she murmured then spun on her heels.

Flabbergasted, Mark followed her through the foyer. "Hey Kel," he called after her. "What's wrong? What did I do?"

Without stopping, she called over her shoulder, "You know what you did."

Mark raised a curving black eyebrow. He had no idea what she was talking about. His baby sister had always been a mystery, and a spoiled brat at that. Chuckling, he put the matter aside. Kelly was probably mad at him for missing her twenty-fourth birthday last month.

Shrugging out of his jacket, he hung it on a coat rack in the foyer, then moved across the gleaming wood floor into the large kitchen. He found his mother standing in front of the stove cooking something that smelled heavenly. His dumbfounded expression changed to admiration for the woman who had raised him.

Dorlinda stopped stirring a pot filled with homemade chili and gasped. "Mark, you're home!"

"Hey, Mom." He grinned boyishly.

Dropping the spoon, she turned and walked over to Mark.

"Welcome back," she said with laughter and a hug.

Mark returned the embrace. "I'm glad someone's happy to see me," he whispered against her cheek, then moistened it with a kiss.

"Let me take a look at you!" she exclaimed, holding Mark out at arm's length.

"I'm still the same…maybe a few pounds lighter."

"Well, it won't take long to fatten you back up," she said with a grin while still admiring him approvingly.

As Dorlinda dropped her arms, a slight frown furrowed her raisin-brown forehead. "Why didn't you tell me you were coming home early?"

Mark turned up his smile a notch. "I wanted to surprise you for Christmas."

Tears of joy welled in her eyes. "I couldn't ask for a better gift. Wait until your father gets home. He'll be so excited." George Saunders, a retired police commissioner, could still be found spending the majority of his days hanging around the precinct.

Mark beamed down at his mother. At fifty-three, Dorlinda could have easily passed for ten years younger. She had large expressive eyes and a smooth complexion that was virtually wrinkle-free.

She turned to Kelly who sat at the kitchen table. "Kel, I think we're going to have to plan an even bigger dinner for Christmas this year." She laced her fingertips together and smiled proudly at her son. "Wait until everyone finds out you're here. They'll be ecstatic."

Kelly grunted rudely and glanced over at the two. "I can think of at least one person who won't be."

Her eyes narrowed slightly. It was a look Mark knew all too well. He had always seen it whenever Kelly didn't approve of something or someone. "Who?" Mark asked curiously.

The room suddenly grew silent. As he returned his gaze to his mother, he noticed a frown settling onto her even features. Stepping back, his eyes shifted between Kelly, who looked ready to chew his head off, to the worry lines that had appeared between his mother's eyes. "Can someone please tell me what's going on?" he scowled.

"How could you?" The words exploded from Kelly's lips. She shook her head briskly, sending her sleek blunt cut swinging across her cheeks. "You knew how Momma was going to feel when she found out. How could you have treated Essence that way?"

His brow arched. "Essence?" Sweet, innocent, Essence Monroe. What did this have to do with the woman who had been the subject of his erotic dreams for the past two years? "I haven't spoken to her since I left."

"I know," Kelly retorted. "She told me." Kelly paused to shake her head, then continued, "I told you if you weren't serious to leave her alone. Essence had just gotten over a bad relationship. But no-o-o, you had to have her just like all the other women. And what did you do? Exactly what I thought you would do—break her heart."

"Where is all this coming from?" he asked, followed by a nervous chuckle. Mark moved to the table and lowered his muscular frame in the seat across from her. Kelly and Essence taught at the same elementary school. *What has Essence told you?* Racking his brain, he couldn't think of anything that would have his sister this upset. "I didn't know I had broken her heart," he began, all humor stripped from his voice. "I was honest with her from the beginning and made it clear that I wasn't looking for anything serious. I thought she understood."

Kelly clucked her tongue against her teeth and murmured, "Maybe that's the way it was in the beginning, but things have changed."

"What things?" Mark asked curiously.

"You know what things," she spat back at him.

Exasperated, he dragged a hand across his face and sighed. *Little sisters.* "What's the point of this conversation?"

Dorlinda crossed her arms underneath her breasts and interjected with, "Kelly, why don't you at least give your brother a chance to explain before you bite his head off."

Mark tilted his head to the right and grinned. "Thanks, Mom. Unfortunately, I have no idea what she's talking about."

Kelly rolled her eyes, then sulked in her chair and waited. For what, Mark wasn't sure. Finally, he looked to his mother for help.

When Dorlinda found her son looking to her for answers, she wiped her hands on a towel, then turned and leaned her weight against the counter. She looked him directly in the eyes as she composed what she was about to say. "I've never made it a secret to either of you about how devastated I was at giving up my daughter thirty years ago. It was the biggest mistake of my life."

Mark nodded. He and Kelly had always known of the existence of an older sister, Calaine. Dorlinda had had an affair with a married man during college. Scared and alone, she had given her daughter up for adoption. It wasn't until two and a half years ago that the two were finally reunited. Calaine lived in Missouri with her husband, David Soul, and their one-year-old little girl, Dominique.

His mother moved over to the kitchen table and sat between the two. Taking her son's hand in hers, Dorlinda stared down at his long calloused fingers. Her head came up slowly, and she met his gaze with a long penetrating stare. "Mark, it hurts my heart that you would turn your back on your own child."

Mark's brow bunched with confusion. "Child! What child?"

"Your son," Kelly offered belligerently. "The little boy you left Essence to raise all alone."

Mark stared numbly at her. "I have a son?" he asked, trying to comprehend what he was hearing.

Dorlinda was puzzled by his question, yet she answered with, "Tyler looks just like you."

The words hit him like the force of a speeding car. He had a son. Mark slipped his hand from her loose grip and sagged against the chair as if all his energy had been drained. There was a child in the world that he had fathered; a child he knew nothing about it.

His eyes snapped across to his sister. "Where's Essence?"

"She's now living in Dover."

He shook his head in disbelief. It couldn't be. Yet…it was definitely possible. They had unprotected sex several times. *Why didn't Essence tell me?* He had deserved to know that he was going to be a father. His eyes darkened dangerously as he tried to conceal the anger and resentment racing through him.

Leaning forward, Mark rested his forehead in the palm of his hands while he forced air back into his lungs. Only after he felt more in control did he look at his sister again. "How did you find out? Why didn't she tell me?"

Kelly met his intense gaze. "You didn't know?" Genuine puzzlement could be heard in her voice.

His gaze narrowed noticeably. "Of course I didn't know. What do you take me for? I never wanted a wife, but I would never ignore my responsibilities."

Kelly's expression softened her features. As if on cue, she and her mother turned to look at one another, releasing anxious laughs.

"Now what's so funny?" Mark snapped.

Kelly offered him a forgiving smile that caused her luminous eyes to crinkle. Rising from her seat, she moved around the table to hug him. "Welcome home, big brother."

"Praise God." Dorlinda smiled, as tears of joy spilled from her eyes. "I knew there had to be a reasonable explanation."

"Yeah, Mom, you were right." Mark didn't see anything funny. "You didn't answer my question, Kel. How did you find out?"

"By pure chance," Kelly admitted as she returned to her seat. "When Essence stopped teaching at Baer Elementary, I thought she had left the state. Then two weeks ago, I ran into her at the mall. She tried to pretend she didn't see me, but I walked over to her. One look at that beautiful little boy she was pushing in a stroller, I knew he was your son."

Mark pulled in a long breath. "Why didn't she tell me?"

Kelly shrugged. "Essence said she wrote you several times, but you never returned any of her letters."

He hadn't received any letters. On several occasions he had considered writing Essence to let her know that she was in his thoughts. The weeks turned into months, and by then he had no idea what to say. When Essence hadn't bothered to write him either, he assumed she had forgotten about him and had moved on with her life.

Mark rose. "Give me her address."

Kelly shook her head. "She doesn't want to see you."

"Too bad. Where is she?" he demanded.

"She lives in Green Tree Meadows. When I took mom to see Tyler last week, she asked us not to tell you where she lives."

Dorlinda nodded. "He is such a lovely child, however, Kelly is right. We have to respect her wishesregarding her home." She paused. "But we can tell you were she works." She paused. "But we can tell you where she works."`

"She teaches at Dover Elementary," Kelly provided.

"Damn!" Mark wasn't sure who he was mad at. He just knew he was mad. He looked down at his watch and saw it was almost three o'clock. Leaning over, he kissed his mom, then headed toward the door, grabbing his jacket along the way.

Essence straightened four little chairs around the last table in her classroom then glanced down at a delicate watch on her slender arm and sighed. It was almost four o'clock. *Another day*, she thought, as her lips curled upward. She loved her job as a third grade elementary teacher and wouldn't have it any other way, even if it meant cleaning up after twenty little people at the end of each day.

Hearing approaching footsteps, she turned and looked over at the door. Her breath halted momentarily. A man had stepped into her room. Or was it a ghost from her past?

*Tyler's father.*

Essence shook her head and raised shaky fingers to her lips. It couldn't be! Kelly had assured her that Mark wasn't scheduled to return to the states until the spring. Apparently, she had been wrong. He was right here. His tall imposing form filled the doorway.

"Hello, Essence."

They exchanged polite smiles, then she swallowed while his voice, deep and sensual, sent tingles to the pit of her stomach. She had almost forgotten how powerful Mark could be. No, that wasn't true. She hadn't forgotten. She had simply tried her best to forget.

Her heart jolted, and her pulse pounded as she prayed that her mind was playing tricks on her. Maybe too many long nights had her seeing things. However, the man watching her was not a figment of her imagination. In fact, her memory had not done him justice. The best way to describe Mark Saunders was by using three simple adjectives—tall, dark and handsome.

Too stunned to move, Essence simply stood there and stared. She found herself momentarily mute as she struggled to get words to form on her lips. It appeared that Mark still had the ability to set her soul on fire with a single glance. His gaze was as soft as a caress, slow and seductive, as his eyes moved from her face to her shoulders, down to her breasts. She took a deep breath in an attempt to get her hormones under control. His topaz eyes were entrancing. She pushedback the need to run into his arms and rekindle a desire that lay dormant for nearly two years. Essence scowled inwardly. Her physical attraction to him was ill-timed and unwanted, considering the circumstances at hand.

Mark stepped into her classroom, moving as determinedly as a soldier. shoulders back, stomach in, and arms by his side. He had an air of cockiness about him that people naturally gravitated toward. It was his spunk that first attracted Essence to him that sunny fall afternoon two years ago....

*She was making copies of the weekly spelling list when Kelly stepped into the teachers' lounge, eyes dancing with excitement. "Essence, I'd like you to meet someone."*

*Essence looked over at the door just as he stepped into the room. At the sight of the handsome stranger, the papers in her hand fluttered onto the floor.*

*Instantly, he moved to her side, knelt, and began scooping up the papers. "Let me help you with that," he offered in a satin-smooth voice that caused a moan to slip between her parted lips.*

*He rose, holding the papers in his proffered hand. Essence stared up at the towering figure and watched as his lips curled into an irresistible smile that almost dropped her to her knees.*

*"Thanks," she managed to say unable to control the shaking of her hand as she retrieved the papers from him.*

*Kelly came over and stood by his side. "Essence, this is my brother,*

Mark Saunders," she introduced with admiration burning in the depths of her eyes. "He came to take his baby sister to lunch."

Essence nodded, although the rest of her body was paralyzed. She took a real good look at him and her mouth became dry. Standing less than two feet away made her keenly aware of his masculinity and handsomeness. She could see the cleanly sculptured curve of his mouth and the small indentation in his chin. "Nice to meet you."

"The pleasure is all mine." His hot breath skimmed her nose before he parted a set of full supple lips and raised her hand to his mouth.

She was conscious of where his warm flesh touched the inside of her palm. The area tingled as if it was on fire. She had no desire to take her hand back. If he hadn't released it, she would have held on forever. She took a deep breath in utter disbelief. She had never been this instantly attracted to anyone, not even Jeremy.

"Would you like to join us?" Kelly asked.

Her co-worker's words snapped her out of her trance. Putting distance between them, Essence moved over to a table and slowly lowered herself into the nearest seat. She shook her head regrettably. "I can't. I have a conference with a parent of one of my students."

Mark stepped forward. His smile increased and two dimples indented his high cheekbones. "Maybe I can convince you to have dinner with me tonight, alone."

"No!" her insides screamed. She couldn't possibly be alone with him. What in the world would they talk about? No, the thought was much too ridiculous to even consider. She took one look at the determination in his eyes and shook her head. "No, I can't."

"Why? Are you involved with someone?"

Other than her two-timing ex-fiancé the answer was, "No, not anymore."

He looked pleased by her answer. "Then, I'd like to change that."

Not only is he gorgeous, he's charming too, *she thought to herself.*

*"I won't take no for an answer." His eyes had darkened and his intentions were quite clear. Mark was more persuasive than she cared to admit.*

*Essence was powerless and felt herself giving in to her desire. What reason did she have not to say "yes," except that she had sworn off men for the durations of her life? Maybe her reluctance was because of the warm fuzzy feeling that swept over her. Mark was determined to make her do something she had never done before—lust for a man. No man should have that much of an effect over a woman, yet as each second increased with his eyes fixed on hers she found herself less in control of the desire running through her. For a split second she almost believed that Mark Saunders was everything she had ever wanted in a man.*

*"Alright."*

*He flashed her a sparkling white smile. "Wonderful. I'll pick you up around seven."*

"You don't look too happy to see me."

Essence jerked her thoughts back from the past to find Mark now standing less than ten feet away.

For months she had been preparing for this moment, rehearsing what she would say, practicing a calm voice, the way she would suck her teeth and act as if it didn't matter that he had returned. But now that the moment had finally arrived, she realized no amount of rehearsing would have prepared her for their encounter. What had happened between them wasn't a scene from a movie, although nothing would have pleased her more than for a director to have yelled, "Cut!" only seconds after Mark had walked out of her life. Instead, she had been left to face reality. The reality that she had been left behind, pregnant and alone.

Meeting his bold gaze, she found herself drawn to a pair of golden eyes that had zeroed in on hers. Essence took a deep breath breaking the sensation, then pressed her strawberry-painted lips together thoughtfully and replied, "You didn't expect me to fall into your arms, did you?"

An easy smile played at the corner of Mark's lips as he tried to end the tense moment. "I wouldn't have been mad if you had."

He appeared amused by his own comment. Essence, however, found nothing amusing and didn't waste her energy on a response. Mark was still as cocky as ever. During the four weeks they had spent together, she had gotten to know him quite well and she refused to feed his inflated ego. Instead, she moved up the aisle, taking the long way so she wouldn't have to pass him, and rounded her desk, keenly aware that Mark was watching her every move. Once behind her desk, she took a seat then slowly raised her eyes to meet his.

His was a face she could not have forgotten, even if she wanted to. Each time she looked at their son, she was reminded of his father. They both shared the same dark raven curls and sweeping black eyebrows. Tyler's hair wasn't quite as thick as his father's, but she knew it was just a matter of time.

She stared across at Mark's clean-shaven mahogany face that was carved in sharp angles and thought about Tyler's chubby little face. Her adorable little boy would some day be just as handsome. As much as she hated to admit it, Mark looked incredible, more incredible than she had remembered. Mark's physique was hidden beneath a bomber jacket, but she knew he had always kept in shape by running three miles every morning. Her gaze dipped from his eyes to his jacket, then lowered even further to find him wearing a pair of faded blue jeans that molded to his powerful thighs and calves.

"How have you been?" she heard him say.

Her gaze snapped to his face again. She took a deep breath, held it, then let it out slowly before responding with, "I've been well, and yourself?"

"A lot better if I had known about my son," Mark said simple and to the point. The way he was about everything.

Essence noticed the way his jaw twitched when he spoke as if ready to go to battle. Mark was mad, but, so was she. Her temper flared quickly. How dare he walk into her classroom, looking calm, cool and collected, then accuse her of withholding information? He didn't have the slightest idea what she had gone through.

Before Mark had even left for Germany, she had suspected that she might have been pregnant and had intended to tell him when they went out to dinner their last night together. However, when he began their conversation with, "let's be friends," all hopes of a future together fizzled. Though Mark had made his feelings clear from the beginning that he wasn't looking for a commitment, Essence had hoped that after four weeks together, he might have changed his mind. She had hoped he would have fallen in love, as she had. But he hadn't, and, in the end, she didn't want him to feel obligated. She decided to keep quiet until she knew for certain that she was pregnant.

She shook her head as if to clear her muddled thoughts, then glanced over at him. "I guess if you had bothered to answer my letters you might have found out sooner," she replied, unable to keep the sharpness from her tone.

Vertical lines appeared between his eyes. "I didn't receive any letters," he insisted in an almost convincing voice.

Essence found it hard to draw a breath as she looked at him, wanting to believe him, but not sure if she could. She knew that if she did, she might lower her guard and start caring again.

"That sounds like a personal problem to me. Besides, it's too late," she added with a shrug. "I've already gone through nine months of pregnancy and eighteen hours of labor without you."

Mark was the first to look away. With his fist embedded deeply in his pockets, he paced across the room. Essence watched him out of the corners of her eyes and knew first hand that her comment hurt him, but she couldn't allow herself to care. Other than her parents and her older sister Tamara, she had been alone and scared. Mark hadn't been there for her. In fact, Mark probably hadn't thought about her at all since he had left. The only reason he had come to see her now was because of Tyler.

She held her breath as he moved toward her desk, where he stopped and took a seat on the edge. The air caught in her chest at the close contact. His eyes, framed by thick, coal black lashes mesmerized her. She wanted to look away but couldn't. There was something in his questioning gaze that was hypnotic. There was already a light in his eyes that was unsettling. His scent, the closeness, both brought back the memories in a rush. With the rapid beating of her heart, Essence knew she wasn't as calm as she wanted to appear. She just hoped Mark hadn't noticed. Pushing the thought away, she tried to regain some measure of control over her emotions.

"I'm sorry that I wasn't there, but it's not too late," he began in an apologetic tone. "I'm here now and ready to be a father to my son."

Essence laughed bitterly as she rose from her chair and reached for her briefcase.

"What's so funny?" Mark asked as he stroked his stubbled chin.

"You," she answered, meeting his gaze and holding it. "You're funny." Folding her hands on her hips, she glared across at him. "How long is this new game going to last before you grow tired of your son and walk out of his life?"

Mark stiffened as if he'd been struck. He couldn't believe Essence thought that little of him. For several long seconds they stood motionless, staring at each other as if they were strangers instead of former lovers. "I would never walk out of my son's life."

"How can I be sure? I haven't seen or heard from you in two years." Unspoken pain was alive and glowing in her eyes.

"That's not my fault," he retorted.

"Then whose fault is it?"

"You should have told me."

"I tried." She paused and exhaled audibly. "Listen," she began. "Why don't you go back to playing soldier. I know fatherhood was never in the plan, but don't worry, Tyler and I are doing just fine."

His expression turned flat and hard, the calm demeanor had long since vanished. "I might not be your ideal choice as a father for your child, but the day you decided to carry him for nine months and bring him into this crazy world, was the day you decided I was going to be a part of his life."

Essence bit down on her lower lip and swallowed the lump forming in her throat. Ignoring him, she began stuffing the leather bag with papers she needed to grade that evening.

"I'll get your address from Kelly, then I'll be by this evening to see my son...and you."

Warning spasms of alarm erupted within her. She wanted to run and escape. She couldn't do this. Essence had believed she was ready, but in all honesty she didn't think she'd ever be.

For two years she had been without this man and without the pain of risking her heart. She had grown content with her simple life and her responsibilities as a single parent. Now Mark was planning to destroy it all.

Her head rose, eyebrows arched in protest. "Tonight is not a good night."

Mark rose from her desk. "Essence. I'm home for a month and during that time I plan to spend every minute I can with my son, starting tonight."

Meeting his penetrating stare, she knew by the fire in his eyes, he meant every word. And nothing in heaven or on earth could stop him.

# CHAPTER TWO

Mark pulled his SUV onto a graveled driveway that ran along the side of a perfect little ranch home. The red brick structure was surrounded by massive trees that had left blankets of leaves across the front lawn and in the small backyard. Essence apparently hadn't had time to rake the yard. With a toddler to raise, the reason was quite obvious.

After shutting his car door, he strolled over and peered into Essence's blue Honda where he found a car seat strapped in the back. Something snatched at Mark's lungs, forcing him to take a deep gulp of cold air. It was at that particular moment that he truly realized the extent of what had happened during his departure. Essence had given his child life, then spent the last sixteen months raising him alone. Shaking his head with regret, he realized he had missed everything. Watching Essence grow round with child, feeling his son kick footballs in her stomach, the birth...damn, he had even missed his son's first step.

He was a father. And behind those brick walls was a child that was half his. He was a life he had helped create.

*A child you might not have ever known about if your sister hadn't run into them at the mall.*

Anger reared his ugly head again. *Had Essence really intended to keep me from knowing about my child?* There was only one way to find out. Pulling his jacket collar up around his ears, he moved around to the front of the house and rang the doorbell.

He had intended to demand his parental rights, but when Essence opened the door, all thoughts flew from his mind.

Essence looked more incredible than she had in her classroom. His heart pounded an erratic rhythm while his gaze moved over her body slowly. She had removed the wool pants suit and now had on a pair of black jeans that hugged her round hips. A long-sleeved T-shirt molded her firm, high-perched breasts then tapered down over a narrow waist.

At school, Essence had worn her auburn hair swept up on her head, showing off the delicately carved bones of her face. Now her hair hung loose and cascaded around her shoulders. Her questioning sienna brown eyes were deep set with hints of gold that could only be seen in the light. Her nose was short and rounded at the tip. He had almost forgotten about a small mole right above her full pouting lips that were outlined in strawberry bringing out the red tones of her cinnamon complexion.

Mark swallowed, trying to control the tingling in his groins. He didn't want to think about how good she looked, considering that she had tried to deny him his child. Yet, standing so close, he wanted nothing more at that moment than to feel her lips pressed against his, while his arms encircled her lush body. Seeing as those were dangerous notions, he cleared his throat and pretended not to be affected.

"Are you going to invite me in?"

Essence cocked her head to one side and stared up at him. "That depends on if you're going to get rid of that frown on your face. You look ready to go to war." She smiled smoothly, betraying nothing of her annoyance. She didn't want him here. Not now. It was much too soon. She had hoped for four more months–plenty of time to prepare.

Stepping closer, his nostrils flared slightly as he inhaled her subtle fragrance, reminding him how sensual a woman she was. "How did you expect me to react, or did you forget the type of man that I am?"

The cold winter air was only partly responsible for Essence's shivering. She hadn't forgotten a thing. Not the smoldering heat in his eyes when he'd made love to her, nor the flash of rage when he was mad. Tilting her chin stubbornly she replied, "I intended to tell you when the time was right."

He wasn't quite sure if he believed her. Too many others had betrayed him in the past. Nevertheless, as he witnessed the vulnerability that shone in Essence's eyes, he began to wonder if she was different. The four weeks they had spent together should have proven that, but, at this point, Mark refused to believe it. The last woman he had allowed himself to trust had broken his heart and he vowed to never let that happen again.

"It's cold out here. Are you going to let me in, or do I have to push my way inside?"

"I guess I'll have to let you in since you haven't giving me much of a choice."

Essence stepped aside, and Mark entered her home. Taking off his jacket, he hung it on an oak coat rack near the door, then moved to the first room on the right.

The living room was spacious and bright with white walls. A lively combination of hardwood and neutral tone carpeting adorned the floors. Ideally located on the far wall was a real wood burning fireplace where several logs crackled behind a black screen.

A small tabletop Christmas tree stood in one corner of the modestly furnished room, with several beautifully wrapped gifts on the floor underneath. When he noticed the toys littering the floor in the corner, he felt as if a hand had squeezed his heart. This was where his child lived. The child, who only a few hours earlier, he hadn't even known existed.

Swinging around, his accusing voice stabbed the air. "Why didn't you try to reach me?"

Essence shut the door then slowly turned to face him with a look of disdain. It was the second time he'd posed that question. "Didn't we already have this discussion?"

"Yes, and until you tell me the truth, we'll keep keep discussing it," he retorted icily.

There was no mistaking his annoyance. Essence found his reaction uncalled for and was now growing irritated as well.

She moved into the living room and took a seat on a matching rust orange chair, then rested her feet on the ottoman before answering. "I did. I sent you three letters, but you never responded to even one." Just looking at him caused her emotions to stir, but she took a deep breath and pushed those feelings to the back of her mind where they belonged.

Standing at the center of the room, Mark's eyes narrowed suspiciously. "Did you mention my son in any of those letters?"

She hesitated, then finally lowered her thick lashes and shook her head. "No."

After quickly analyzing her reaction, Mark rubbed a frustrated hand across his head trying to curb his temper. "Why not? Why didn't you try to reach me through my unit?"

*Because I wanted you to contact me because you missed me, not because of Tyler.* "I didn't want you to think I was trying to trap you. You made it perfectly clear before you left that you weren't looking for a commitment. So I respected your wishes."

"Wishes?" he gaped. "We're not talking about a commitment. We're talking about my son!" he shouted.

Essence shot him an icy glare. "Can you please keep it down before you wake him?"

Mark's expression softened as he suddenly remembered that his son was somewhere in the house. "Where is he?" he asked in a hushed voice as he peered down the long hallway.

"He's asleep."

He met her gaze. "I want to see him."

Essence didn't miss the eagerness in his eyes or voice and almost regretted shaking her head. "Tyler's cranky if he's disturbed. He spent the day with my parents. They took him to the mall to see Santa Claus." She paused to smile. "He was so excited. By the time I pulled out their driveway, he was fast asleep. He'll probably sleep all night, so why don't you come back tomorrow?"

Mark's expression was grim. He didn't want to wait, but considering the circumstances, he didn't have much of a choice. "I'll just wait here until he wakes up." He moved over to the couch and lowered himself against the cushions. Giving her a sidelong glance, he made certain she understood he wasn't leaving until he had seen his son.

Essence sat across from him with her slender fingers tense in her lap, not sure what to do or say next.

"What did you tell your parents?"

His question had caught her completely off guard. "About what?"

"About Tyler's father?"

She shrugged nonchalantly, portraying an ease she didn't really feel. "Nothing more than they needed to know. I am grown, or have you forgotten?"

"I haven't forgotten," he murmured as his eyes riveted over her face. "I also haven't forgotten that your father is a Baptist minister."

She hesitated, measuring him for a moment. His suspicions were starting to get on her nerves. "I figured I'd try to find you when it was time."

His burning eyes held her. "And when would that have been?"

"Before Tyler had gotten old enough to start asking questions," she snapped, infuriated by his tone.

His jaw hardened as he tried to curb his anger. He was angry that he was getting turned on sitting across from her. Warmth skittered the length of him and splintered inside his chest, sending shafts of heat dancing through his body. Pushing his desires back to the corner of his mind, he replied, "I want to provide for my child."

The intensity of his eyes and the concentrated energy of his stare startled her. "I don't need your help," Essence replied, stiff with dignity.

"What about what I need?"

Her brow rose. "And what is that?"

"To be a father. If it were up to you, I wouldn't have even known I had a son."

She was quiet, her expression blank. Mark leaned over toward Essence drawing her attention. "Talk to me Essence." His voice had softened considerably. "How come you didn't tell me about my son?"

"I tried," she answered, turning her face away from him.

Mark shook his head violently. "No you didn't. Even if I hadn't responded to any of your letters, which by the way I never received, you could have contacted the Army. They would have told me I had a baby on the way."

She looked across at him again. "Then what would you had done?"

"I would have stayed in contact with you all these months."

Her heart sank. It was only because of her son. When Mark had reported to duty in Germany, he had no intentions of keeping in touch with her. But now because of Tyler, all that might have changed.

"Tyler is my son. I have a right to be his father," he reiterated.

Essence was silent. Mark was right and she knew it. Even though guilt had weighed heavily on her heart, she would have denied him his child for a number of years had not fate stepped in. A moment ticked by before she spoke, her words tumbling over one another. "You're right. You do have a right to know your son. I just didn't know how to tell you. I...I was so afraid you would have rejected him...that you wouldn't have cared."

He shook his head. "How could you think so little of me?"

She reluctantly met his gaze. "I really didn't know what to think."

Mark tried to hide his disappointment. Selfishly he had hoped that memories of their time together still burned fresh in her mind. "I guess once I left, you never gave me a second thought."

"That's where you're wrong. How could you think that? I thought of you the entire time your child was growing inside of me. While I was in labor with my mother by my side, I screamed out your name and cursed you under my breath for leaving me to go through the entire nine months alone. I couldn't have erased you from my mind if I had wanted to because every time I look at Tyler, I see you."

Essence dropped her eyelids. She remembered being angry with him. At first she had been angry because he simply hadn't bothered to stay in contact, and later because he wasn't around to share in the responsibilities of their son. Eventually, she adjusted and grew to accept things as they were—a four-week affair with no strings attached.

Oh, she blamed herself. She knew she never should have had unprotected sex. Not because their coming together had created Tyler, because she could never regret her darling little boy, but because Mark's touch had left an imprint that she still felt clear down to her soul. Too bad the feeling wasn't mutual. "It's apparent you haven't thought about me even once."

Mark may have been busy the past two years, but more than a fleeting thought of those four glorious weeks together had past through his mind time and time again. He hadn't forgotten, seeing her again brought all those memories front and center. Essence had a special innocence about her that turned him on. He hadn't forgotten her soft surrendering sighs or her calling his name at the top of her lungs. He even remembered the taste of her warm and wet against his tongue, the feeling of being buried deep inside her. He groaned inward. He was driving himself crazy just thinking about it.

There was a noticeable pause before he replied, "You might not believe it, but I spent many nights lying in my bed thinking of you."

Essence swallowed and stared across at him, wishing what he said was true.

They were both quiet and content for the moment. Essence knew they both needed to somehow put the past behind them and decide on a future. There was an invisible thread that bound them, even if she wished it wasn't so. It was what had drawn them together in the first place.

After growing uncomfortable with the prolonged silence, Essence rose from her chair. "I'd better try to straighten up a little, then get Tyler's bottle ready before he wakes. Here..." she handed him the remote control, "...make yourself at home."

With that, Essence acted as if he wasn't there. She moved around the room, picking up the mail that was scattered on the coffee table. A basket of laundry was sitting in the corner near the television, waiting to be folded. Toys were in disarray, and Mark could see a shoe peeking out from beneath the chair. His brow rose curiously. Essence had always been such a meticulous person. But as he watched her scrambling around the room, gathering the toys, and putting things where they belonged, it hit him. *When does she have time?* With a toddler running around the house, chances were she barely had time to sleep, let alone clean her house.

Essence obviously would rather spend quality time with their son than take time away from him to do housework.

Tilting his head slightly, Mark looked at Essence clearly for the first time since his arrival and noticed the strain of being a single parent.

The puffiness under her eyes was an obvious sign...one he hadn't noticed before.

Mark dropped the remote back on the coffee table and rose. "Let me help," he offered.

Essence, touched by his offer, glanced over at him and shook her head. "Oh no. I don't need any help."

"I insist." Mark reached for the basket of clean clothes and, despite her protest, began folding them in a neat pile on her couch.

"Would you like something to eat?" she asked as she moved toward the kitchen.

He shook his head. Since he'd found out about his son, food had been the furthest thing from his mind.

Essence nodded, then paused when Mark reached into the basket again. Her cheeks warmed as she watched him fold one of Tyler's bibs followed by a pair of her silk panties. She waited for his reaction, and when she didn't see one, she sighed, then turned and left the room.

Mark waited until she departed before he looked up again. Desire shot through his loins, and he quickly took a seat before Essence returned and witnessed the obvious. Closing his eyes, images of her standing before him in a pair of panties similar to the pair in his hand came to mind. She had worn them on their last night together...

*He lay back across the bed in awe as Essence emerged from the bathroom.*

*"What do you think?" she asked as she poised in the doorframe.*

*Mark's eyes traveled from her face to the low scoop of her neck. Deftly, she slipped the dress off her shoulders, and it fell to the floor. Essence stood breathlessly before him, clad only in a matching peach bra and panties. Gazing into her eyes, he saw the same smoldering need that claimed his body, obliterating rational thoughts from his mind.*

*Dragging in a breath, Mark took in every voluptuous curve. Only thin* lacy material kept him from her lush body. "Come here," he commanded in a powerful whisper.

Essence sauntered over and stood near the edge of the bed. She released the pins from her hair, then silky strands fell to her bare shoulders.

Mark sat up on the bed and slid his hands up the length of her legs. Completely aroused, his hands explored the soft lines of her waist and thighs, traveling to her slim hips to cup her bottom. He rose pulling her closer to the heat of his body. Their eyes met as he stared down at her with intense desire burning in their depths.

His demanding lips met hers, warm and persuasive. Essence, surrendering to the need building inside her, pressed her open mouth to his. Their tongues twined and merged in a hot, wet assault. As he ignited her passion, his own grew stronger. His mouth moved down the smooth line of her neck to her collarbone and then to her full throbbing breasts. His lips covered the thin silky fabric, teasing her nipples to tingling peaks.

He seared a path up her spine to the center of her back where he unhooked her bra. Essence spilled into his hands, and he covered her breasts, squeezing gently. Lifting one to his mouth, his lips touched her nipple possessively, suckling and teasing until it was pebble hard before moving to the other. His other hand glided down to cup her buttocks, pulling her flush against him. He reached up to the band at her waist, sliding her panties down off her hips and finally down around her ankles.

A soft cry from the back of the house filtered through Mark's thoughts, bringing him back to the present.

Essence reappeared. "I believe your son is awake."

All thoughts of her naked in his arms went up in smoke as Mark pushed the basket aside and followed her down the carpeted hallway to a small room on the left, decorated in caricatures of *Scooby Doo*. However, Mark wasn't interested in the décor, only the boy who stood up in his crib.

Everything in him went still as Essence reached over into the crib. A soft smile curved her lush lips as she lifted the baby with his fat little legs, pumping in the air. The child squealed and Essence held him close. "Meet your son, Tyler."

Mark felt his heart fill and explode at the sight of his son. He stepped closer, letting his gaze move over him. Round-faced and healthy, Tyler had dark curly hair like his, eyes like his, but his beauty belonged to his mother. With his head tucked under his mother's chin, Tyler stared at him with wide golden eyes; reminiscent of Dorlinda's. No wonder Kelly had been so certain he was his son.

*My son.*

"Hey, Champ." He barely managed to speak, his throat thick with emotion.

Love shone on Essence's face, and he couldn't help being moved by it. She could have terminated the pregnancy, but she hadn't. Instead, she had given his son life. The mere unselfish act touched him in ways he couldn't begin to describe.

Tyler lifted a fist and rubbed his eyes. Mark reached out to touch him just to make sure he was truly real, and in an instant, one of his tiny hands latched onto his finger and held on tight.

And just like that Mark fell in love.

Essence watched Mark. Nervousness she'd never thought to see in him came to the surface. For goodness sakes, he was an officer in the United States Army! They were trained to be strong and brave, but he approached his son with a hesitancy that touched her heart.

"He's handsome," he replied after studying him for a long moment. It was almost impossible to take his eyes off of his son.

"Yeah," Essence replied as he ran a fingertip along Tyler's arm. The baby simply continued to stare at Mark as if he knew who he was. "Just like his father," she murmured, her gaze meeting and holding his.

Mark moved as close as he could, their baby between them. "Look at what we made, Essence," he whispered in awe.

Essence's heart swelled just a little. She'd been alone with Tyler for so long that sharing him with Mark felt strange, yet sweet. She hadn't known what to expect from Mark's first encounter with her son, but watching him fall in love with Tyler in less than a minute wasn't it.

"You want to hold him?" she asked.

"Yes, but I don't want to scare him," he admitted softly.

The corner of her mouth twitched. "I don't think he'll mind."

Essence watched Mark hold out his arms. Tyler hesitated momentarily then leaned over toward his father.

Mark drew him to his chest, feeling his little heartbeat. Nothing he had ever experienced could have prepared him for his son. He leaned down to kiss the top of his head, inhaling his smell of powder and innocence. Tyler stared up at him, and Mark found he was perfect in every way. From his curly hair, down to his ten little toes, he was his son. Whether he would have had nine fingers or two heads, he was still his son and he would have loved him just the same.

Tyler began to fidget, then with a whimper he leaned over for Essence to hold him again. With reluctance, Mark handed him back to his mother. While letting go, his fingertips slid up Tyler's arm tucked against his mother and Mark accidentally brushed Essence's breast. Heat ripped through him as he heard her breath catch. He looked at Essence with the same intensity he had with their child.

Mark slanted her a long glance. "I'm here and I'm staying. I'm going to be in his life whether you want me here or not."

Essence simply nodded and said, "I know."

"Do you have any objections?"

She swallowed hard and lowered her voice a notch or two. "I'll get used to it."

Nodding, Mark stroked the top of Tyler's head, loving the way he watched him. "Have you forgotten how good we were together?"

Essence nearly came undone when he nailed her with his penetrating eyes again. "No, I haven't forgotten."

He curved a hand under her chin, and raised her face to his. "Good. Neither have I."

Lowering his head, Mark pressed a tender kiss at the corner of her mouth. Her lips flamed from the brush of his lips while his masculine scent swirled about her. *What was it about Mark Saunders that made her weak when he touched her?* He devoured her mouth like a thirsty man taking his first drink of water after being denied for days. She tried to retreat, but he wrapped his massive arms around her and their son and held tight.

Tyler fussed, then reached up and touched his face. Mark felt something new and strong possess him, and he increased the pressure on Essence's mouth, overwhelmed by the feeling yet wanting to shout when he felt her respond.

The instant she did, he drew back. She was breathing a little harder, and her eyes appeared glassy. *Victory looms on the horizon*, he thought. However, he knew he would need all of the patience he could muster for the challenge.

He hadn't intended to kiss her, however, his curiosity had taken over. He wondered if he would have the same gut-level reaction if he kissed her again.

And he had.

"Expect me in your life, Essence," he warned in all seriousness. An intimate warmth had traveled up his arm and spread through his body, leaving him momentarily unsure of his chosen course.

Touching the top of his head, Mark looked down at Tyler and realized that the little boy was the best thing to have ever happened in his life. Suddenly, tears welled in his eyes and he struggled to conceal them. He attempted to collect himself, but lost the battle as a lone tear rolled from the corner of his right eye. He would have never imagined that the emotion of having a child could be so overpowering. He needed to get away fast.

Mark dropped his gaze from her view, then pressed his lips to his son's soft skin and whispered, "See you tomorrow." He then spun on his heels and left the room.

Essence gripped the crib rail because her knees threatened to give out. Hearing the front door close, she exhaled and realized she had been holding her breath. She dropped a kiss to Tyler's cheek then lowered him back in the crib.

"Well, Tyler, that was your Daddy. What did you think?"

Tyler began gurgling and blowing bubbles all at once.

"Yeah, he has that type of affect on people." *Even me.* Although Mark was no longer holding onto her, she still felt his touch clear down to the bone. Mark Saunders was back and stirring up all kinds of thoughts and *what ifs* that she rarely let herself dwell on anymore. Nevertheless, she had asked herself several times during the course of the evening, if she had told him two years ago that she was pregnant, would things have been different?

She scowled at her thoughts. *Why am I even pondering that possibility?* She made what she thought was the right decision. Mark had never told her he loved her. He had never promised to keep in touch. Instead, he left and never once looked back.

*Then why do I feel so guilty?*

Tyler laughed, drawing her attention. He was fascinated by his new Elmo doll. She grinned. Tyler was such a good baby. She couldn't have asked for a better child.

It was only on nights like tonight, when she stared down at Tyler's smile that was so much like Mark's that she thought about the choice she had made. Essence honestly believed that she had made the right decision by not telling him about Tyler. Despite the fact that her older sister Tamara had lectured her on numerous occasions to get in touch with him.

"He has a right to know," Tamara would insist.

"I know…I know," Essence would say.

With that in mind, she had wrote him three letters. When she never heard back, she felt confident she had made the right choice, and never tried to contact him again.

She really hadn't believed Mark to be "father" material, but after watching him tonight, she began to have doubts. She even felt a little guilty that she had never given him a chance.

Tyler tossed the toy aside and began to whine. She reached for his bottle in the crib and positioned him down on his side. Stroking Tyler's hair, she stared down at his handsome face; a face so much like his father.

She didn't need help to see Mark was still an attractive man. As a soldier, he had a strong body that proved he was hardworking. However, it was his personality that had reeled her in that first night. He was charming and had a wonderful sense of humor. She loved it when he laughed. His laughter was full and robust. His eyes would sparkle and his smile would light up the room.

With a frown, she tossed those superficial thoughts away. She tried to ignore the pang of longing that always occurred when she thought of him. Unfortunately, seeing Mark again brought back a rush of the good times they shared, but which now she'd rather forget.

Forcing her mind away from their stolen kiss, she focused on her son whose eyelids had grown heavy.

She didn't need this kind of complication right now. Tyler was her world. Her attention had to be devoted to him. Anything else would just be a distraction that she didn't need. The only way to keep her attention focused was to keep her distance from Mark. However, now that he knew about Tyler that was going to be virtually impossible.

"What are we going to do?" she whispered.

Her son didn't offer any solution and Essence didn't have one either. All she knew was that Mark Saunders could turn her life upside down with a single glance, and after that kiss…she knew she was headed for trouble.

She wasn't going to fall for him again. *No way…no how.* But while she dreaded his re-appearance in her life, a small part of her knew that she couldn't wait to see how things would develop.

# CHAPTER THREE

After Essence escorted her class to the gym for Physical Education, she moved down the hall to the teacher's lounge where several of her co-workers sat sipping coffee.

"Speak of the devil. Here's the lucky lady." Gretchen's green eyes lit with excitement when she entered the room.

Essence looked around the room to find six pairs of eyes staring at her, and smiled. "No wonder my ears were burning. What's going on?" she asked, as she moved toward the cabinet, reaching for her mug.

Tiffany, a chubby, middle-aged first grade teacher, snorted with laughter. "We should be asking you that question. Those are for you."

Essence's eyes followed the direction of her finger to find a beautiful floral arrangement on the table. "Oh, my!" she murmured, clearly surprised. She quickly filled her mug with coffee and moved over to the table to look for a card.

"It's right there," Sandra offered, her large dark eyes fixed on a small pink card hidden behind a branch of baby's breath.

Essence groaned inwardly, certain that all of them had taken a peek.

She reached for the small envelope and opened it. Despite her intentions not to, a smile tipped the curve of her lips. It was from Mark.

*I want the total package.*

A back draft of heat surged through her veins, eliciting a tingling in her breasts. The note was his way of letting her know that she was in for the ride of her life. Why did that possibility scare her? *You know why*, she told herself. All Essence had to do was close her eyes and Mark was there. She could actually feel his hands on her body, his lips on her mouth, his hardened manhood pulsing up against her thigh. If the rapid beat of her heart was any indication of how the message made her feel, she was in big trouble.

"So, who's Mark?" she heard Gretchen ask. "I thought your boyfriend's name was Malcolm."

*Malcolm!*

In all of the excitement of Mark's return, she had forgotten all about Malcolm Cole: sweet, dependable Malcolm.

She had met him while attending a Labor Day barbecue hosted by Tamara. He was not only a good friend of her brother-in-law Paul, but also a partner at his law firm. Finding that they had a lot in common, she and Malcolm instantly hit it off and had been dating off and on for almost three months. Unfortunately, he was ready to take the relationship to the next level but she wasn't. Essence wished that she felt the same. He was good to her and Tyler. But when Malcolm kissed her, she felt nothing remotely close to the way she had felt in Mark's arms last night. His kisses caused her toes to curl and melted her insides, while Malcolm's kisses were mild and engendered only platonic feelings. There would never be any passion between her and Malcolm. She was positive of that.

"Are we going to get the 411, or what?" Tiffany asked, cutting into her thoughts.

Essence forced a smile for her audience. "Sorry, but I don't kiss and tell." Without another word, she dumped her coffee in the sink, reached for the vase and carried it back to her classroom.

Essence was trying to comfort Tyler who was ready for dinner, as well as load laundry in the washing machine, when she heard a knock at the door.

"Who could that be?" she asked.

Tyler cooed in response.

"You're right, probably nobody, but I'd better check anyway. Who knows, it may be Ed McMahan." She handed her son a slice of a banana. "I'll be right back." Propping the laundry basket on her hip, she moved to the front door. When she opened it, she frowned at the man she found standing there. "Mark."

"Good," he smirked. "I was afraid you had forgotten my name."

*Like that could ever happen.* Just looking at him made her want to pull him to her and taste his mouth until she purred his name. However, she couldn't do that. Was she crazy? The whole idea was insane. She tried to ignore how her heart lurched, but it was useless. Every time Mark was around, Essence found she couldn't think straight. She met his golden gaze and almost shuddered under the intensity. The attraction was just as strong now as it had been almost two years ago. Mark had a way of provoking the most intense physical response she had ever experienced. She felt the heat even while standing in the drafty doorway.

While drawing a deep breath, she stared at the smile plastered on his face and scowled. She shouldn't have been at all surprised to find him standing outside her door.

"What are you doing here?" she asked as if she didn't already know the answer.

"I came to see you and my son."

Essence ran a hand through her hair and flashed him a look of sheer irritation. "I'm really busy."

Mark didn't appear to be the least bit affected by her cool behavior. "Then I guess you aren't up for Grotto's Pizza?" he asked as he held up a cardboard box.

Essence inhaled the delicious tangy scent and smothered a groan. It was her favorite pizza and Mark knew it. He was fighting dirty. The offer was tempting, but if she let Mark in now he'd only expect to be able to drop by whenever he felt like it.

She sighed. After a long and difficult afternoon with her students, she was just too tired to have to deal with him right now. "No thanks. I've already eaten and Tyler's food is warming."

As if Tyler had known he was being discussed, he took that moment to exercise his lungs. Not waiting for an invitation, Mark stepped in from the cold and followed the sound of his son's voice. Essence was on the verge of screaming as she watched his retreating back. Who did he think he was walking into her house? She sighed with irritation, wondering how she could get him to leave.

After shutting out the cold wind, she followed him and found herself annoyed that she was admiring how well his backside looked in a pair of gray sweatpants.

"Hey, Champ," Mark greeted.

Essence stepped into the kitchen to find Tyler grinning up from his high chair at his father. How could she deny her son such pleasure? Planting her free hand firmly to her waist she hissed, "Alright, you can visit for a little while, but I like to get Tyler bathed and in bed by eight."

Mark grinned. "Good, then we can talk."

She made a rude sound that drew his attention again. "No-o-o-o. Then I get to clean up the kitchen, iron my clothes for work tomorrow, take a hot bath, and then try to get some sleep."

Besides the apparent attitude, Mark found her face showed signs of fatigue. "It's tough isn't it?"

Her spine stiffened. She didn't want him to think for a minute she couldn't do it on her own. "I manage and will continue to do so long after you're gone."

"Hey, I'm not trying to take over," he said in an even tone as he set the pizza box on the table. "I'm just bringing food and coming to spend time with my son." He raised his hands, palms forward.

She frowned. Mark had a smooth way of making her feel like the bad guy. "You should have called first."

"Listen, Essence," he began as he stroked his son's hair. "Tyler is my son too. I barely got a chance to look at him yesterday."

Another small twinge of guilt poked at her chest and before Essence knew it, she heard herself say, "Then I guess you better get him fed."

With a grin a mile long, Mark shrugged out of his jacket and draped it over one of the kitchen chairs. He then removed Tyler's plate from the microwave and pulled up a chair in front of him.

With a dejected sigh, Essence moved toward the laundry room, directly behind the kitchen.

"Essence."

She stopped and looked over her shoulders to find Mark staring at her.

"We still need to talk before I leave," he said with dangerous softness.

Essence stared, once again lost in those golden eyes. Ignoring the sinking feeling in her stomach, she quickly nodded and looked away.

She stepped into the laundry room and lowered the basket to the floor. Leaning against the clothes dryer, Essence briefly dropped her eyelids as his deep sexy draw lingered in her ears.

"Damn!" she mumbled under her breath as she set the dial on the washing machine.

Yesterday she had made the mistake of letting Mark kiss her. Tonight she was annoyed for being turned on by his presence. A part of her hoped for a repeat of last night. *What is wrong with me? Will I have to keep reminding myself that this was the same man who had walked away two years ago and never looked back?* It was against her better judgment to spend any great length of time alone with him. Nonetheless, Mark was right. They did need to talk. Maybe then she could finally get past some of the uneasiness surrounding them.

She loaded Tyler's clothes in the washing machine with a vengeance followed by a splattered capful of detergent. *Get it together*, she told herself, then quietly moved back into the kitchen.

Leaning against the doorframe, she watched Mark put a clean bib around Tyler's neck, securing the Velcro strap. The other, covered with slimy banana, he had set on the kitchen counter. Mark wiped off both of his hands and then took his seat. He tested the temperature of Tyler's food with the back of his hand and offered him his first spoonful. "All right, Champ, show your Dad how a real man puts away a meal."

Kicking his chubby legs, Tyler eagerly accepted the spoon that wa placed before him.

Essence could not resist a smile as she listened to Mark hold a co versation with Tyler as if they had been together from the start. Ty spit his food and squealed as he tried to communicate back. Witnessi the entire episode, she tried not to notice the fluttering of her he Despite her best intentions, she found herself fascinated by the r who seemed to be a natural at fatherhood. She'd had no idea that M had had any experience with children.

Tyler looked over at her and gave her a wide grin with meat drool running down his chin. It brought tears to her eyes and it w that moment she realized that Mark was something she could ne to her son—his father.

Certain that Mark had everything under control she reach the dirty bib and tossed it in the washing machine. She grabb s pizza box and moved to the living room. Plopping down on the couch, she propped her feet on the coffee table. For the first time in as long as she could remember, she watched the six o'clock news. Twenty minutes into the program, she tossed the box aside and stretched out across the couch. And with little effort on her part, she drifted off to sleep…

*The waiter appeared with their food and then disappeared. When Essence tasted a morsel of the blackened catfish, she couldn't help moaning with pleasure as the spicy flavor burst in her mouth. It was delicious.*

*Mark's eyes sparkled as he smiled. He seemed to be enjoying the meal as much as she was. It was incredible. Had anything ever affected her the way his golden eyes did? She doubted it.*

*Other than minimal small talk, they virtually ate in silence; each watched the other as the minutes passed. After dessert, Mark suggested a walk around the block and Essence agreed.*

*Outside they were met with a warm October breeze as they strolled across Silver Lake. There was a full moon and several stars overhead that sparkled across the water. They had barely gone twenty feet when Essence stopped to slip off her high-heeled sandals.*

*"These shoes are killing my feet," she groaned.*

*Mark's brow quirked in amusement. "Then why wear them?"*

*"Because they're new and they make my legs look long," she explained.*

*He chuckled, his pearly white teeth flashing under the streetlight. "Leave it to a shrimp to try and find a way to appear tall."*

*Essence punched him playfully in the arm and giggled. "I'm not that short."*

*"If you say so."*

*As they resumed their stroll, Mark reached for her hand and linked their fingers together. A current of electricity flowed from her hand and up her arm at his touch. Looking down at his long fingers clasped around hers, she thought they looked right together; felt right.*

*While they moved up State Street through the historical district of Dover, Essence tried to make sense of what she was feeling. After only one evening, she liked Mark. She liked having dinner with him. She liked looking at him. She even enjoyed holding his hand as they strolled at a leisurely pace.*

*Mark whistled, drawing her attention. "Man, look at that house."*

*She turned to look at a grand Victorian style home with a large wrap-around porch.*

*"It's lovely," she replied in a dreamy voice.*

*"Some day I plan to buy a house on this street," Mark declared confidently.*

*"These houses are expensive."*

*"And so is my taste."*

*He looked down at her and there was no mistaking the desire she saw in their depths.*

*"Right now, I'm curious how a short little woman tastes."*

*Lightly, he brushed his lips over her forehead and Essence's eyes fluttered shut as she savored the warm, sweet feeling. She tilted her head up and stared into his golden eyes that sparkled from the reflection of the moon. Her mouth parted, a silent, seductive invitation. His mouth accepted and softly covered hers.*

*Mark's lips were like an intoxicating drug, making her light-headed. His tongue was slow as it ran against her bottom lip before moving inside. Their tongues merged, and she could taste the wine in his mouth. Somehow it tasted better this way and was just as potent. She felt him slide his hands down her back and over her hips, causing her to arch against him. Caught in the rapture of passion, they were wrapped in each other's arms, tightly hanging on to each other and the new wonderful feeling they had found.*

Essence felt someone tapping her shoulder. Slowly, she opened her eyes to find Mark sitting on the couch near her right hip, hovering over her. His face was inches from hers, his gaze taking a slow perusal of her features. Despite the tightening of her breasts, she fought her body's response to his closeness.

"Where's Tyler?" she asked softly, still unable to take her eyes off of him.

"Sound asleep. After his bath, the little man was tuckered out."

She gasped. "You bathed him?"

He flashed her an irresistible smile. "You look surprised. I have lots of younger cousins. Back in the day, I was the best babysitter in the neighborhood."

"You?" It was hard to believe a pretty boy like him babysat.

"You better recognize. During the summer when all my homeboys were flipping burgers at Mickey D's, I was hanging out at the park with the kids from my neighborhood whose moms had to work. At a buck fifty an hour, I was making more than my friends were and I got to have fun at the same time."

Essence couldn't do anything but shake her head and smile. Mark Saunders was a mystery to her. "You're something else."

"Yes I am," he responded without conceit.

There was a noticeable silence before either of them spoke again.

"Thanks for the flowers." She stared at him through her lashes, unaware of the seductive gesture.

His grin deepened. "You're quite welcome."

Casting a nervous glance toward the clock on the mantle, she groaned, "Oh no, it's after nine! How could I have slept that long?"

"You were tired." He was so close, closer than she had realized until his warm breath feathered over her nose and lips.

She wrinkled her nose. "I'm a mother. We don't have time to be tired. I've got clothes to dry, and a kitchen to clean before I can shower and go to bed." She tried to rise but Mark kept her firmly on the couch.

"The clothes have already been dried and folded, and I spent the last thirty minutes cleaning the kitchen."

Momentarily she was stunned by his act of kindness. "Thank you."

"You're welcome." He reached out and caressed her cheek. His touch was so soft and gentle, causing her breathing to increase. Instantly, she knew she was in trouble.

"Now if you'd like, we can retreat to the shower. That way we'll have plenty of time to lay under the sheets and talk."

She gaped at his face. He was serious! "No thank you, Casanova. I like sleeping alone."

Angling his head, he winked. "No you don't. You said so yourself."

Yes, she had after they had spent four consecutive weeks together sharing her bed. The mere thought of the things they had done caused a stir between her legs.

A look of distress marred her beautiful face. "That was long before Tyler was born."

"All the more reason. We were good together. I know that it can only get better."

She swallowed, finding herself speechless. Every time she looked directly in his eyes, she found a mixture of desire and impatience inside them.

"...That way Tyler can wake up to find both his Momma and Daddy together—the way it should be."

Tearing her eyes away from his golden gaze, she blinked twice. "What did you say?"

"You heard me." His hand came to rest at the curve of her waist.

Essence observed flickers of desire darken his eyes. He wanted her. The need was written all over his face. When Mark leaned closer, Essence knew he was going to kiss her again. She had made that mistake last night and knew she was about to do it again. Part of her felt she should get up and move as far away from him as possible, but, despite the consequences (and she knew there would be plenty of those) a part of her couldn't wait. When his lips lowered and their mouths met, the kiss was nothing like the one the night before. This time it was filled with glorious heat and hunger, no baby wedged between them. His full, supple lips teased and coaxed her full cooperation.

Essence tried fighting for control but instead she met his lips with firm, demanding pressure of her own. She tried pushing him away but when she placed her hand to his hard chest, the feel of his firm muscles melted any further resistance.

The intense kiss sent her senses spinning. Her mouth opened easily under his probing tongue and when she moaned, he responded by deepening the kiss. His tongue plunged into her mouth, sliding seductively against hers.

She expected to have felt the memory of their past but those were a weak comparison to the real thing. She felt a rush of heat flow through her body followed by a vibrating liquid between her legs. His large hand glided down her waist, across her hips, and down to cup her bottom. What was happening was spiraling quickly out of control, leaving her gasping for air.

Mark was the first to pull back. When his warm lips left her, Essence became annoyed that she hadn't found the energy to be the first to pull away. Instead, she was left feeling weak and lightheaded.

"Now, are you ready to talk?" he asked breathing heavily.

She nodded, unable to speak. What was wrong with her? Annoyed at him and herself, she swung her legs off the couch, then moved over toward the edge trying to put as much distance between them as possible. "All right. What do you want to talk about?" she spat impatiently.

"I have only known my son one day and already I love him. I want him to be a part of my life. I want him to have all the pleasure I had as a child."

A muscle twitched at her jaw. "What are you trying to say? That I'm incapable of providing for my son properly?" she asked defensively.

"Not at all." He reached for her hand. "I think you've done a fabulous job. What I'm trying to say is Tyler needs the love of two parents."

Trying to ignore the heat generating from his fingers, Essence pulled in a deep breath then let it out again. "I agree."

"Good," Mark said, drawing the words out slowly. "Then you won't have any objections."

Her brow furrowed with confusion. Had she missed something? "Objections to what?"

"To marrying me."

# CHAPTER FOUR

The heavy lashes that shadowed her cheeks flew up. Essence looked at him as if he'd lost his mind. She couldn't have possibly heard him right. Not now. Not two years after he had suggested that they 'just be friends.'

"What did you say?"

A dimple showed as he smiled. "I asked you to marry me."

"No," Essence said without any further hesitation. "But I appreciate the offer."

Mark appeared annoyed by her abrupt response. "Couldn't you at least think about it before you give me an answer?"

She was tempted to laugh at his question. If he had only known how many times she had thought of being Mrs. Saunders.

She had waited what felt like an eternity to hear those magical words until she finally had given up hope and faced reality. Hearing them now was meaningless. "There's nothing to think about. My answer will still be the same."

Mark leaned forward, resting both elbows on his knees. "Essence, be reasonable."

Essence, having recovered from the shock of his proposal, replied, "I am being reasonable. I'm also curious to know when you came up with this idea. Before you found out about Tyler or after?"

Mark shrugged, "What difference does it make?"

"It makes a big difference. You feel obligated to ask. I wouldn't even begin to consider saying *yes* to someone who doesn't really want to be married."

"Who says I don't?" he asked defensively.

She folded her legs underneath her bottom then rolled her eyes. "Mark, don't insult me. If Tyler wasn't between us, would you have come to see me?"

"I've been home for two days and I've spent the majority of the time here. What do you think?"

"I think your avoiding the question. I think you want to do the honorable thing and I appreciate the gesture. But I don't need it. I don't want to marry you just because I'm the mother of your child. Marriage is tough enough as it is."

"I'll be a good father."

"Oh, I know you will," she said gently. "But you don't have to marry me to be one."

Essence was surprised at how calm she acted, especially with her stomach was all tied up in knots.

Shifting slightly on the couch, Mark thought of his own father. His parents had fallen in love in high school. He and Kelly were products of that love. He wanted Tyler to have the same. "I insist. You can't continue to do this alone."

"Oh, so now it's time to come to my rescue!" she barked with laughter. "Do I look like a damsel in distress?"

"No, you look like the mother of my child and that child needs me. I want to give him my name."

"He already has a name. Tyler Dane Monroe," she managed to state in an even tone. "It sounds perfectly fine to me."

Mark covered his face with his hand. "Why are you being so stubborn?" he whispered bitterly between his fingers before raising his head to look at her again.

"This isn't the 'ole days. I don't *have* to marry my baby's daddy if I don't want to."

Reaching over, he cupped her chin, turning her face so that she had to look at him. "Is marrying me such a bad thing?"

"Yes." She couldn't go through life married to a man who didn't love her. She didn't want to live with the constant uncertainty of "does he want me for myself," or "because I'm the mother of his child?" Or because it's the right and honorable thing to do?

Mark let her go, dragging his hand over his head then his face again. "You know…you are about the strangest woman I know."

She snorted. "I couldn't have been too strange. You couldn't wait to get me in your bed."

"That's not true."

"Yes, it is. But I can't blame anybody but myself. Kelly warned me that you were getting ready to go overseas, but I was so caught up in the moment I couldn't think of anything but what was happening right then. I willingly gave myself to you that first night. For four weeks, birth control was the farthest thing from my mind. All I could think about was how good you made me feel, how much I loved—" she stopped suddenly, realizing she had said too much.

Mark's eyes snapped to hers. "You love me?"

Essence schooled her features not to reflect what she was truly feeling. "Don't get excited. I said I *used* to love you. I've gotten over you a long time ago."

He was speechless. Never in his wildest dreams would he have considered the possibility that she had fallen in love with him. But now as he looked back, her feelings were so painfully obvious he wondered why he hadn't realized it before. *You jerk!* He couldn't blame her for turning down his proposal. He'd romanced her for four straight weeks, slept in her bed every night then, just like *that* he had walked away for two years. He'd had his reasons, but of course that didn't do him any good now. Any other man probably would have accepted her response at face value. Unfortunately, he wasn't one to give up that easily.

"If you loved me once, you can love me again," he stated confidently.

"You are too much," she said, laughing. He was cockier than ever. "Can I ask another question?"

"Sure, anything."

"Do you love me?" She blurted out before she lost the guts. When Mark didn't answer quickly enough she began again. "If you don't love me Mark, then just say it. I'm a big girl."

"I won't lie to you. No, I don't love you," he answered softly.

Her heart fractured. *Well, at least he was honest.*

He squeezed her hand. "But I do know that what I feel for you is strong enough that you have invaded my mind for the last two years."

She snorted rudely. "And I guess that's why I never heard from you."

"I made a mistake," Mark said and leaned closer, his mouth a fraction from her. "We're good together. Denying it isn't helping."

*Oh no, not again.* Essence could feel his breath on her lips. Almost taste him. She leaned out of his reach. An instant before his mouth brushed hers, the phone rang.

At the possibility of falling in his arms again, the interruption was the bucket of ice water she needed. She dashed off the couch and into the kitchen to answer it before the noise disturbed Tyler.

"Hello," came out in a croak and she had to clear her throat. "Oh, hi Malcolm."

Mark had followed her into the kitchen. Essence glanced across the room in time to see his eyes narrowed dangerously.

"Busy? Uh…actually I am." She turned away from Mark's intense stare then dropped her voice down to almost a whisper. "Sure. Bye."

"Who was that?" Mark asked the second she hung up.

While fidgeting nervously with the phone cord she murmured, "A friend."

"What kind of friend?"

She didn't miss the edge in his voice. Swinging around, she pursed her lips and glared at him. "The none-of-your-business kind of friend."

He shook his head. "I can't believe you're dating."

"Any reason I shouldn't?"

The pupils of his eyes darkened. "Yes, I can think of two reasons— me and Tyler."

He was jealous. It was written all over his face. What Mark didn't know was that he was more dangerous to her than Malcolm could ever be. She could barely recall the color of Malcolm's eyes, but there wasn't a thing about Mark she had forgotten.

Finding that her throat was suddenly dry, Essence moved to get a drink of water. She turned on the tap water and allowed it to run for a few seconds. When she was certain it was cold, she reached for a glass and filled it.

Mark was suddenly standing behind her, his hands on her shoulders, his thumbs rubbing the bare flesh of her collarbones. He leaned closer and the heat of his body eased into hers just as he pressed a kiss to the back of her neck. Swallowing the water in her mouth, Essence took several deep breaths and tried to stay perfectly still. It was impossible. The hand holding the glass had begun to tremble.

"I want another chance."

She felt his warm moist breath feather over the nape of her neck. Her shaking became much more violent as his hands slid down her arms. One moved around to cup her waist. The other, he dropped down over her stomach, then lowered until his hand rested between her legs. There, he pressed gently. With a groan, Essence lowered the glass to the counter.

"Are you in love with this guy?" he whispered.

His breath was so close to her ear that his lips actually brushed it. She shivered uncontrollably, ripples of something she had never experienced before shimmered all through her body. Her mind was unable to actually grasp what he had just said. She leaned back into him, her breasts rising and falling quickly now.

"I, um…" she gasped with surprise as his lips closed on the rim of her ear. His hands clasped her waist gently, bringing her further into his embrace. He did some dark and mysterious things to her earlobes that had her turning into putty in his hands. Moaning mindlessly, she let her head drop limply back against his chest. She wasn't quite sure what he was doing, but she couldn't seem to find the mind to care. It felt so damned good, she hardly noticed as his hands inched their way up over her ribs, to climb the mounds of her breasts.

"Does he make you feel like this?"

A second moan slipped from her. She arched into his touch, her breasts pushing against the cloth that bound them. Her hands came up to cover his, cupping them closer against her flesh. Unconsciously, she twisted her head and sought his lips with hers. When his mouth covered hers and his tongue slid out to trace her lips, urging her to open to him, to give him complete access, she made a tiny sound of pleasure in her throat, causing a hungry groan to slip from her mouth into his. He turned her in his arms, mindlessly seeking a closer embrace. Mark's hips pinned her against the counter.

"Tell me you want me to leave and I'll leave," he whispered as he nuzzled his nose against hers, then kissed her eyelids that had fallen close. "Tell me you don't want me here kissing you, touching you, yearning to be inside of you."

Caught by her shoulders, Essence allowed Mark to lead her over to the wall and press her back against it. He wedged a knee between her thighs, pushing forward and upward then tugged at her shirt and freed the buttons. Essence wasn't wearing a bra, so access was instant. She felt the cool air on her nipples, like a caress, before his hands covered them. His lips left hers to travel down her throat, then in search of a hardened nipple. Gasping and moaning, Essence pressed her bare shoulders back into the cool wall, pushing her breasts out as he plucked at them with his fingers and licked at the bare flesh he had revealed. It was like some sort of madness. She wanted and needed him with a violence that would have terrified her had she seen it coming.

As if hungry for his touch, she arched toward him, pressing closer, moving against him, encouraging him. Mark responded in kind, catching her hair in his fingers and tugging her head back as far as it would go. Then he gave her the kiss she wanted, devouring her mouth with a passion that stole all her breath and left her panting and gasping. He tugged her right leg impatiently upward and she felt herself further inflamed by that touch.

"I want to make love to you."

His voice caused her eyelids to fly open. Shaking her head in an effort to try to clear her mind, she lifted both her hands, palms out, to put some distance between them. What in the world was she doing? Was she going to be a doormat for the rest of her life?

"No," she cried.

"No?" he repeated. His gaze moved over her features as surely as a caress.

A whisper of goose bumps raced along her spine but Essence ignored them. "You heard me, no."

"You know you want me," he countered and to her fury she saw that he was laughing at her.

Steeling herself, Essence said, "Regardless. Everything I want isn't always good for me."

"It's good. It's damn good and you know it."

He was beside her again at once, his hands grasping her waist. He turned her in his arms and tortured them both with another searing kiss that left them gasping and breathless. Essence released a cry. For a moment her body seemed to sing with joy as it felt his nearness and touch again. At that point Mark could have thrown her across the kitchen table and taken her right then. She pushed him away with all the strength she could muster up.

"Leave now."

Essence looked up into his eyes and caught a glint of anger shining in those golden depths. *Well, better anger than the desire that had been there moments before.*

"The only man that is going to raise my son is me and if that means I have to keep his mother away from anyone else, then so be it."

Before she could find the strength to shout, "Who the hell do you think you are?" Mark reached for his coat and left.

Long after he was gone, Essence sat on the couch, staring at the Christmas tree. The house was quiet. The lights were off except for the ones that were strung around the three-foot evergreen.

After he had left for Germany, she prayed nightly that Mark would come to his senses. However, as the weeks turned into months, she realized this was one fairytale that wasn't going to end *happily ever after.*

Everyday she had gone to the mailbox hoping for a letter that was never there. Every time the phone rang, she prayed for the call that never came. Eventually, it had become so unbearable, she had packed up and moved back in with her parents. Too hurt and distraught to return to the same elementary school where Kelly also worked, the place where everyone knew she had fallen in love with a military officer, the school where they would have all pitied her when they found out she was pregnant, Essence waited until Christmas break, then broke her contract with the school district. She spent the next several months deeply depressed and feeling sorry for herself. It wasn't until after Tyler was born that she finally pulled herself together for the sake of her son.

Her temper flared. Mark had a lot of nerve thinking he could just show up and start over where they had left off. She had not forgotten the last two years. She had not forgotten her broken heart.

She had refused to marry him because she had once loved him and she knew that she could love him again. But that meant taking a risk at getting hurt again and that scared her more than anything.

Mark was a handsome man and resisting him wouldn't be easy. It wasn't just his handsome face. As they spent those four unforgettable weeks together, she had found him to be quite impressive. He was a strong, no-nonsense sort, who was sharp and smart, very goal driven—traits she possessed herself and could appreciate. However, it was his personality that she had found herself initially drawn to. Mark had a funny little smile where one side curved up and sort of bent downward. She liked it when his eyes sparkled with laughter, especially when she made him do so. He had a nice laugh—full, deep and robust.

And damned if he wasn't the finest kisser. He had left her lips numb, then tingling, long after he had gone.

Frustrated and weary, Essence finally decided to go to bed. She slowly moved down the hall to her room and changed into her gown.

Climbing under the blankets, she ignored a strange ache lurking around her heart.

Mark took the long scenic route back to his parents' house, hoping that when he arrived they would have already turned in for the night. He wasn't in the mood for talking.

He still could not understand why Essence had refused his marriage proposal. He believed that marriage was a partnership, two people striving together to reach a common goal. For them, they shared a son and that alone was reason enough for him. So, what was the problem? He and Essence got along, well…at least they used to, and they would again if she would let her guard down and allow their relationship to evolve once more. Not to mention they were sexually compatible. What more could she possibly want? He scowled already knowing the answer to that question. *Love.*

Essence was being unreasonable. She believed love and marriage went hand in hand but, like the song goes, "What's love got to do with it?" Love was overrated.

A love ballad came blaring through the speakers and Mark reached down and changed to another radio station. He stopped turning the knob when a popular rap song came on the air.

He thought Essence would have been happy that he had proposed and that he was ready to share in the responsibilities of raising their son. But no-o-o! Outside of Tyler, Essence didn't want to have anything to do with him.

Maybe his pride bothered him and he wasn't used to women saying no. Women were drawn to his good looks, and they loved a man in uniform. He had always been the one to end the relationship, never the other way around. *Except for Carmen.* He frowned at that thought. The woman had done some serious damage to a brother all in the name of love. As a result, he refused to ever travel down the same treacherous road again.

Mark had fallen in love with Carmen James when he was twenty-five. He remembered meeting her like it was yesterday. He was leaving the mall when he saw her, an exquisite creature he thought to be perfect in every way. After one look, he knew he had to make her his wife. Theirs was a whirlwind affair and within a matter of weeks, they were engaged. It was a disaster from the start and ended as quickly as it had begun. After their break-up, Mark vowed he would never fall in love again, at least not head-over-hills like he did for Carmen. He never wanted to feel that consumed with anyone ever again.

He hardly thought of Carmen anymore. Nevertheless, if he allowed his thoughts to drift in that direction he found the pain, betrayal, and humiliation was still there. He refused to allow another woman to get that close.

Since Carmen, he'd never had a relationship that had lasted longer than a month. He traveled a great deal and preferred it that way. He didn't want a woman waiting for him to come home. He'd rather just be forgotten.

Only this time he was the one who couldn't forget. For two years, his mind had been filled with images of Essence Monroe and the two of them locked in a full body embrace.

He had arisen this morning in a fine state and with a serious hard-on. All he could think about was how beautiful a person Essence Monroe was. What man in his right mind would let such a fabulous woman go? She was intelligent, charming and independent, different from so many military wives who depended on their husbands for everything. Essence had been a single parent for over a year and had done a fabulous job raising their son on her own.

However, despite all those things, Mark had to admit that her independence scared him. Because now he wanted her to need him as he needed her.

*Need her?* He frowned. Mark Saunders needing a woman? No, that wasn't possible. All he needed was to be a prominent fixture in his son's life, even if that meant marriage. And he had better not forget that. Otherwise, if he wasn't careful he would find himself traveling down the same road he had gone with Carmen, and he wasn't about to let that happen. Now, if only he could forget the four weeks they shared, then he could keep his mind focused. Just as he had with any other woman whose bed he'd shared.

Only Essence wasn't just another notch in his belt. She was the mother of his child.

*And she is seeing someone else.*

He wasn't sure when he had ever felt as jealous as he had tonight. Essence was involved with someone and he didn't like it one bit. He knew he had no right, but that did nothing to change his feelings. What had he expected? For her to sit around twiddling her thumbs for two years? Of course she was going to see someone else. Nevertheless, even though Mark knew that, it didn't mean he had to like it and he sure as hell didn't plan to sit back and accept it. Essence and Tyler were his family and he damn sure wasn't going to let anyone else stand in his way.

# CHAPTER FIVE

Over the top of his newspaper, George Saunders watched his son staring out the window into the backyard as he sipped his coffee. It had been at least ten minutes since he'd last spoke.

Last night over a glass of rum, the two had talked extensively until the wee hours of the morning.

From the long look on Mark's face, George could tell that he was still dealing with conflicting emotions. During their discussion, he had detected a hint of censure in his son's tone. A muscle clenching at his jaw confirmed that he was still overwhelmed with confusion.

George had hoped that after being gone for two years his son would have gotten over the pain from his past and would open up his heart to love again. So far it didn't appear that time had healed any wounds.

*All because of one woman.*

While scratching his salt and pepper beard, he remembered the first time he met Carmen James. Even then he had known she spelled trouble. He had never seen a more beautiful woman with long black hair, large almond-shaped eyes and smooth golden skin. The girl knew exactly how to use those assets to her advantage. She had led his son around by the seat of his pants and, in a matter of weeks, she brought Mark to his knees. When she ran off with an Air Force pilot, George didn't think Mark would ever recover.

*Until now.*

Last night he saw something that he hadn't seen in his son in a long time—love for another human being. Mark had spoken nonstop about his baby boy.

"Son," he finally said drawing his attention.

Mark glanced over at his pop and smiled. "Yeah?"

"What's on your mind?"

His father narrowed his cocoa bean-colored eyes behind his glasses as if he was seeing more than Mark wanted him to. Mark wondered if his father had noticed the worry marring his features, especially the strain that had settled in around his eyes.

"Nothing in particular." *No one but Essence.* She had been on his mind all morning long. He woke up still feeling her lips on his. Nothing tasted like her...nothing. He thought he had forgotten the feel of her mouth, but it was not the case.

Mark wasn't sure how he had lived the last two years without grazing his mouth against her silky skin. He could still feel her arms wrapped around him, her fingers in his hair, her body molded to his, hear herr gasps and sighs or groans and moans as he licked her eager flesh. Dear God, just the memory aroused him. He had tortured himself with those thoughts for hours as he had pondered all night the possibility of making love to her again. In the car, on her table, in her bed, he didn't care where as long as he was buried deep inside of her, pumping in and out of her wet center.

"What are you planning to do today?" his father asked, breaking him from his erotic thoughts.

Shifting uncomfortably, Mark finally rose and removed a gallon of milk from the refrigerator. "I'm thinking about getting some Christmas shopping done this morning."

George creased his paper in half and sat it on the table. "Mind if I join you?"

He smiled. "I'd love it."

Mark reached for a box of cold cereal in a cabinet above the sink then returned to the table. Glancing across from him, he tore his thoughts away from Essence long enough to noticed how much his father had aged in two years. His hair was completely gray and his face had developed fine lines around his warm eyes and mouth. Last night he also noticed how much slower his father moved.

"When do I get to finally meet my grandson?"

"I'll arrange it with his mother so I can bring him over. I don't think she'll mind."

"Good, I can't wait."

Mark saw the happiness on his father's face. He knew his parents enjoyed being grandparents. His sister, Calaine, had finally granted them their wish when she had given birth to Dominique.

More and more, Mark realized it was a good thing he had returned. His parents were aging and he wouldn't fool himself into believing they would always be around. He wanted to spend as much time with them as he could, which was the principal reason why he had originally requested Ft. Mead, Maryland as his next duty station. Thank God he had. Now while he tried to convince Essence to marry him, he'd be close enough to see his parents and his son.

Mark looked toward the door as Dorlinda strolled into the room. "Good morning," she greeted in a cheerful voice.

Dressed in a purple sweat suit, she had spent most of the morning walking on her treadmill in the basement. She credited her good health to regular exercise and a sensible diet.

"Good morning, Mom."

She planted a kiss on the cheeks of both men, then strolled toward the refrigerator and removed a cup of yogurt. Moving toward the table, she noticed her son eating a bowl of her husband's sugar coated cereal and frowned. "What would you guys like for breakfast this morning?"

"Nothing for me," George replied.

"Me either, Mom. Cereal is fine," Mark said between chews.

She took the seat directly across from him, not even trying to hide her displeasure. George couldn't resist a knowing smile.

"Have you asked Essence to marry you yet?" Dorlinda asked as she removed the lid and dipped her spoon into the cup.

*Leave it to Mom not to beat around the bush about anything,* Mark thought with a wry smile. That was her style. He should have known when he had voiced the idea to her the other night she wasn't going to let it rest. He hesitated long enough to swallow. "Yes, and she declined."

She dismissed it with a wave. "Well, what do you expect? You've been gone two years without a word. Did you really think the girl was sitting around waiting for you to return?"

"No, but I didn't think she'd be this stubborn either."

"Give her time. She'll come around."

"Your mother's right. Love takes time," his father said.

*What is it with everyone's obsession with love?* The only thing Mark was obsessed with was being present in his son's life.

Essence pulled her car in the driveway and shut off the engine. *Lord, but it is good to be home,* she thought as she unfastened her seat belt and unlocked her car door. She was really looking forward to a quiet evening with her son. She planned to cook a light dinner, then play with Tyler until it was time for his bath.

*What if Mark drops by?* she pondered as she climbed out the car. Mentally, she didn't think she could handle being in his company three nights in a row. Emotionally, she felt overwhelmed. She'd had a difficult enough time recovering from their last brief encounter.

Before last night, Essence had been so certain that she had gotten over her emotional attachment to him. That is, before she made the mistake of letting him kiss her *again*. When he had pulled her into his arms, lowering his lips to hers and caressing her mouth, she had felt herself weakening. Even in contemplation, she could still feel the intimacy of his kiss. The encounter had her almost believing they might have a chance of making it together. He made her feel something she hadn't felt in years—desire. She had come so close to reconsidering and accepting his proposal of marriage. It was at that moment she had to fight her own personal battle of physical restraint. She reminded herself that the last time she had allowed herself to believe in fairytales, the heartache that followed was almost more than she could endure. Thank goodness her momma hadn't raise a dummy, she thought as she stuck her key in the door. She had come to her senses long before she had given in to the passion and allowed Mark to carry her off to her bed and make love to her.

Essence had barely stepped into the house, when a wonderful smell coming from the kitchen met her in the foyer. She had only had a tuna sandwich and a bottle of water for lunch. Removing her coat, she hung it on the coat rack and moved toward the kitchen.

She could honestly say she wasn't disappointed that Tyler's babysitter had cooked. On numerous occasions, while Tyler was napping, Liz would prepare dinner for her family and she always made extra for Essence.

"Liz, whatever you're making smells heavenly."

"I agree," the older woman said before Essence stepped fully inside the kitchen. "Unfortunately, I didn't make it."

Essence stopped in her tracks, going still with anger. "Mark."

Standing in front of the stove, he glanced over his shoulder and winked. "Welcome home, sweetheart."

His beautiful smile caused her pulse to skitter. "What are you doing here?"

"I'm showing off my culinary skills in your kitchen," he said. His back was to her while he stirred something in a pan.

"How was your day, dear?" Liz glanced up at her with motherly interest.

"I spent most of the day making Christmas ornaments with my students and the other half practicing for the Christmas assembly next week." She crouched down and kissed Tyler on the cheek. He was in his high chair making excited noises while Liz fed him his dinner.

Rising, Essence glanced over at the stove again. "Mark, you still have not answered my question. Why are you here?"

Liz glanced from Essence to Mark and back to her employer again, feeling a heat that wasn't radiating from the stove. "I guess I'm partly to blame. Mark had called and asked if he could drop by and I didn't see any harm." She shrugged. "You said so yourself this morning that Tyler's father was home for the holiday. Quite naturally, he would want to spend that time with his son."

Essence hated being reminded of the conversation they'd had. However, she couldn't be angry with Liz. Mark was to blame and she would deal with him later. "It's all right, Liz. I'm sure Mark charmed his way in."

Leaning back against the counter, Mark chuckled. "Not hardly. Liz read me my rights before she'd let me in the door."

"I most certainly did," Liz said, joining in with his laughter. "Nevertheless, he is the child's father. I will never deny a man his child."

Now Essence looked irritated, impatient. "Yes, he is Tyler's father. But this is my home, Mark."

"And my son's."

"I didn't invite you here."

"He did. Isn't that right, Tyler?" Mark asked. Pushing away from the counter, he leaned down to the baby. Tyler grabbed his face and rubbed peas across his cheeks.

Seeing the look on Mark's face, Essence couldn't resist a laugh. Liz wiped his hands, also finding the entire scene quite amusing.

Essence ruffled Tyler's hair, loving his infectious giggles as he started blowing bubbles. "Good for you, sweetheart."

Mark joined in. The sound of his laughter was deep, warm and rich, then with an incredibly sexy grin, he turned back to the stove. He reached for an oven mitt and removed a batch of golden brown biscuits.

"All gone sweetheart." Liz told Tyler as she gave him the last spoonful of macaroni and cheese." With an amused sigh, Liz rose and pushed her chair back to the table. "I'll see you in the morning," she said.

"No!" Essence said far too quickly. She reiterated calmly, "Liz, you don't have to leave so soon."

"Oh, yes I do." A mysterious smile softened her mouth. Liz moved over to the counter where Mark had prepared a large pan covered in aluminum foil for her to take home. "Thanks so much for dinner."

"Any time." He winked.

Essence swore she saw a sly glint in Liz's eyes when she added, "Glad you're finally home." She rolled her eyes. The look exchanged between the two was as if they shared a secret.

Essence knew good and well a scheming mind lurked behind that innocent-little-old-lady look. Liz had tried on several occasions to fix her up with one relative after another.

"Are you trying to impress me?" she asked Mark after Liz was gone.

Their gazes met, fusing as he studied her through lowered lashes. "No, but if my cooking is what it'll take to get you to relax around me then…" he purposely allowed his voice to trail off.

"I am relaxed," she snapped.

Mark moved over to her and before she knew what he was doing, he pushed his hands into the soft tangle of her curls. "No you're not. However, you do look very nice today."

She stood stiff as a board trying to fight the powerful tremor flowing through her veins. "Don't touch me."

He chuckled. "You're supposed to say thank you when someone compliments you."

"You're supposed to leave me alone. There will be no repeat of last night."

He nodded. "I understand completely. Now is not a good time."

She stepped back away from him. "Not now, not ever. You are here for Tyler and Tyler only."

Crossing his arms over his chest, he angled his head. "Are you daring me?"

"I'm setting boundaries."

"Boundaries are made to be broken."

"Not this one. I'm already involved with someone."

Mark chuckled again. "The man is a cop out; just another way to hide your true feelings."

She felt a headache coming on. She pinched the bridge of her nose with a thumb and forefinger. Would this nightmare ever end?

"How would you know? You've never even met him."

"I don't need to. Your kiss told it all. If you truly cared for him you wouldn't have kissed me with such passion."

She glared at him wishing she could tell him that she was indeed in love with Malcolm. Maybe then Mark would leave her alone, but she had never been any good at lying. "My love life is none of your business. Now if you'll excuse me, I was looking forward to a quiet evening *alone*."

Essence kicked off her heels and left them under the kitchen table. She went over to Tyler, lifting him out of his high chair and cuddled him close. "Your Daddy thinks he can just come over whenever he wants. Well, he can't," she mumbled as if Mark was no longer standing there.

He moved away from the stove and wiped his hands on a towel. "I'm on leave, Essence. I have nothing to do all day while my son is here with a baby sitter. What's wrong with me getting to know Tyler? I can already tell he likes being around his Daddy."

"Da Da."

Essence gasped. "Oh my God! He called you Daddy!"

Mark's expression stilled and Essence could tell he was experiencing the same feeling she had felt the first time Tyler had called her *Ma Ma*.

Her mood softened and she found herself grinning at his stunned expression. "I guess I can't argue with that. It seems that Tyler likes spending time with his Daddy, too."

"Da Da."

Closing his eyes, Mark let out his breath slowly. He stepped forward gripped by emotion when he leaned down and kissed his son on the cheek. "Thanks, Champ."

Tipping her head to one side, Essence watched Mark. When he noticed, they stood and grinned at each other foolishly for several seconds before she tore her eyes away. Their son had removed the tension in the room. Giving in for the moment, she took a seat at the table with Tyler, watching Mark chop vegetables for a salad. Mark resumed cooking and she noticed how at ease he was in the kitchen. "I didn't know you could cook."

"There's a lot you don't know about me," he said without turning around. He reached for a pot from the stove and poured steaming hot pasta into a strainer. "My mom insisted that I learn how to cook when I was in grade school."

"Really?" she said, as she reached down to retrieve a carrot stick. She handed Tyler a piece of tomato.

"Yep. Tuesday's were my night to cook. I would spend hours pouring over cookbooks trying to plan a meal. Then I had to prepare a grocery list and go shopping with my mom for all of the ingredients. Every week I tried to out do Kelly."

"That sounds like a lot of fun."

"And a lot of work," He paused and smiled with fond memories. "But it paid off. Now I like to show off whenever the opportunity arises."

"Well I have never been any good at cooking."

"Oh, I haven't forgotten." His eyes sparkled with a teasing light.

Essence groaned at the reminder of a time she had tried to impress him in the kitchen. Mark had arrived just as the fire truck was leaving. "I can honestly say I tried," she replied with a giggle.

Curiosity got the better of her and Essence rose, moving to the other side of the counter where Mark was stirring a red sauce that was bubbling with flavor.

Essence snatched a piece of fried catfish draining on a paper towel while he worked on the pasta. Popping a chunk into her mouth, she moaned, "Oh, man."

"Good?" he asked with a quick glance.

"Incredible. Fish is my favorite."

"I know."

She paused to look up at him. Was there anything he hadn't forgotten?

*He forgot about me.*

"Why don't you go change into something more comfortable," Mark suggested.

Nodding she took a step away then stopped to look back at him. Mark moved around in her kitchen as if he'd always been there. But the fact that he had invited himself back into her life, her home, made it perfectly clear he wasn't going to be pushed out. If he was here for Tyler, she'd never deny him. But Essence had a sneaking suspicion Mark had a plan she'd have a tough time fighting. He was trying to make himself indispensable.

She sighed. Right now, she was tired and hungry. So if he wanted to cook, let him, she thought.

"Go on, Essence." He turned and looked her way.

As she left the kitchen and headed to the bedroom with Tyler, Essence couldn't help notice how he gurgled loudly for his daddy.

Mark watched her leave the room and groaned under his breath as his gaze lingered on the rounded curves of Essence's swaying hips. He adored the way she looked: businesslike, confident and sexy. His body reacted to her lush figure. Everything about her teased him, from her full breasts to her round hips. He was glad she had left when she did because his arousal had become quite evident.

He knew she would be angry to find him here in her house, invading her space. Mark also knew that by doing something nice, like cooking, she was less likely to bite his head off. She was so stubborn he was tempted to bend her over one knee. *Wasn't her spirit one of the many things that had drawn you to her in the first place?*

He reached into a cabinet next to the sink and removed two

plates. Reaching for the strainer, he put pasta on each, then ladled a generous helping of sauce on top.

Mark knew he was being a little devious, but after the way Essence had reacted yesterday, he knew she'd try her best to keep him out of her life. That scenario wouldn't work because he wanted in and nothing was going to stop him. He told himself it was so he could be with his son, that he'd already missed too much of his life and needed to catch up. However, the truth had much more to do with Tyler's mom.

He used his son as an excuse, but that was only half his dilemma. He felt an overwhelming need to make Essence's his. Lust. Although it had been a long time since he'd been with a woman, two years to be exact, he wasn't sure if that was the sole reason. He nodded his head. That's it. Celibacy. It certainly couldn't be anything else.

However, while he prepared a tossed salad, he found himself contemplating the possibilities even further. He didn't like it. He didn't like it at all. The only other woman he had felt this drawn to was Carmen and he refused to allow another woman to have that kind of power over him.

Last night after he had cleaned the kitchen and moved to the living room, he had stopped in his tracks when he found Essence fast asleep. The flames from the fireplace danced across her face, highlighting the gold tones of her skin. Her breasts rose and fell with her breathing. He felt a stirring within his chest that might have been his heart. But how would he know? Other than Carmen, he never allowed another woman in his life to affect him emotionally. He never stuck around long enough for the relationship to come to that. He never felt the need or the desire. Until now. Or did he?

He didn't like his weakness, nor did he want to act on his desire unless he knew for certain she was willing to accept the terms. But he wasn't sure how long he could remain strong in her presence, emotionally and physically.

Fifteen minutes later he still hadn't come up with an explanation when he heard footsteps coming down the hall. Shaking away the tormenting thoughts, he carried their plates over to the table.

Essence stopped as soon as she stepped into the kitchen with Tyler on her hip. "Everything looks great."

"Thanks."

She moved toward the refrigerator and removed a bottle off the shelf. In soft lounging pants and a gray long sleeve shirt, she looked delectable. Her hair was pulled up in a simple ponytail, making her appear young and vulnerable. Tyler was growing sleepy and he rested his head on his mother's shoulder.

Mark felt a swell of something close to pride as he watched her warm his bottle. Essence whispered to Tyler, rocking him gently. She had him already bathed and dressed for bed.

Mark didn't want his son to be sleepy. He had already missed so much. *Missed so much from both of them*, he thought. He missed out on being the first one to know about the baby. He missed seeing Essence grown round with their child, and being there to comfort her when she was scared. He knew it sounded selfish, but as far as he was concerned he'd already missed sixteen months of seeing him grow up. He didn't want to miss another minute.

Essence handed Tyler his bottle and he accepted it eagerly.

"Hungry?" Mark asked.

She nodded. "Yes, but let me feed him first, then I'll eat."

Mark held out his arms. "Here, give him to me."

"Aren't you going to eat?" she asked.

"Later." He took his son from her. "Now sit before you insult the cook."

Essence's heart did a flip when Tyler curled against his father with a content sigh. They both took a seat and while Mark held their son, he encouraged Essence to eat before her food grew cold. She reached for her fork and sampled the red sauce. It was heavenly.

"Oh, Mark," she moaned. "This is fabulous."

Mark cleared his throat and shifted uncomfortably on the seat. She had no idea what that sound did to him. He envisioned her lying beneath him with him between her thighs.

Tyler lifted his head to stare at him. Wide eyes skimmed his face, trying to understand who he was and why he was here. Mark smiled then kissed him. Satisfied with that, Tyler laid his head back against his chest.

Mark thought that nothing in this world would ever touch him as deeply as the feel of his child in his arms, trusting him to love and to protect him.

"Aren't you having any food?" Essence asked. "I can fix you a plate. At least you can eat with your right hand."

"In a few minutes. Right now I'm enjoying holding my son."

Essence grinned knowingly. Tyler looked so small against Mark's wide muscled chest. The arm cradling him was almost longer than his entire body.

When he met her stare, Mark's eyes were brimmed with tenderness and love. "I would never have imagined I could fall in love with him so fast."

"Neither did I," she said, and felt a catch in her throat.

It warmed her heart that he had. Mark could have easily shunned his responsibilities or have done the less than honorable thing and offered to pay child support without having once laid eyes on his son. Either reaction would have made Essence hate Mark. Although she had denied him the first sixteen months of his life, Mark had always been welcome to be a part of Tyler's life. He just didn't know it.

Essence brought the pasta to her lips, savoring the flavor while she watched Mark shift Tyler comfortably in the crook of his arm. Tyler opened his eyes briefly then, feeling safe, closed them again. It appeared that Mark had already made an impact on his life. A bond between father and son had already been forged...a strong bond that she could never put a wedge between. She thought she would have been jealous. After all, she had been raising Tyler alone since he had arrived. But she wasn't. In fact, despite all the animosity and ill feelings she felt about Mark's rejecting her, she wished that he had been there to share those precious moments, such as his first word, his first tooth, and his very first unaided step.

Essence swallowed hard and bit back tears. Looking down at her plate she tried to pull her emotions under control. She was confused and struggling with her decision not to marry Mark. Essence wondered if maybe she was making a terrible mistake. She wanted love, but did she want it at the expense of depriving her son the opportunity to be raised by his father on a permanent full-time basis?

As she chewed her food, Mark could tell something was wrong with Essence. Her head was lowered and she was extremely quiet. He wanted to offer her comfort for whatever was bothering her, but just didn't want to take the chance of her biting his head off. Since Tyler had called him daddy, the two of them had been getting along just fine and he didn't want to ruin that.

"Tell me about your students, Ms. Monroe."

When Essence looked up, Mark saw a trace of sadness she tried to hide behind a smile.

Propping an elbow on the table she rested her chin in her cupped hand. "Well...I'm still teaching third grade even though I'm working for a different school district. This year I have a very special blend of students."

"How so?"

"I have two sets of identical twins." Her eyes danced with pride.

"Two?"

She nodded and giggled. "Donnell and Ronnell, and Gretchen and Gertrude. The boys I can tell apart because Donnell is a few inches shorter than his brother. The girls, however, are hard to distinguish unless they are both in front of my face," she said between chews. "They are both blonde with blue eyes and speak with a lisp. Thank heavens Gretchen has a slight gap between her two front teeth, which is the only way I can separate the two."

"I thought they usually separate twins."

Essence paused as if considering that for a moment. "They do, but their mother asked if her daughters could be together. Apparently, the two were separated shortly after birth. Their parents went through a bitter divorce and the judge gave each parent custody of one child."

Mark's brow quirked. "You've got to be joking."

She shook her head and swallowed. "I'm afraid not. The father moved to another country just to keep his ex-wife from ever seeing Gretchen again. It wasn't until the twins were five, that he was involved in a fatal car accident. The girls were reunited shortly thereafter."

"What an incredible story."

"I thought so," Essence agreed, as she reached for her glass of ice tea that had watered down considerably.

Mark couldn't believe he felt a since of relief at the death of the selfish man. Who could keep a child away from his mother or father? He glanced up at Essence. She hadn't intentionally kept him from his son, he told himself. That he was now certain.

Mark finally agreed to a plate of food. Essence also fixed herself a second helping. They engaged in light chitchat and within the next half hour, Tyler drifted off. Mark removed the bottle from his mouth and sat it on the table next to his plate. However, he did not move to put him in his bed. Instead, he reached up and used the corner of his napkin to dab traces of milk from Tyler's mouth.

"Let me ask you something," Essence began. "What would you have done if you had known I was pregnant?"

Her question surprised him. Nonetheless, he was pleased she had brought up the topic on her own. She had asked the question calmly, yet he sensed her intensity as she focused on his reply.

"I would have come home and married you."

"That's a nice thought, but I still wouldn't have married you."

"I'd have convinced you to marry me."

"It wouldn't have worked." She gave him a half smile. "It has nothing to do with you. I think you are great with your son. It has to do with what I want."

"So, tell me what will it take to convince you that I sincerely want to marry you?"

"Love," she replied, hesitantly.

Mark grew quiet. She was still determined to put love before their child's well being. He just couldn't understand it.

As if reading his mind, she added, "I can't marry a man for the sake of a child."

"Do you deny that we are good together?"

"There is no question of sexual compatibility, however I want more than that. Now, can you please pass me the pepper?" Her tone indicated an end to the discussion but Mark wasn't ready to stop. He hadn't started the conversation, she had. Nevertheless, what she had said was true. During the four weeks the two of them had spent together, they had spent more time in the bed than out. They had never gotten the chance to really know one another. However, Mark doubted time would have changed his feelings.

When he spoke again, his deep voice held an uncharacteristic cynical note. "People use the word love too much. Don't you realize that people marry everyday for love and nine times out of ten it doesn't last?"

She shrugged a delicate shoulder. "True, but it's a foundation. Without love what is there?"

"A mutual commitment to raising our child." When she didn't answer, he added, "I know it would work if you'd give us a chance," he said with a hopeful expression. "My son needs me in his life."

"I agree. Tyler does, but his mother doesn't."

Mark settled back in the chair, disappointed. Her words had hit him far below the belt. He released a long overdue sigh. Essence was going to be one tough cookie to crack.

Tyler fussed. Mark pushed away from the table and rose. "I'll put him down," he said when she tried to reach for him.

She nodded.

Mark turned and walked down the hall. He wondered if he was overreacting. He knew he was pushing her and couldn't help it. The longer his son didn't have his name, the angrier he grew. He tried to see reason, but one look at his child and he couldn't.

Growing up, he had several friends that came from single parent homes. He remembered the baseball games when his father was there and theirs were not and the look of sadness on their faces. He never wanted Tyler to be subjected to that.

He lowered Tyler in the crib, and pulled the cover up to his chin. Staring down at his precious face, he saw one thing and one thing only—his future.

He was frustrated because he didn't know what approach to use on Essence. Badgering didn't help. Pretending it didn't matter would drive him up the wall. He was leaving in less than four weeks and still nothing had been resolved.

Staring out the window in the corner of his room, he watched snow flurries dance around his windowsill. There was no accumulation predicted, but as soon as there was, he was buying a sled and heading to the park with his son.

*My son.*

What was he going to do if he couldn't see his adorable face every-day? He shook that thought away. Right now that possibility wasn't even an option.

He returned to the living room to find that Essence had turned on the Christmas lights around the windows and on her small tree. Leaning against the wall, he watched as she bent over to turn on the stereo, giving him an unobstructed view of her rear. He had to fight images of the two of them in the shower and entering her from behind. Thoughts of their past sexual relationship were dangerous.

Essence tuned into a local radio station that was playing R&B Christmas songs. He felt the music soothing the rough edges of his mood.

"I'll back off if you want," he finally said.

Essence's head jerked up. "What?"

"I'll stop pestering you to marry me." *For now*, he thought. "But I want to be in Tyler's life and on that I'm not budging."

Essence's gaze locked into his. She nodded. "Okay."

His golden eyes glittered in the shadow of the dim lights. "Good."

Essence stood up straight pulling her shoulders back. Unaware that the motion brought Mark's gaze to the outlines of her bare breasts pushing against the cotton fabric, he swallowed. She wasn't wearing a bra and her nipples had hardened.

"Why don't you come over during the day?" she suggested.

He forced his eyes to her face. Her comment was easy to decipher, come over when the sitter was here, while Essence was at work. "You're setting limits."

He walked slowly toward her and Essence felt her heartbeat quicken at the strange unsettling light in his eyes.

"No, it's just that—"

"You can't handle being near me?" he interrupted. "Afraid you'll like it?" He knowingly took another step closer.

"Of course I can handle it."

"Good, because I have four weeks leave and this is the only place I plan to be."

Her traitorous heart fluttered at the possibility of getting to spend another four weeks with him.

Mark walked directly to her and stopped just an inch or so before actually touching her. She stared up at him, studying the strong lines of his jaw, the stubble on his chin, his wide soft mouth. Everything in her ached for him to reach out, grab hold of her and pull her into his arms. Bringing a hand to the back of her neck, she stepped back and sighed.

It would be a disaster to give in to her desire, to let old memories and rekindled yearning team up to weaken her resolve. She couldn't let him kiss her again. And yet as she thought of him she tingled with awareness that it was exactly what she wanted him to do and more. She took another step backwards before she did something stupid like ask him to make love to her.

His gaze roamed over her beautiful face, noticing her apprehensions. "Are you all right?" He smiled at her, yet his gaze looked serious, questioning.

"I'm fine," she finally managed to say. "Just tired, that's all." It was impossible to think clearly when he was around.

"That's because you've been doing it alone for too long. Let me help you."

A long silence passed between them as he cupped her cheek and rubbed a thumb back and forth across her jaw. He was standing so close she could count every dark lash framing his eyes, every hair blanketing his jaw.

"I'll be here tomorrow."

She shook her head. "You don't have to do that."

"I didn't say I had to," he said softly. "I said I'd be here." He flashed her a sexy stubborn grin.

She read the determination in his golden eyes and knew even before she started arguing with him, she would lose.

"Thanks," she said sincerely. Essence squeezed her eyes shut, overcome by emotion. Mark loved his son. What more could she ask for? And when she felt Mark's strong arms circle her shoulders, she simply leaned into his strength, giving a quiet thanks he was there.

"You don't have to be alone anymore," he told her.

She felt the brush of his breath across the top of her head. "I know and I thank you."

He pulled back a bit and when she looked up at him, she saw a slight frown, tugging at his lips.

"You don't need to keep thanking me. Tyler is my son also."

"But—"

"No buts," he interrupted.

She felt his arm tighten around his waist. "Ok."

While she was staring up at him, Mark's frown vanished, and was replaced by a warm grin. She watched his eyes. Desire, hunger, and compassion flit across their surface and her insides twisted. "I'm glad you're home."

He nodded slowly, keeping his gaze locked on her upturned face, admiring her flawless complexion. "Good. Because the only reason why I'm here is because here is where I want to be."

One corner of his mouth twitched up into a mere shadow of the full glory that was his high voltage grin and even that caused heat to pour through her vein.

Turning her head, she laid it on his firm chest and listened to the steady sounds of his heart beating against her cheek. Mark's chin rested lightly atop her head as he nestled her in his arms. She closed her eyes, inhaled his strong masculine scent and surrendered to his caring and protective embrace. The heat of his body flowed into hers. He touched her, stroking her arm tenderly up and down, making her shiver with pleasure. As much as she fought it, regardless if she never admitted it, she was happy to share the love of her son with his father. It was such a relief to know that even though they would never be anything more than friends, he was willing to take part in his son's life, not because of obligation, but because of an emotional attachment.

What was happening to her? For years, she struggled against these feelings and now she was allowing them to surface and run out of control. What was she going to do? Did she really have the willpower to do anything about it?

Her mind was telling her it was too soon, but her body was urging her to give into her desires. A sigh broke and she did the only thing she knew she could do. She forced herself to step away from his embrace.

Looking up at his questioning expression, she ignored her desire to kiss him and forced a smile. "How about some butter pecan ice cream for dessert?"

Mark nodded, and together they walked back into the kitchen.

His fingers tensed on the steering wheel as he pulled up to the house and shut off the engine. He didn't get out. His mind was still tripping over ways to get into his son's life, and his mother's.

When Mark had taken Essence in his arms, he was instantly aware of the slenderness of her waist and the warmth of her hips. Burning heat had rushed through his body and settled at his loins. He wanted to make love to her all through the night, but he knew better than to even try and kiss her again. Essence was beginning to trust him and he didn't want to blow it.

He just hadn't realized how much he had missed her. How much he needed to be with her...until now. The desire he felt for her was just as strong, possibly even stronger, than it had been two years ago. Never in his thirty years had he ever been so completely aware of a woman.

*Man*, he thought, rubbing his face. Essence Monroe didn't look like a mother. He swallowed hard as he imagined her belly swollen with his baby, and when he did, something sparked inside him. Longing? Did he want her in his life because of the baby?

He checked that thought off the list in an instant. He'd done nothing but think about her for months, long before he even knew Tyler existed. If only he had known about his child. It would have changed so much. *Hell. Look at the flip side.* He would have gone nuts if he'd known Essence was carrying his child. He would have wanted to be there with her, for her. He'd have done anything for that chance, even ended his tour early.

But dammit to hell, he had missed it all.

Sighing with resignation, he left the car and headed into the house. Mark didn't notice his mother sitting on the couch in front of the television. He didn't notice that she was watching his favorite program *Law and Order.* All he saw was Essence, holding his son to her breast, stroking his little spine.

Tyler was his son. His flesh and blood. And he was going to give him everything he'd had…including his name.

# CHAPTER SIX

"Is something wrong?" Essence asked. She had noticed all through dinner that Mark had become increasingly quiet.

He had taken her to a fancy restaurant on the Baltimore Harbor and had asked her to dress in her best outfit. There was something he wanted to tell her. She had a gut feeling about it. She had waited all through dinner and she couldn't wait any longer.

As if he could read her mind, Mark reached across the table, and grasped her hands. He raised his head to meet her eager gaze as he replied, "There's a plane leaving Dover Air Force Base in the morning. I have orders to be on it."

"What! B-but I thought you had until the end of the week."

"I thought I did too, but things have changed."

Essence dropped her eyes so he wouldn't see the tears that were beginning to cloud her vision, but Mark placed a hand under her chin and raised her eyes to meet his again.

"Hey..." he gave her a wide grin, trying to ease the moment, "...we still have tonight."

Swallowing, Essence forced a smile that she didn't feel.

Their waiter returned with two slices of strawberry cheesecake. When he left, she reached for her fork and shoveled a large bite in her mouth.

She was noticeably quiet and it wasn't long before Mark lowered his fork and leaned across the table. "Just because I'm leaving doesn't mean we can't remain friends."

Following a slight hesitation, she found the nerve to ask, "Is that all I am to you?"

*Mark leaned back in his seat then dragged a hand across his face before answering, "Essence, I've tried to be as honest as I possibly can. I'm not looking for a relationship. I travel a great deal so my job makes it almost impossible to be in any one place for any length of time."*

*She nodded and forced a lump down her throat. She was dying inside, but there was no way in the world she was going to let Mark see her fall apart. "You don't have to explain. I understand perfectly well. Long distance relationships never work."*

*"I agree." He grinned as he extended his hand. "Friends?"*

Essence was awakened by the sound of sharp knocking on her front door. Her bedroom was dark and the clock on the nightstand showed it was barely five-thirty in the morning. Who could be knocking at her door this early?

She slowly climbed out the bed. Slipping into her robe, she tied it tightly around her waist, then moved to the door and looked through the peephole. It was Mark. What was he doing here?

She turned the lock and cracked the door open. "Mark?"

"Good morning. I hope I didn't wake Tyler."

*What about waking me?* She shook her head. "No, although he'll be up shortly. Why are you here?"

"Did you forget I was coming to spend the day with Tyler?"

When Mark said he would be by in the morning, she had no idea he meant this early in the morning. However, Essence was certain she had made it clear he was to come over *after* she had left for work. "I said to come over when Liz is here."

"And I told you, you are setting limitations. Besides…Liz isn't coming." He lightly pushed on the door. Essence stepped back and allowed him to enter.

"Isn't coming?" she repeated, gasping. "Why not?"

He shrugged out of his jacket and hung it on the rack. "Because

I gave her the holiday off."

"How could you do that?"

"I told you I plan to spend all my time with my son and I meant it."

She shook her head. "You had no right."

"Yes, I did. I paid her plus gave her a nice Christmas bonus."

"I can't believe you!"

Mark shrugged his broad shoulders. "No point in arguing about it now. Liz wanted to spend time with her daughter and since I don't have anything else to do for the next couple of weeks, I told her to go."

"She never said anything to me about wanting to visit her daughter." Liz's daughter and her family lived in Denver.

"Because she knew you needed her here to help with Tyler."

That wasn't true. She could have asked her sister or even her mother to watch him. Besides, after next week, she would be off for the Christmas holiday and wouldn't return until the day after the New Year.

Liz hadn't taken a day off since she'd started watching Tyler. Even when Essence made the suggestion, Liz insisted she didn't need the time off, but if she did, she would ask. Only she hadn't. Essence frowned. They were going to have a long talk when she returned. Liz was in cahoots with Mark and she didn't like it one bit.

Essence took a deep breath. It was much too late to argue. "I guess I don't have much of a choice."

"Nope. Now if you'd excuse me I hear someone waking up." With nothing further to say, he dropped a kiss to her cheek and strolled down the hall.

Essence didn't know if she should yell or be grateful. She raised her hand to her cheek where he had kissed her and unconsciously her lips curled into a faint smile.

*What am I going to do with him?* Mark definitely had a mind of his own. Shaking the thought, she put on a pot of coffee then returned to her room.

Her alarm wasn't scheduled to go off for another ten minutes. She yawned then headed toward the master bathroom. *Might as well get my shower out the way.*

The previous owner had a garden tub installed. It was one of the things that had drawn her to the five-year-old house. With a toddler, she didn't get to utilize her tub as often as she liked, but when she did it was heavenly.

Moving to a separate shower stall, she pushed open the sliding glass door and turned on the hot water. While the water heated, she washed her face and brushed her teeth, then stripped and climbed into the shower.

While she lathered her body, she thought about how well behaved Mark had been last night. Not once had he tried to kiss her.

After dessert, he insisted on loading the dishwasher while she kicked up her feet and watched "Miracle on 34th Street." As soon as he was done cleaning the kitchen, he had joined her. Essence thought she would have been anxious for him to leave, but instead she had enjoyed his company. They spent a little better than an hour discussing Tyler's future. Mark planned to open a savings account for him. Essence told him about the college plan she had started when he was only a few days old.

She reached for her jasmine body wash and squirted some on a towel, then lathered her body. She rubbed across her nipples and they hardened on contact. She had little control over her body these days. Every time she thought of Mark, her breasts had that kind of reaction.

When the movie had ended, she had pulled out several picture albums from the top shelf of her closet. They spent the next several hours, recanting the last sixteen months of Tyler's life. Mark listened to everything she had to say, from carrying him for nine months, up until the day before he walked back into her life. From the somber expression on Mark's face, she could tell it bothered him deeply that he hadn't been there. He was so interested in their son's life that it brought tears to her eyes. If she hadn't known before how wonderful and amazing Mark was, she definitely knew it now. Tyler was lucky to have him as a father.

Stepping forward, she allowed the warm water to spray across her face while she cleaned her ears. She didn't want to speculate on her feelings for him. Not yet. She was afraid that she was beginning to care about Mark again and she wasn't quite sure yet if she was ready for that.

Turning off the water, she slid open the door and reached for a large bath towel. As she strolled into her bedroom, Mark's laughter coming from across the hall, drew her attention. The deep, genuine sound caused her to shiver with awareness. Hearing Tyler laugh along with him, caused her to join in. *The men in my life.* That was what Mark was, whether she liked it or not.

Essence moved to her closet and searched through the hangers. She finally decided on a simple brown suit and carried it over to her bed. Reaching for a bottle of scented lotion, she then spread it generously over her body. Essence was smiling as she realized this was the first morning she'd had in months to take her time getting ready for work. Usually she balanced Tyler with one arm while she tried to use a curling iron with the other. Having Mark around was definitely proving to be an asset. If she agreed to marry him, they could share the responsibilities of raising him together. But that wasn't going to happen. She wondered what Mark would say when he finally realized she wasn't going to change her mind.

He wasn't going anywhere until Uncle Sam called him home, but even then, no matter how near or far, he would always be a part of her life. She just wasn't sure yet how involved she wanted him to be. Sure he had asked her to marry him, but she wasn't going to fool herself into thinking it meant anything beyond obligation. So if she didn't marry him, which she wasn't even considering, how would they both manage being in Tyler's life? Her son had every right to have his father around. Mark had just as much right as she had. How would they manage it? That was one question she didn't know how to answer.

Mark fastened a diaper to Tyler's little bottom, then pulled his footed pajamas up to his waist and fastened them to his pajama top. Tyler squealed when he lowered him onto the floor. Instantly, he dashed for the door and down the hall. Mark, surprised at how fast he could move, picked up the soiled diaper and followed close behind.

He loved time like this with his son. These were the days that he would always hold dear to his heart.

As they neared the kitchen, he scooped Tyler into his arms, laughing and blowing bubbles as he secured him in his high chair.

"Well, let's see what's for breakfast this morning." He reached into the cabinet for a box of instant oatmeal. In the meantime, he handed Tyler a banana to occupy his time.

He found a small pot at the bottom of the stove, filled it with water and placed it on the stove. The smell of fresh brewed Hazelnut coffee filled the air. He removed a mug from the cabinet and filled it.

"Why don't we fix your Mommy something to eat," he suggested.

"Ma Ma!" Tyler squealed in agreement.

Mark reached into the refrigerator, pulled out a carton of eggs and a few vegetables and commenced to make two omelets.

Reaching back into the cabinet, he removed a can of juice and filled Tyler's cup and handed it to him. The little tike quickly forgot about the banana he had smashed on the tray and eagerly brought his own personal drink cup to his lips. Mark took a sip from his mug, then lowered it onto the counter and reached for a knife.

While he chopped onions, green peppers and tomatoes, he thought how much he felt part of a family. Not that he hadn't felt part of one before. However, this was different from being part of the Saunders family. This was his son.

Last night, Essence had spent hours recanting the past two years and he felt more connected to her than he had ever felt before. She proved to be a beautiful woman inside and out and the perfect mother for his child.

He added the vegetables to the skillet, sautéed them, and cracked four eggs in a bowl. By the time he poured cereal in the boiling water, the vegetables were nice and tender. He poured in half of the scrambled eggs. By the time Essence walked into the room, he had slid the second omelet on a plate.

"Good morning, sweetheart."

Thinking she might have been speaking to him, Mark swung around from the stove to find Essence smiling down at Tyler.

She leaned over and kissed him on the forehead. "How is my darling this morning?"

"Ma Ma," he cooed.

After giving him another kiss, she moved to the cabinet, removed a mug and carried it over to the coffee pot and reached for the carafe.

She glanced at him. "Would you like a cup?"

Mark turned, carrying both plates to the table. "I already have a cup, but some sweetener would be nice."

She gasped. "Those are beautiful."

"You're beautiful." Actually, that was an understatement.

She found herself smiling as she reached for the last canister on the end and removed two sweetener packages.

"Go ahead and eat while I feed Tyler his breakfast."

She shook her head. "Why don't you eat and I'll feed him?"

"Because you have to work today and I don't." He pulled out a chair and signaled for her to sit.

Essence obeyed. She appeared amused as she reached for the fork dangling in his hand.

Tyler became fussy and Mark quickly prepared him a bowl of hot cereal and poured sugar and cold milk over it.

"I think you better hurry. Tyler doesn't like to be kept waiting."

Mark didn't miss the amused expression still on her face. He pulled a chair in front of Tyler and took a seat.

Essence took a sip of her coffee, savoring the flavor. Turning sideways in her chair, she asked, "What do you have planned for today?"

"Well, I think I am going to play it by ear," he said as he spooned the cereal in Tyler's awaiting mouth. "Maybe go to the mall, pick up some chicks. What do you say, Champ?"

He squealed in agreement.

Essence giggled, then dug into her eggs and watched as Mark fed their hungry son.

Mark tried not to stare at her legs that were right before his eyes. However, they were there and he was a man who loved beautiful legs. She wore natural colored pantyhose and had chocolate pumps on her feet. He loved the things pumps did to a woman's legs.

"Are you sure you can handle him by yourself?"

With a smirk, he raised his right hand. "Scout's honor."

With reluctance, Essence went over Tyler's schedule as she ate.

Essence hesitated. "…He usually goes back to sleep around ten thirty. And if he cries, he probably wants his rabbit, Floppy. Give him a bottle, but make sure it's water. Make sure to lock the side of his crib and never—"

"I can handle it," he interrupted. He glanced over and saw the panic in her eyes. "If I have any questions I'll call you, otherwise I can call Your Highness, Dorlinda Saunders. She has the answers to all of our worries." He winked, then rose and carried the empty bowl to the sink.

Essence sipped the last of her coffee, looking unconvinced. Mark waited for her to protest further, but she didn't.

"Why don't you give me your keys so I can warm up your car?"

She pointed to a set of keys hanging on the end of a corkboard underneath the phone.

"How come you don't park in the garage?" he asked, curiously.

"Because the door is old and heavy and too much trouble."

Mark simply nodded. He reached for the keys and went to slip on his jacket.

While he was gone, Essence put her mug in the sink and reached for a washcloth in a drawer near the stove. She kept a supply close by for when she needed them. After running it under the faucet, she moved to clean Tyler's hands and face. Tyler squealed and she smiled. He looked so much like his father when he smiled. Same dimples and all. Maybe if he had been a girl she wouldn't feel so guilty. Boys need their fathers. They need their mothers also, but fathers were just as, if not more, important. She wanted to share this time with Mark, she really did; it was just that she was beginning to feel a little left out. It was starting to bother her that she had been raising Tyler alone for so long, and then Mark walked in as if he'd never left. He stepped perfectly into the picture. He seemed to be taking control over her and Tyler's lives, and she was letting him. She just couldn't understand why she was allowing it to happen. Was it really guilt or was it something else? She just wasn't sure yet.

She lifted Tyler from his high-chair laughing as she swung him into her arms.

"Kiss Momma goodbye." Tyler planted a super wet one on her lips, but she didn't mind. She smoothed his curls back. "Be good, sweetheart." She carried him into the living room and gave him one final kiss before she lowered him into his playpen.

Peering out the frosted window, she found Mark scraping the ice off her car. She felt a warm sensation every time he did something nice for her.

It was as if he belonged here with her and Tyler. He was making her decision not to marry him more difficult by the hour. However, she was going to stand by her belief. She wanted love and marriage or nothing at all.

Walking back to her room, she checked her make up, applying another coat of lipstick, and ran a brush across her hair pulling back the strands that had escaped from her bun.

When she returned, Mark was wiping his feet off on the rug in the foyer. He looked up when he saw her.

"Has your car been winterized?"

She was surprised by his question. "Well…no."

He frowned. "I'll make you an appointment. Tomorrow you can drive my car."

"My car is just fine."

"No it isn't…so don't argue with me. If you don't want to do it for me, do it for Tyler."

His last statement ceased any further disagreement.

"Well, I guess I better get to work. I'll call later." She removed a long camel wool coat from the hall closet. Mark helped her into it. "Thanks." She picked up her briefcase and after giving Tyler one final look, finding that he was busy with his toys, she headed toward the door.

"See you later, Mark."

Mark lowered his hand to the knob and paused before opening it. "Is that how you say good bye?"

Before she could prepare, he pulled her in his arms and kissed her on the mouth. A deep, delving kiss. A meeting of lips and tongues. Her entire body came to life, every nerve, every muscle. He held her close and kissed her the way she had wanted him to since he had entered the house. The way she had wanted him to last night.

Before she lost control, she stepped back letting her arms fall to her sides.

"Have a nice day," he said as he opened the door.

She simply nodded and a stunned Essence Monroe walked out to her car.

Essence sat behind her desk sipping a cup of coffee while eating a slice of Nana's banana bread. Nana Jackson was the school librarian. She moved to Dover ten years ago from Biloxi, Mississippi. The woman could burn in the kitchen and it was always a treat when she took the time to spoil the staff.

Taking another bite, Essence chewed the moist cake as her thoughts filtered back to Mark.

Her relationship with Mark was beginning to develop into something much more than she had imagined. She was beginning to wonder if she was strong enough to fight it.

Last night he had managed to keep his hands to himself, then today he had kissed her. She didn't know what to think or to suspect. She didn't know if he was going to keep his hands to himself or pull her into his arms. What was really bothering her was what she knew she truly wanted.

She wanted Mark. She'd always wanted him. He was under her skin, in her blood, whatever, but he was there. Two years of trying to pry him out of her mind hadn't done much good because she still wanted him. Whenever she closed her heart to him, he always seemed to open the door.

He was invading her life and her space and she knew that unless she held her ground, it would only be a matter of time before he broke through her barrier and recaptured her heart.

Hearing laughter, Essence looked up to find that her students had begun to trickle into the classroom.

"Good morning, Ms. Monroe," Gretchen greeted, as she moved to hang up her coat.

"Good morning, Gretchen."

Essence rose, knocking the crumbs from her lap and moved to the front of the classroom. Putting on her best smiling face, she was prepared to begin her day.

Essence opened the front door and dropped her keys on a mahogany table in the foyer. She removed her coat and hung it on the hook, along with her purse, then stepped into the kitchen where she found a note on the refrigerator. *Gone to the mall to see Santa Claus*

*again, dinner is in the oven.* She smiled as she moved over to the stove and found a pan of lasagna in the oven. Mmmm, she couldn't wait to try it. She removed it from the oven and was about to cut a slice when the telephone rang.

Picking up the wall phone, she answered the call, "Hello?"

"Hi, sweetheart."

"Hi, Mom." Taking a seat at the table, she kicked off her shoes and settled back to talk to Julia Monroe.

"I haven't heard from you in a couple of days. How have you and Tyler been?"

"Fine."

"I hear a lot more than just fine in your voice. What's going on?"

There was a slight hesitation before she finally answered. "Mark's home."

"Oh!" Julia gasped with surprise. "And how is that going?"

"Actually better than I had imagined. He fell in love with Tyler the minute he saw him."

Her mother chuckled. "Well that's easy to do…he is a little ham. How does he feel having his dad around?"

Essence rested her chin in her palm and smiled. "He already knows the word 'daddy.' Mark gave Liz the holiday off so he could take care of Tyler."

There was a brief silence before she asked, "And how do you feel having him around?"

She released a sigh. "Relieved, happy, confused."

"How so?"

Essence hesitated. Did she really want to tell her mother that Mark proposed? Not really because she knew her mother would disagree with her decision. But she really needed to talk to someone about what she was feeling. "Mark asked me to marry him."

Julia took a deep breath. "And?"

"And I told him no."

"I thought you loved him?"

There was a moment of silence before she spoke again. "I do, or at least I did. But regardless of how I feel, he doesn't love me." It felt strange but it was the first time she'd confessed what she had been afraid to admit.

"How can you be so sure?"

"He told me so…the only reason he proposed is because he doesn't want Tyler to be raised without a father."

"Is that so bad?"

"Yes, it is. I won't settle for anything less than love."

"Maybe deep down in his heart he does love you."

"Maybe, but I'm not willing to take that chance."

"Well, I trust you to follow your heart. You know what's best. Just remember you have to consider what's best for Tyler, too."

She released an audible sigh. "I know."

Julia was certain she had given her daughter enough to think about for one night and decided to change the subject. "Your aunt Tina's coming up for Christmas."

"Oh, that's great." Tina was her mom's sister from Louisiana. "Is she bringing anyone with her?"

"As many as she can load in her van," she chuckled. "You know they know how to put away some food, so I am expecting all the help I can get for dinner."

"I'll be more than happy to help. In fact, I'm sure Mark wouldn't mind pitching in either."

"Oh, really?"

"Oh, Mom, he's a wonderful cook! I've come home the past two days and found delicious homemade meals, not Hamburger Helper."

"I see."

"I don't remember when I have eaten so well and I don't see how he managed it after spending the entire day with Tyler, but he did. He also washes dishes and washes clothes."

"And this is the guy you refused to marry? Maybe you do need to lend him to me for a couple of days."

Essence gasped suddenly, realizing how she probably sounded as she sang Mark's praises. "Well, anyway, just let me know what you need and I'll take care of it."

Julia chuckled knowingly. "I'm sure you will."

Essence groaned inwardly and was suddenly anxious to get off the phone. "Mom, I...um...just walked in the house and haven't even had a chance to change out of my clothes."

"Sure, dear. I'll talk to you this weekend." Her mother was still chuckling as she hung up the phone.

*Now you've done it,* Essence thought as she hung up the receiver. Her mother was going to tell her father everything and then there would be no end to the pressure he would place on her.

She was still scolding herself when her eyes traveled to the end of the counter where she spotted a small remote control. She reached over and picked it up. Turning it over, she pushed the button. Her eyes grew large when she heard the loud noise coming from the garage.

"Oh, no, he didn't," she mumbled as she moved to the side entrance door. She swung it opened and stared. Mark had installed an electric garage opener. Her heart pitter-pattered at the kind gesture, making it impossible to be mad. He was so thoughtful. What was she going to do?

"I'll tell you what you're going to do," she said aloud to herself. "You're going to put back on your shoes and go outside and park your car in the garage." With the remote in her hand and a smile on her face, she slipped into her pumps and headed out into the hall for her car keys.

# CHAPTER SEVEN

The following afternoon Essence was sitting behind her desk when Mark strolled into her classroom carrying Tyler in his arms.

"What are you doing here?" she asked, completely surprised.

"Someone missed you."

Glancing up at him, she saw the twinkle in his eyes and was tempted to ask him which one of them he was referring to but thought better of it.

Mark lowered the squirming toddler to the floor and Tyler quickly took off. Essence rose and bent down just in time to scoop him in her arms and hugged him close to her bosom. "Oh, hello, sweetheart," she murmured, and he giggled excitedly and squeezed her back.

"We went to visit my parents this morning. Since we were in the area I thought we would surprise you and drop by," Mark said as he took a step closer, his gaze roaming leisurely over the navy blue designer suit.

She returned to her chair with Tyler in her lap. Reaching up she unzipped his coat then removed the hat from his head. "You missed your mommy?" she cooed. Tyler bounced on her lap and banged his hand on the desk.

"How about going out to lunch with us?" Mark suggested.

"Sounds tempting." She grinned and reached for an ink pen Tyler was only seconds away from putting in his mouth.

She pressed her lips to her baby's head. The idea of spending a few minutes with the two of them was quiet appealing. Essence stared at Mark's rugged build in a pair of blue jeans and a cream sweater, watching his gaze sweep around her classroom before returning to her.

"Come on," he encouraged with a sexy smile.

Essence's heart hammered against her chest. She wondered if being alone with Mark was a good idea. Tyler was a baby. Mark's baby. The three of them together would feel too much like a family. Once again, she would be treading on dangerous ground.

At her continued silence, Mark arched a brow. "Scared to be alone with me, Essence?"

Her defenses rang out like a chime. "Lead the way, Captain." This was so she could spend time with Tyler, she told herself. She rose and lowered Tyler to the floor and he dashed across the room.

Mark grinned. "Don't act tough on my account."

She rolled her eyes and moved to the closet for her coat. "Give it up, Mark."

*Not a chance*, Mark thought.

He followed her and Tyler out in the hallway, his gaze dropping to her cute behind. He bit back a groan and the urge to drag her back inside the classroom and learn what color lingerie she wore underneath her power suit. The idea was quickly drenched when several staff members rushed over to see their son.

Essence saw the speculative gleam in her co-worker's eyes as the women gave Mark the slow once-over. Inwardly she sighed, knowing that sooner or later they would want details about the gorgeous man standing beside her.

A few looked curiously at him, their eyes traveling from Mark to Tyler and then back to him. Mark kept silent as Essence showed off her son and she was grateful. After she told another teacher on her team that she was going to grab a bite to eat while her class was in PE, she urged Mark to follow her to the door.

An older woman sitting at the reception desk stopped them, cooing at the baby. "I just have to say you have a gorgeous family."

"Thank you, Linda," Essence said, proudly looking down at her son. Tyler bounced in her arms.

"He has his father's eyes. You and your husband should be proud."

Essence's mouth opened to tell the woman Mark wasn't her husband, then closed it again.

Mark stepped in and said, "We are very proud. Thank you,"

He ushered Essence out the door and to his vehicle. After Tyler was settled in his car seat, he climbed in and drove off. Beside him, Essence was quiet.

"Does it bother you what that woman said?" Mark asked.

Essence shrugged. "No, it's a logical assumption. Tyler does look like you."

"Hair and eyes maybe, but he reminds me of you."

She appeared pleased by his comment. "You think so?"

"He's also good-looking, stubborn, and unaware of what is happening right before his eyes."

Her eyes moved to stare out her side window. "I'm aware. I'm just content with my life the way it is. I have a beautiful son and have already begun to build a life for the two of us."

"Won't you even consider building a life with me?"

She grinned as she turned to look at him. "Mark, you are beginning to sound like a broken record."

His fingers gripped the steering wheel. "Damn it, Essence! I never thought I'd have to beg a woman to marry me. Just give me one good reason why you won't."

"I've already given you several reasons. You don't have to marry me to be Tyler's father. These past few days have proven that. Marriage for the sake of giving a child his father's name is not necessary."

"It is if he's my child."

She glanced at him, wondering why he couldn't just leave well enough alone. They had been getting along so well and, as usual he had to ruin it. She twisted in the seat to check on her son who was happily chewing on a cracker and making a mess in Mark's SUV. "I really don't think Tyler minds."

Mark had a stony expression on his face when they pulled up at the drive-thru window at Popeye's. As soon as someone came over the intercom asking for his order, he looked to Essence. "You still like spicy wings, dirty rice and biscuits with honey?"

She turned her gaze to him in amazement. "How did you remember?"

His lips pursed. "I told you before, there isn't much about you that I have forgotten."

*Except for me,* she thought, as he placed their orders.

He pulled up to the cashier and remained quiet as he waited for their food.

After prolonged silence, Essence added, "You're angry."

"Yes, dammit! I'm not used to a woman turning me down," he said after he handed the cashier a twenty-dollar bill. "It's not something that happens everyday."

He sounded angry but his eyes told her otherwise. He was hurt. He deserved to know it all. "I almost married once for the wrong reason."

His gaze pivoted to her. "You've been engaged? When?"

"It was a guy I was dating before I met you."

Mark reached for the bag the cashier handed him and gave it to Essence. They had never talked about their past relationships before. He had never asked and she had never offered, but then he had never spoken of Carmen either. "What happened?"

Essence looked inside the box, pulled out a couple of loose fries and handed them to Tyler. "I was in love and he wasn't."

He pulled away from the window and over to a parking space at the back of the lot. Once the car was in park, he turned in his seat and asked, "How long were you engaged?"

She made a sound that might have been a sound of regret. "Long enough for my father to have announced the prenuptial during one of his sermons."

"Ouch." He could image how embarrassing that must have been.

"His wife had died of cancer, leaving him to raise two toddlers. He only wanted a mother for his sons, not love."

"That man was stupid."

"No...marriage for the wrong reason is stupid."

Mark held his temper. She was comparing him to that moron. Was that why she thought marriage would be a bad choice?

"How did you find out that truth?"

She held his gaze, wondering if he'd still be around if it wasn't for the baby they shared. She'd always wonder that and it was a bigger reason not to marry him. "I found him in bed with another woman."

"Bastard."

She shrugged a slender shoulder. "He said that he didn't love me. He was only marrying me for his kids."

Mark heard the hurt in Essence's voice even though she obviously tried to hide it.

She wrapped her arms around her body in a protective gesture. "So I went on with my life...and then I met you."

He tossed her a look. "I'm not like him."

Her expressive eyes blazed. "And you think that's a good reason to propose to me?"

"Yes."

"No it isn't. Clark didn't love me, so his infidelities were inevitable. I'm just glad it happened before we were married. You don't love me either, so what's to say it won't happen again?"

"Because I'm not him."

Essence stared silently at him. Recognizing the faraway look in her eyes, he wondered if perhaps she was thinking about the way their relationship had ended two years ago. He couldn't blame her if she was.

After a moment, Essence let out a breath and took a bite of her chicken. " I love this chicken." Her brow rose, her smile genuine.

Hearing happy noises coming from the back seat, she glanced over her shoulder. "I think somebody back there is enjoying his fries."

They shared a smile before Essence looked away.

"How's it been being a father?" she asked, slightly shifting the conversation.

"Scary. Wonderful. Proud," he replied honestly.

"How so?"

His smile broadened. "It's frightening to know that I'm responsible for someone else's happiness."

She met his gaze and nodded.

"Essence, when I leave I really want to take both of you with me."

She was quiet for several seconds before asking, "Do you know where you're going?"

"I have orders to report to Ft. Mead the day after New Years."

She smiled. "You'll still be close by."

"But not close enough. I want you to consider joining me."

She sadly shook her head. "You don't love me. That's the key here. So, don't tell me that marriage will make things just magically work out because they won't."

"It can if you give it a chance."

"I am giving you a chance, a chance to build a relationship with your son. I'm not about to marry you so that Tyler can change his name."

"It's more than a name," Mark said, grinding his teeth.

He knew for certain, Essence was protecting herself and her heart. She'd already had her heart broken once and didn't trust her feelings enough to put faith in them. She truly believed there wasn't a chance for her and him beyond a name on a license, and she just couldn't risk getting hurt again.

But she was right in a couple of ways, he didn't love her. He was honest enough with himself to admit that. However, what he felt for Essence was more that just lust and memories of great sex. Even if Tyler weren't between them, he'd have hunted her down. He'd have done it to satisfy his ego that she hadn't forgotten him and to see if the dreams that plagued him were just that, dreams. At the rate they were going, she wasn't going to give him a chance to find out.

"Essence?"

She turned and gazed softly at him. The unshed tears swimming in her eyes were like a stab in the heart.

"Honey, talk to me." He raised his hand to her jaw and cupped her face in his palm.

She swallowed, shook her head. "I-I can't marry you, Mark. Please don't ask me again. I know it would be better for Tyler, but you and I will have to live with the decision and so will he."

"Listen to me, Essence," he whispered. "I'm sorry that I wasn't there for you. But I'm not Clark. If I take a pledge to love, honor and obey, I will take those vows seriously." He pressed a finger over her lips to stop a protest. "Shhh. Don't say anymore. I can accept how you feel. I don't have to like it, but I can accept it." *For now*, he added silently. He wasn't going to give up.

For some strange reason, Essence felt a twinge of disappointment that he was willing to accept her refusal. She did want him. She just didn't trust her heart. She'd missed him terribly the past two years and now that he was here, she was the one pushing him away. She felt it was necessary, but she didn't like it.

When they had made love, she and Mark had actually become one, and the world ceased to exist. For just a moment, she allowed herself to remember the passion that only Mark was capable of evoking from her. His touch in all the right places, the magical way they rode the storm as they came together. They were precious memories that she would always hold dear and near to her heart, but it was the "never knowing" factor, that helped her keep her distance. Never knowing if he could love her the way she'd dreamed, instead of as a ball and chain that had taken away his freedom.

Mark could almost see the thoughts churning in her eyes, the nervousness in her expression. He was the cause of her pain and he didn't like that one bit. "We can be friends. No strings."

She nodded.

"Just consider me a full-time father for the next couple of weeks," he said and smiled across at her.

Her expression softened. "Friends then," she agreed after finally finding her voice. It sounded hollow and lack luster. *But that's what you wanted, right?* a voice in her head whispered.

Mark whistled under his breath. "Well I'll be damned; it's snowing."

She looked past his head and out the window behind him. "Yes it is," she said, smiling.

He returned her smile. "It's going to be a white Christmas after all."

"Yes, it appears that way." Essence glanced down at her watch and sighed. "I guess I need to get back." Her class would be returning in the next fifteen minutes.

Mark started the car and pulled out of the parking lot in the direction of the school. Ten minutes later, he pulled up in front of the building.

Essence turned to find that Tyler had dozed off with a french fry hanging from his parted lips.

Mark turned his head. Essence's face was within an inch of his and if he moved a fraction, their lips would meet. Her rapid breathing and parted lips indicated shock. Her warm breath swept over his nose. His body reacted so quickly that he feared losing control.

"Thank you so much for him," he finally said.

The caressing sound of his voice made her tingle and she returned the smile. "You took part."

"Yeah, but I didn't carry him for nine months alone. I didn't suffer the pain to get him here so I could love him."

Essence cast her eyes downward, then back up at him again.

Mark eased back a bit and gently brushed a strand of hair off her face. "Maybe you'll tell me about it?"

"Yeah, some day." Maybe one of these days she would show him the video her sister had taken of Tyler's delivery.

At a lost for words and time, she turned away and opened the car door. Mark was there in an instant offering a hand. Her fingers slid easily into his and he tugged her closer. "See you this evening?" she whispered.

His gaze raked her features. "We'll be there."

A blast of cold wind slapped at them. Essence tipped her face into it, closed her eyes and inhaled deeply. Mark simply stared at her, lips parted in awe. Her high cheeks were rosy, auburn hair tousled by the wind. Her gentle overwhelming beauty brought his untried senses to life.

He swore he wasn't going to do it, swore he'd back off, but he couldn't resist. Just one kiss, that's all he needed. Essence was taking his breath away by the second and he needed to touch her. Before he had a chance to talk himself out of it, he leaned forward and brushed his mouth over hers.

Instead of pushing him away, Essence closed the door, then her hands gripped the smooth fabric of his jacket. It's all right, she told herself. It was only a kiss, nothing more. A delightful shiver of wanting raced through her limbs, leaving them trembling with excitement. Mark altered the kiss with a subtle easing of pressure. The dampness of his tongue nudged at her mouth until she gave a tiny, involuntary gasp.

The moment her lips parted, his lips recaptured her, more demanding this time. He plunged deeper into her mouth, stroking her tongue, teasing it to play. He wrapped his arms around her and continued to kiss her with a finesse that sent heated blood pounding in her head, sweeping downward through her body to the passage between her thighs. She kissed him back, feeling the warm, relaxed firmness of his body, drinking in the comfort of his nearness. The throaty moans coming from him made it harder and harder to hear the voice of reason. Her feelings for him had nothing to do with reason. The loneliness of the past two years swallowed up inside her and at that moment everything she wanted was right here, right now.

Her gloved fingers stroked over his face and behind his head where she wrapped her arms around his neck. She wanted to absorb him within her. Instinctively, she pressed herself to him, reveling in the heat of his body against the soft curves of her own.

Finally, and only because she knew she needed to return to her classroom, she regained her senses and pulled back. Shaken by the way she'd allowed herself to so completely lose control, her voice came out shaky. "See you later." She forced herself to turn and walk into the school. Her steps were a little less steady. Her pulse was well out of control.

*Oh man*, she thought pushing through the door and ignoring the glances from her staff as she walked down the hall. She went directly to her room and sat in her chair. Pressing her forehead to the desk, she let out a long shaky breath. She was getting in way over her head.

# CHAPTER EIGHT

Tamara blinked her eyes several times, surprised. "Now let me get this straight, Mark has asked you to marry him not once, not twice, but three times, and each time you've turned him down?"

"Don't even go there," Essence warned her older sister.

She shook her head. "Girlfriend, I can't understand you. You've been waiting for this man for years, turned down almost every double date I've set you up on and the minute he returns to town you decide you're no longer interested."

Essence looked up from her lunch with a look of denial. "I haven't been waiting for him."

"Oh, yes you have," Tamara laughed. "No man has ever been able to put a finger on the phenomenal Mark Saunders."

Essence rolled her eyes heavenward. "I don't know why I even tell you anything."

"Because you know I'm going to tell you like it is," she retorted, then reached for her hamburger and took another bite.

She glanced over at Tyler who was sitting in a high chair, eating french fries with his fingers. He would soon be sleepy. At her sister's insistence, they had been shopping at the Dover Mall since it opened. Essence would have preferred waiting until next week when school was out before beginning her shopping so that the stores would have been less crowded. Shopping on the weekend was a big mistake. Trying to push a baby stroller through a crowd of customers was even worse.

She had spent most of the morning shopping for her picky mother before she had finally decided it was safer just to get her a mall gift card. Her father was always happy to receive another bottle of cognac and a box of expensive Cuban cigars. Picking out gifts for her niece and nephew was a piece of cake. Aaliyah was thirteen going on twenty-five and loved the latest fashions and CDs. For her nephew Cameron, she bought a couple of new video games. With her sister's help, Essence picked out a tie and dress shirt for her brother-in-law Paul. Tamara's gift she would decide on when she wasn't around peeking in her bags.

Every Christmas the family drew names for the following year and Essence had pulled her father's sister, Geraldine. The sixty year-old widow was a collector of angels. Essence had found her a priceless sculptor created by the African-American designer, Thomas Blackshear.

After passing several men's clothing stores, Essence had debated buying Mark a gift from Tyler but thought it would seem too much like a gift from her. Not wanting him to read anything in the thoughtful gesture, she decided against it.

During the course of the afternoon she had been trying to pull her scattered emotions together and still wasn't able to make heads or tails of what was happening to her. Unable to come up with a solution on her own, she waited forty-five minutes for a booth at Ruby Tuesday's before spilling her guts to her big sister.

"So little sis, what are you going to do?"

Tamara's question shattered her wayward thoughts. Essence closed her eyes and mumbled, "Nothing. I'm not going to marry him."

"Give me one good reason why not?"

Opening her eyes, Essence stared at her sister's awed expression. "Because I think I'm still in love with him," she confessed.

Tamara leaned back on the bench and cackled. "Tell me something I don't know." She continued to chuckle as she reached over and aided her nephew with a piece of steamed broccoli that kept slipping between his little fingers. "Ain't that right, Tyler. Your mommy loves your Daddy."

"Da Da."

"See even Tyler knows." Tamara couldn't control her burst of laughter. "I don't see what's the problem. Mark wants to marry you and you're in love with him. It sounds like the perfect solution."

Essence speared a shrimp then turned and looked away. She hated when her sister tried to give her advice, especially when all she really wanted her to do was listen. "I don't think I've ever stopped loving him. I want him in my bed so badly it's driving me crazy." She gazed at her in despair. There was no mistaking the frustration in her voice.

"After two years, sex is long overdue," she offered between chews.

She frowned at Tamara. "There is more to a relationship than sex," she scolded softly. Dropping her fork, she rested her chin in the palm of her hand. "I love Mark, yet he doesn't love me."

Tamara gave her a skeptical look. "How do you know?"

"He told me so."

Tamara shrugged a slender shoulder. "Men say anything. I don't think Mark would have asked you to marry him just for the hell of it."

Essence shook her head, her brow creasing with thought. "He asked me because of Tyler. He wants his son to have a stable home environment with two parents."

Her sister's full ruby lips curled in a beautiful white-toothed smile. "I can't argue with him there. I don't know what I would do if Paul and I weren't together."

Essence snorted and reached for her fork again. "That's not about to happen. I've never seen a couple more in love than the two of you."

Her sister had married her high school sweetheart and on her thirty-fourth birthday, the couple would celebrate sixteen years. It was sometimes hard for her to believe especially when her sister wore her raven black hair in a simple ponytail and bangs that made it almost impossible to tell her age. Like their mother, Tamara was the color of Colombian coffee beans, with large dark eyes the color of a midnight sky.

Essence reached over to assist Tyler with his drink cup. "Mark doesn't believe in commitment. He told me so. Why do you think I never bothered to tell him about Tyler?"

Tamara shrugged. "People change."

Vertical lines appeared between her eyes. "If I marry Mark I'll be shortchanging myself. I want a man who loves me."

"Like Malcolm?" Tamara retorted with the roll of her eyes. "Girl, I have never met a man that's more wrong for you than him."

Essence lowered her arm back onto the table. "True, but you have to admit he loves me and Tyler."

"And that makes it right?"

Essence was quiet for a tense moment, then sighed and replied, "No, but it is definitely something to work with."

Placing her elbows on the table, Tamara laced her fingers together. "I disagree. You deserve to be happy and even though I still haven't met Mark, I know you'll be happy with him. It's written all over your face. Every time you mention him your eyes dance."

Essence reached down for her last onion ring and popped it in her mouth. She knew her sister was right. Malcolm definitely wasn't the right man for her, but was she willing to short-change herself and marry Mark? She just didn't know. What she did know was that since his return she barely slept a wink. And when she did, every gesture and facial expression, even the timber of his voice, replayed again and again in her mind.

"I wish I didn't love him so much," she replied softly.

Tamara gave her a half smile. "Girl, there's nothing wrong with loving a man."

"It is when he doesn't love you."

A wry smile tilted the corners of Tamara's mouth. "Then make him love you."

She studied her sister thoughtfully for a moment. "And how am I supposed to do that?"

Her penetrating gaze caught and held Essence's eyes. "Throw some of that Monroe whip appeal on his behind. He won't know what hit him."

Unconsciously, Essence stirred the iced tea with her straw. Tamara just didn't know how close she and Mark had come to making love. The only thing that had held her back was her stubborn pride.

"What you need to do is give him some," Tamara suggested then reached for her glass of lemonade and took a sip.

Her mouth dropped open at how calmly and easily Tamara had made the suggestion. She used to think her sister was such a prude. Over the years, she'd learned otherwise. "Girl, you are crazy. Some of us have more important things on our mind."

"What you need to be thinking about is how to hook Tyler's Daddy," she said raising her perfectly arched eyebrows with exaggeration.

"Da Da."

They both turned to him at the same time and chuckled.

The corners of Tamara's mouth turned up a notch. "See, even Tyler agrees."

*Texas!*

Mark still couldn't believe it. He had received word last night that he was to report to a military intelligence unit at Ft. Hood, Texas the day after New Years.

*Damn it!*

Mark fell back on the mattress and stared up at the ceiling.

He would be hundreds of miles away from Tyler. *And Essence.*

He had planned to be on the east coast within driving distance. That way he could see the two of them as often as he liked. Now that idea had been shot to hell.

He had three weeks left. Now what was he going to do?

Essence still refused to marry him.

He cupped his hand behind his head and allowed his eyes to travel around the room as he tried to make some sense of it all. Why did she have to be so stubborn? He had offered to make a home for them. He wanted to raise their son together. He had even promised to be faithful to her. So what was the problem? *You know what the problem is.*

His eyes traveled to the baseball bats that bordered the blue walls. When he was ten his mother had surprised him by decorating his room for his birthday. Twenty years later, the room still looked the same. It would be perfect for a little boy.

Mark couldn't help but smile as memories of his little man flooded his mind. Yesterday after receiving five inches of snow, he had gone and bought a sled. He had taken Tyler to the park and together they had hit the slope. Tyler's laughter was priceless. Worn out and hungry, they had gone to Chuck E. Cheese for lunch.

As he drove to and from Essence's home, Mark would find himself smiling and laughing at something Tyler had done. His feeling for his son surpassed anything he had ever felt before. He never thought he'd be prepared to take a stray bullet for someone other than his family. For Tyler, he was willing to give his life if he had to.

What about Essence? Never before had a woman affected him the way she had. He now knew for certain it wasn't lust. It was something else. He was convinced it had a lot to do with the emotional bond they shared. She wasn't just another woman. Essence was the mother of his child.

Mark inhaled a ragged breath trying to get rid of the raging emotion within him. Sitting up in bed, Mark rested his elbows on his knees. It was the same thing he did every evening when he left her house. He would lie awake at night thinking about their kisses, aching for a release that only she could give him. No one else would do.

He could feel her lips, her body against his.

He had three weeks to convince her to accept his offer. He would have to use every minute to remind her how good they were together. Mark knew he had a fight on his hand but he was a captain in the United States Army and was up for the challenge. There was no doubt in his mind that she was going to continue to try to push him away. It wouldn't be easy but nothing worth having ever was.

Essence was a stubborn woman, but then he was a stubborn man.

As he lay there, Mark realized he was going to enjoy every single minute it took to make her change her mind. He would have to prove to her that he was indeed the man for her and she the woman for him. He had come to realize that without the two of them his life was meaningless. If that meant he had to open up his heart and allow love

**115**

in, then so be it.

❧

After leaving the mall, Essence dropped by the grocery store to pick up a few items. It was around four when she finally turned into her driveway. When she pressed the button on the small remote control of her visor, her lips curled upward. She was still getting used to the idea that she could now, thanks to Mark, park in her garage and it amazed her every time. On cold winter mornings, she no longer had to worry about scraping snow or ice off her car. All she had to do was raise the garage door and drive off.

Climbing out the driver's seat, she shut the door then turned and glanced in the back seat. She smiled down at Tyler, who had fallen asleep during the drive back. He was so sweet and beautiful, she thought. To this day she didn't regret, nor would she ever, the time she'd spent loving Mark. How could she when the result had been a gift this precious?

She opened the rear door, ducked her head inside the car and reached down to smooth back his dark baby curls. "We're home, handsome," she crooned, and proceeded to unfasten the safety belt of his car seat. After slipping his arms through the straps, she lifted the sleeping darling into her arms.

"Need some help?"

Essence swung around to find Mark standing there. Now where did he come from? Her heart turned over in response, causing her to grow angry at her vulnerability toward him.

"It's the weekend, Mark. What are you doing here?" she demanded, taking care not to raise her voice and wake Tyler.

"I thought I'd come and spend some time with my son," he remarked as he shut the car door.

"Tyler had a full day at the mall and is now sound asleep," she replied. *Why didn't I close my garage door behind me?*

He grinned, his white teeth set off against his warm brown skin. "Well, it looks like you've got a car load so why don't you let me carry him inside for you?"

And before she could object, Mark had removed Tyler from her arms and was carrying him toward the side door entrance. Essence hurried after him, unlocked the door then followed Mark inside.

He moved through her house with a familiarity that made her ill at ease. It was apparent things were getting out of hand. The time had come for them to have a long talk.

She hurried in the room ahead of him and pulled back the comforter on Tyler's bed.

"He's a real soldier," Mark murmured.

*Like his father*, Essence thought, as she watched Mark place their sleeping son in his bed.

"Should I take off his shoes?"

Essence nodded and watched as Mark eased off one shoe and then another with a gentleness that never failed to surprise her. It had been this gentle caring side of him that snagged her heart the first time. It was his caring side that was trying to reel her back in.

She observed Mark as he gazed down at his son. Hesitantly, he ran his index finger over his tiny hand. She saw undeniable love reflecting from his beautiful golden eyes. *A father's love.* The gesture made her heart swell. She was reminded of his offer of marriage and how easy it would be to have given into that emotion. If only Mark could give her the one thing she desired most, then the decision would be easy. If only he had offered his love.

She pressed her lips firmly together. Maybe she was being selfish. Maybe she would regret her decision after he had left to report to duty. But she just wasn't ready to risk her heart when she knew he would never come to love her. Swallowing hard against the sudden emotion, Essence glanced over and said, "Mark, we need to talk."

Mark straightened and stepped away from Tyler's bed. "Sure, just let me know when you're ready," he said, and without waiting for her response he left the room.

Essence started to follow when a whimper from Tyler's bed brought her back to his side. After she calmed him and he drifted back to sleep, she turned on the baby monitor then shut the door quietly behind her and went in search of Mark. She found him carrying in the last of her things from the car.

"You didn't have to do that," she admonished and wanted to wince at the sharpness in her voice. "I mean…I was going to get the bags from out of my car."

He leveled his golden gaze on her. "I thought I'd save you the trouble. Where do you want these?" he asked, holding up several plastic bags.

His dimpled smile warmed her in places only he had the ability to heat. "You can leave the groceries on the counter. I'll take the bags in your hands." She strolled over and retrieved her Christmas gifts.

"Would one of those be for me by chance?"

She noted the teasing light in his eyes as he smiled. "Don't flatter yourself." Bags in hand, she pivoted on her heels and moved to her room before her resistance totally evaporated.

When Essence returned, she stood near the door and watched him put a gallon of milk in the refrigerator and found herself growing increasingly uneasy at his familiarity with her house.

She leaned back against the door with her arms folded across her chest. "Mark, you want to tell me what is going on?"

"Going on?" he repeated, all innocent and charming. She knew the man was far from innocent and she was determined to resist his charm no matter how susceptible she might be to it.

"What are you doing here?" she asked with what little patience she had left.

The teasing light in his eyes died as swiftly as the smile on his lips. "I'm here because you're here and so is my son. I'm here because I told you I planned to spend every minute I can with Tyler," he said, moving closer, and mesmerizing her with his eyes. "I also wanted to spend some time with you."

Essence looked at Mark as if he'd spoken a foreign language. "With me?" He was doing it again. Ruffling her feathers and she was letting him.

His gaze zeroed in on her lips before he again locked her eyes. Head-to-toe chills traveled downward, and heat settled low in her belly.

"I plan to show you how much I want to be with you."

Essence was caught between wanting to slap him and kiss him. Shaking her head, she wondered what on earth she was going to do with him. He was so hardheaded.

"Mark, please don't make this situation difficult."

He pushed away from the counter and strode toward her, causing her breath to catch and her heart to leap. "I don't plan on making it difficult. Instead, I plan to show you how much I truly need you in my life," he said in a warm honeyed voice, thick and seductively sweet.

"You're kidding?" she chuckled, thinking he meant it as a joke. However, the look on his face told her otherwise.

He rubbed a hand over his shaved jaw and answered, "Do I look like I'm kidding?"

She quickly got over the shock. Her expression changed to contempt as she dropped a hand to her waist. She sighed impatiently, her eyes narrowed in anger. "And I guess you think that if you wear me down, I will accept your offer of marriage?"

"That's the plan," he smirked.

"It won't work," she replied, fighting the challenge in his eyes. Despite her indifference, her heart pounded wildly against her chest.

A smile crooked the corner of his lips. "Yes it will."

Essence shook her head, then dropped her eyes. Awareness that he was watching her sent electricity racing along her nerve endings. She couldn't believe anybody could be so arrogant. She also couldn't believe that this particular trait was arousing her. "No it won't. I thought I made myself perfectly clear about my reason for not marrying you."

His grin deepened. "You did, but I plan to change you mind about us, and about me."

Silence stretched between them, her glaring and him grinning. Essence's magenta lips were pursed in a thin line. Her arms were folded beneath her breasts. The orange cashmere sweater she wore showed ample cleavage, causing his loins to stir.

He watched her, waiting for some kind of comeback, but his eyes traveled down to her shapely legs in a pair of black jeans that fit her like a second skin. She was a tempting sight. He wanted nothing more than to pull her into his arms and kiss her until they fell to the linoleum in a tangled knot of hungry hands and arching bodies.

He fought the urge to take her in his arms. There were still a lot of things they needed to work out, a lot of things he still had to make her understand. He needed to think with his head, not with his other body part. That was what had gotten them in this mess in the first place.

Only he couldn't help himself.

Mark eased up to her until their hips connected, savoring the contact of lush breasts and legs.

"Don't," she whispered, but with little force behind the word. His hand rose and tipped her face up to his.

"Let it happen, Essence," he murmured, barely touching his mouth with hers, drowning in the feeling.

Mark buried his hands in her hair and kissed her so deeply she almost forgot how to breathe. His lips were demanding, his embrace possessive and strong. When he leaned his hips against her body, he was undeniably male. He challenged her with his kiss, wordlessly demanding that she acknowledge the tension and heat that existed between them. A heat that was capable of welding two hearts into one. Desire shuddered through her so intensely that she moaned, confused and afraid. Essence knew it was dangerous to enjoy his touch, too risky to permit what could surely become addictive pleasure.

Essence jerked away, her nostrils flared. "We've been getting along so well, why'd you have to go and ruin it!"

"Damn it, Essence! I only have three weeks left," Mark argued, and followed swiftly behind her as she started down the hall.

She swung around. "I thought you were going to Ft. Mead?"

"I...I am," he lied. "But that's beside the point. I want to come home to you and Tyler each night, not to cold and empty quarters."

She waved a dismissive hand. "Listen, I've had a long day and I would like to get dinner started before Tyler wakes up. So if you don't mind leaving..."

"Not yet. I brought Tyler something."

She threw up her hands in a gesture of dismissal. "Fine." She turned and entered her room, slamming the door behind her.

Once inside, Essence stood very still. Her knees were trembling as if she'd been peddling on her stationary bike for more than thirty minutes. Her heartbeat pounded heavily in the sudden silence. One kiss, she thought numbly. How could one kiss turn her life upside down?

*Because you love him.*

That reason alone was going to be her downfall.

When she finally found the nerve to come out of her room, Mark was lugging a Christmas tree through the front door.

She was appalled. "What are you doing? I already have a tree."

Mark peered around the pine branches and replied, "Don't get me wrong, your tree is cute, but kids like big trees."

"I really don't think Tyler is old enough to care," Essence mumbled while she rubbed her arms and shivered.

"Maybe not, but with all the lights, he'll be quite fascinated. Besides, I'm a kid at heart," he smirked causing her heart to hammer foolishly. He shut the door then reached down in a brown sack and removed a tree stand.

Essence remained quiet as he set up the tree in the corner next to hers. The little tree looked like a weed in comparison.

As she watched, something in his manner soothed her. Instead of wrapping her fingers around his neck and demanding that he listen to reason, she simply leaned against the wall with her arms wrapped around her middle and watched.

As if sensing her mood, Mark glanced over his shoulder and said, "I promise to leave after Tyler and I have dinner and decorate the tree."

Essence noticed the heart rendering tenderness of his gaze when he spoke of their son. It was moments like that that made it difficult to stay mad with him.

She nodded, even though she had a strong suspicion his leaving wouldn't be that easy.

# CHAPTER NINE

Essence tried to busy herself in her room so that Mark and Tyler could spend time alone together, but an hour after Tyler's nap, curiosity had gotten the best of her. She followed the sound of their voices into the living room. Inhaling deeply, she braced one hip against the doorframe, and kept her gaze locked on her son and the man who had somehow become quite important to her.

*Mark...important? Impossible.* She didn't need him in her life. Not now. Not ever.

Mark was on the couch with Tyler on his lap. He held the book open while Tyler stabbed at the pictures with his index finger.

"Cat."

"Dog," Mark corrected gently, then smoothed one hand over the back of the child's head.

"Doggie," Tyler repeated.

"Good boy." A deep chuckle rumbled in his chest.

While Mark read the story, Essence stood by and listened. His voice, strong with a velvet edge, vibrated through her. She swallowed hard, trying to calm the tremors she was experiencing. His thermal shirt pushed up at the sleeves revealed skin threaded with masculine hair. *Why'd he have to be so compassionate and good looking?* she thought angrily. If he were selfish and uncaring, resisting him would be so much easier.

Mark grinned, and as if sensing her presence, he turned his head to meet her gaze. Essence felt the power of that stare right down to the soles of her feet.

"We're reading," he informed her.

She dragged her eyes from his and held up the paperback in her hand. "So was I."

Actually, she had tried to focus on a new romance novel she had bought while at the mall, but just knowing that Mark was somewhere in her house made concentrating virtually impossible.

Darned if they didn't look like father and son. So cozy and comfortable with each other. *Don't go there*, she warned. But she couldn't help it. Mark made Tyler happy. Her admiration for him increased, and nothing seemed to stop the feeling of unrestrained warmth from flooding her insides.

*And that's why you should marry him.*

Essence moved and took a seat in the chair near the fireplace. She tried to force her thoughts in another direction, but that was becoming impossible. She glanced over at the eight-foot tree. The lights were blinking and the red and white balls sparkling. "The tree looks great," she commented.

Mark smiled but didn't answer. Again, he affected her, the hypnotic stare pulling her in. She could very well come apart at the seams if he didn't stop looking at her that way.

She dragged her eyes away and buried them in her book. However, while sitting across from him, her attention was captured by his patience and affection for their son. *What will happen after the holidays were over and everything returns to normal?* She already knew the answer to that. Tyler was going to miss having him around. He was going to be hurt when he was gone.

*And so will I.*

"Ma Ma," Tyler called, snapping her out of her delirious state.

"Hey, sweetheart, whatcha doing?" she asked, resting her chin in her palm, an affectionate smile on her lips.

The little boy tipped his head to one side and pointed to the page. "Doggie."

Her head bobbed up and down as she giggled. "Yes, that's a doggie."

"Doggie," he mimicked.

Mark looked up from the book and across at her. "Have you ever thought about buying him a dog?"

Essence nodded. "My parents have a yellow Lab that Tyler adores. I would love to get him one, but I don't have the time or the patience to train it."

"I'll train him," Mark offered.

Tyler held out his arms to her and Essence drew him onto her lap. "No, I couldn't let you do that."

"He's my son and I would love to do it."

She gave him a sidelong glance. "How do you plan to train a dog all the way from Ft. Mead?"

Mark looked like he might argue, then changed his mind. Instead, he handed her the book, then propped his elbows on his wide spread knees. "I'll find a way. You know there isn't anything I wouldn't do for my little man."

She already knew that. He'd developed a special relationship with Tyler and though it worried her a little, she was also pleased. It was good to have Mark around, even for a little while.

A knock at the front door shattered her train of thought. She handed Tyler back to his father then rose. She moved to the door and opened it. Seeing the man standing on her porch, her gaze widened. "Malcolm!"

"Hey sweetheart." He pulled her into his arms and kissed her on the mouth before she had a chance to protest.

By the time he released her, she had turned pale with shock. "When did you get back?"

"Two hours and fifteen minutes ago. I couldn't wait to see you so I came straight over from the air—" Stepping into the house, he stopped short when he saw Mark. He looked from Essence to Mark, then back to Essence again. "I'm sorry, I didn't know you had company."

Essence closed the door then moved into the living room beside him. "Um…I'd like you to meet Mark."

Mark lowered Tyler onto the floor. "I'm sorry, I didn't catch your name. You are…" He rose and extended his hand, the solemn expression never changing.

"Malcolm Cole, criminal attorney," he said as he met him halfway, then reached for the proffered hand.

"Well, pleased to meet you. I'm Captain Mark Saunders…Tyler's father." He didn't miss the shock on the face of the man he towered over by at least five inches.

Malcolm looked as if he was trying to decide if it was a good or a bad thing finding the two of them together. "So…you're finally home," he drawled with sarcasm.

One corner of Mark's mouth lifted in a tight smile more grimace than grin. "Something like that."

Malcolm wrapped a possessive arm loosely around Essence's waist. "Well, you have a great son."

"I know," Mark replied.

Essence didn't miss Mark's obvious examination and disapproval of Malcolm. She stepped aside, moving out of Malcolm's embrace and gave a nervous laugh. "We had just finished decorating the tree."

Mark gave her a look that said, "We?"

*Okay maybe I hadn't helped but Malcolm didn't need to know that.*

Tyler was toddling around the room. Malcolm crouched down and called, "Come here, Tyler."

Tyler looked from him to his father, then turned and ran. "Da-Da!"

He held out his arms to Mark. The special bond and affection he had already begun to feel for the little guy exploded into full-fledge love in that instant. "Daddy's right here." Mark swung Tyler up into his arms and balanced him on his hip.

Essence saw undeniable love reflecting from his eyes. *A father's love.* She cleared her throat. "Tyler has grown quite fond of his father," she said by way of an explanation.

Malcolm gave a rude snort. "I find that quite amazing, especially since he's never been around before."

Mark noted the sarcasm in his voice. "Some things couldn't have been helped. But now that I am, I plan to stick around *permanently*."

Essence heard the challenge in his voice and decided it was time to intervene before the two went to blows. "Mark didn't you have somewhere you needed to be this evening?"

Mark shook his head. "No, no where at all, but don't mind me. You and Malcolm make yourself comfortable while I go and give my son a bath." With that, he raised Tyler onto his shoulders and headed down the hall, leaving them to stare at his backside.

As soon as he was no longer in ear's range, Malcolm turned to Essence. She could see the glint of wonder in his eyes. "How long has he been back?"

She hugged her arms to her middle. "A little over a week."

Malcolm shook his head. "You should have told me he had returned, I could have cut my trip short. I'm sure these past couple of days have been quite difficult for you."

*More than you'll ever know.* Her heart pitter-pattered at the thought of the sexual tension that had been vibrating between them since Mark's return.

Her eyes roamed over Malcolm's face. He prided himself on his good looks. He was a perfect gentleman and a perfect choice for any woman but her.

He was, in his own unique way, quite handsome. Malcolm had a round face with large dark satin eyes that were emphasized by the longest lashes she had ever seen on a man. His nose was wide and his mouth full, complementing a rich milk chocolate complexion. He was a few inches taller than her, with a lean body that he kept in shape, running several miles like clockwork every morning. Even though he had just gotten off a plane, he was dressed as if he'd just attended a court hearing. He was wearing all black from his suit jacket to his tie.

"He has a lot of nerve showing back up after he abandoned you," he hissed, his eyes flat and hard.

"Yes, well, we've worked through that." *Not that it's any of your business.*

"Is he staying here?"

"Heavens, no!" she gasped. "He's staying with his parents."

A satisfied light came to his eyes. "Good." Malcolm curved an arm around her waist again, pulling her closer to his side and planted light kisses to her hair. Being in his arms caused her to feel increasingly uncomfortable.

She managed to pull back slightly, then sighed. "Malcolm, this is really not a good time. I'm tired and I'd like to get Tyler in bed so I can send Mark on his way."

"Would you like me to help you?"

She looked at the man she wished she had stronger feelings for than friendship and shook her head. "No. I can handle it."

Malcolm hesitated, flashing a warm smile that didn't quite reach his eyes. "All right. Only if you and Tyler promise to have dinner with me Tuesday night?"

A soft smile parted her lips. "Okay."

"Good, I'll pick you up around six." He brushed a light kiss over her lips. To her disappointment, the kiss did nothing except make her wish it were Mark. *Damn him for upsetting my comfortable world.*

When Essence finally got Malcolm to leave, she went in search of Mark. She followed the sound of Tyler's laughter down the hall to the bathroom where the door was ajar. Mark was kneeling in front of the tub with his back to her, minus his shirt. "Okay, Champ, let's get those legs."

The picture he made bathing Tyler combined with her baby's delighted laughter, nearly undid her. The muscles across Mark's back, flexed as he moved. Essence shook it off, reminding herself that the only man she was even vaguely interested in had just walked out the door.

Tyler was playing with his boat in the tub. "What is my favorite man doing?" Essence asked as she lowered the toilet seat and flopped down.

Mark continued to keep his back to her. He swooped his hand through the water like a wave, sending the boat rocking back and forth. "Your boyfriend didn't have to leave on my account."

"He's not my boyfriend," she countered angrily.

He glanced over at her. "Then what is he? After all, you made it perfectly clear a couple of days ago that the two of you were involved."

Essence pressed her lips firmly together, but didn't bother to comment.

"Okay, Champ. Let's get you out before you shrivel up like a prune." Mark raised the lever in the tub and the water gurgled down the drain. He then wrapped Tyler in a large towel and lifted him out of the tub. His back still to her, he placed Tyler on the rug, he'd been kneeling on and proceeded to dry him. "You want to hand me a diaper?"

**130**

Essence reached for the diaper lying on the sink top and handed it to him. Then she watched as he got Tyler dressed for bed. It was a ritual, until recently, she had handled alone.

Mark slipped the shirt over Tyler's head, then rose himself and turned to face her.

Essence's mouth went dry. Her brain turned to mush. The sight of Mark standing there bare-chested, wearing low riding jeans, sent all thoughts straight out of her head. She inhaled deeply, feeling as if she were on fire. Mark was gorgeous. Lean muscles defined his torso. Taut muscles spanned his abdomen. She took in his wide quarterback shoulders, skin the color of bronze and the dust of dark hair that covered the space between his nipples then narrowed down his middle and disappeared inside his jeans.

"Essence."

"What?" She snapped her eyes back to his face and found his smile just as disarming as the rest of him.

"I said a cup of hot cocoa would be nice. Do you mind putting on some hot water while I put Tyler to bed?"

"Uh…sure." She tried to respond but couldn't quite reclaim her voice. She couldn't think straight with him standing before her looking like he just stepped off the cover of *Ebony Man*.

Although she knew better, her gaze traveled back to his chest. The muscles on his abdomen clinched as he towel dried Tyler's hair. She had the overwhelming urge to touch it to see if it felt as comforting as she remembered. His magnetism washed over her, and sparked her thoughts to those memorable nights in his arms. *Nothing wrong with fantasy*, she guessed, as long as she didn't confuse them with reality.

The spell was suddenly broken when reality took hold. "On second thought," she began, focusing her eyes above his neck. "I'll put Tyler to bed."

"I can do it."

"And so can I," she countered. She felt incredibly selfish when she held out her arms. "Come on sweetheart. It's time to go beddie-bye."

Tyler moved to stand behind his father's leg and clung tightly to his calf.

"Tyler, come to Mommy," she said sternly. When he didn't budge, she added, "Don't you want me to finish reading the doggie story?"

He shook his head and continued to hold onto Mark's leg.

"Tyler, please come give Mommy a kiss," she said with as reasonable a voice as she could manage considering the fact her son preferred his father over her.

Mark looked down at his son. "Tyler, go to your mother."

Tyler stuck his lips out in a pout and when the tears surfaced, Essence caved in. "It's okay, honey. Mark, you go ahead and put him down."

Mark must have noticed the pained look in her eyes, because he made the suggestion, "How about we do it together?"

She nodded. Her shoulders sagged with relief when Mark reached for his shirt and lowered it over his head. She wasn't sure how much more she could resist.

When he scooped Tyler into his arms, she followed them into his room.

She flopped down onto a bench seat at his bedroom window and listened to Mark read to Tyler while they sat together in his rocking chair. Sucking on a bottle of warm milk, it wasn't long before he drifted off to sleep. His little hand clung to Mark's arm, seeking a sense of security. Tyler had quickly grown attached to his father and had earned a special place in his heart. If only Mark could open up his heart and learn to love her, she could willingly accept his offer of marriage. Then their family would be complete. Instead, Tyler would be torn between two people. She wasn't sure how he was going to react when he no longer saw his father every morning.

There had been very few men in her son's life. There was his grandpa and Liz's husband who came over with his wife on occasions. There was also Tamara's husband, her son and yes, Malcolm.

Tyler was a friendly child and he liked Malcolm some of the time. Some days he didn't mind him being around and other days he didn't want to share her. But his attachment to his father was instantaneous. Tyler liked Mark from the start.

Essence frowned. She hadn't anticipated her son becoming so attached to his father so quickly. After his episode in the bathroom, she was concerned. What would happen when Mark left? His leaving nearly destroyed her two years ago. What would his leaving do to their son?

"I think he's asleep," Mark whispered breaking into her thoughts. He rose from the rocking chair with Tyler in his arms. Moving over to the bed, he laid him gently onto the mattress.

She rose from the window and moved over to his crib. Glancing down at Tyler, she grinned. "Yes, he is." She adjusted his blanket then brushed a hand over his dark curls before she pressed a kiss to his head and exited the room behind Mark.

"He was one tired little guy," Mark commented as they stood outside the door of his room. Now that Tyler was asleep, they were finally alone.

Nodding, she added, "He had a full day at the mall."

"I can tell."

A reluctant grin curled at the corners of her full mouth. "And don't forget the Christmas tree. I have to admit that was a good idea."

Mark massaged the back of his neck and smiled. "Thank you."

She moved to the living room and glanced out at the night sky. Small flakes were falling again. She watched them stick to the ground as she searched for the right words. "I'm concerned about Tyler."

"Concerned about what?"

She inhaled deeply as she realized Mark had come to stand directly behind her. She lost her train of thought when she felt the warm heat of his body against her. He wrapped his arms around her midriff and rested his chin on her shoulder.

"Baby, tell me what's bothering you."

She couldn't ignore the electric current that his touch generated through her entire body. She braced herself against the impact he had on her senses, steeled herself not to respond when his mouth brushed against her neck.

Mark turned her slowly around. She gazed up into his eyes and found his face was tense and the look in his eyes was serious. His breath fanned her face, fed the flame now spanning the length of her. "I want to take all your problems away."

Before she took her next breath, he leaned down and covered her mouth with his own. He took things slow, teasing and coaxing her lips apart, tasting her and encouraging her to taste him. And before Essence realized what she was doing, she was reaching up and had placed her arms around his neck. He pulled her snuggly against his erection, letting her feel his long hard length pressed against her pelvis. Pleasure and heat began flowing through her body and settled between her legs. She found her senses spinning as she lost herself in the soft kisses that teased and tantalized. Suddenly aware of what was happening, Essence froze and pushed Mark away.

"Essence, what is it?"

"Don't." She held up her hand to stop him from reaching for her again. "Don't touch me. I can't think straight when you touch me."

He frowned, then his mouth turned up into an earth-shattering grin. "You have a similar effect on me, only mine is much more obvious."

She tried not to look down at the obvious bulge below the waistband of his jeans, but her gaze was drawn to that area just the same. He looked as if he was straining for release. She wanted so badly to lower the zipper of his jeans and stroke him.

"Mark, please be serious. We need to talk." She looked away, not able to bring herself in full contact with his powerful golden gaze. "I didn't realize how quickly Tyler is becoming attached to you."

His look was intense when he said quietly, "He should. I'm his father. Would you rather he be frightened of me like he is with your boyfriend?" All the teasing was gone from his voice and expression.

"He's not afraid of Malcolm. Tyler just preferred to be around you today. He acted the same way with me." She wasn't jealous, she told herself. She was thinking about what was best for her son. "The problem is what will happen when you leave? How do you think that's going to affect him? One day you're here and the next you're gone."

"Who said I'm going anywhere?"

She braced her hands on her hips. "We both know that after the holidays you have to report to Ft. Mead."

"And I plan to still be around. Tyler is my son. If you'd stop being so stubborn, you'd see reason and marry me. Then I can spend the rest of my life with the two of you."

The sincerity of his offer touched something deep inside her, a part of her that had once dreamed of hearing those words. To have him say them to her now out of duty and not love, hurt much more than when he'd said nothing at all.

"I wished you'd get it through your thick skull, I will not now or ever marry you."

Mark stared down at her for a long moment, his eyes growing dark with contempt. "You know what?" he finally said. "You'll never have to worry about me asking you to marry me again." He then turned and stormed out the door.

# CHAPTER TEN

They fell into a strange routine. Mark showed up in the morning early enough to have coffee with Essence and he was there when she came home after work. He cooked something fantastic every evening. Happiness would fill her as they dined together, laughed, and chatted until it was time for Tyler's bedtime story. Then the moment he was fast asleep, Mark would take her in his arms and kiss her until all the strength had drained from her body. Her breasts would tingle and the area between her trembling thighs would throb. Then he would pull away and leave with a casual, "See ya."

It was tough being around him. Essence was left feeling frustrated, disappointed and mad as hell. She found herself wishing he'd hang around a little bit longer, even though she knew that would only lead to trouble. Nevertheless, desire blazed through her. She wanted so much more from him that every part of her was on the constant edge of anticipation. When she was in his arms, he would grind against her, making sure she was well aware of his erection. Every time he was within a foot of her, she felt her insides clench and pull. She tried to act as if it didn't matter, as if she didn't feel anything. However when Mark left and she was alone, she felt only the torment of need.

The sexual tension was becoming unbearable. She felt it and knew he did too. Despite the freezing temperatures, the air around them sizzled with sensual heat. Feelings of lust began to consume her and even though she tried to deny it, that didn't stop the feeling.

Mark didn't even have to kiss or touch her anymore. The moment she saw him, Essence's body began to blaze with desire. When he accidentally brushed against her in passing, a jolt of desire shot through her like lightning. There was no fighting it, the reaction to his scent, his closeness, even the stubborn memories of his kisses wouldn't go away. At first she had tried to avoid any situation he might take advantage of, but now she sought them all out.

Nighttime was even worse. She dreamed of being crushed within his embrace, having him buried deep inside. Each episode made her more miserable. She was quickly approaching the breaking point.

She and Tyler had met Malcolm for dinner on Tuesday, and at the end of the evening she tried kissing him, but it didn't work. With him there was no warming desire or rush of arousal. It was like trying to substitute hamburger for steak. She didn't want just any man. Only Mark would do.

After being on an emotional roller coaster, she called Tamara on Wednesday. Talking to her sister was her undoing. She poured out everything that had been happening between them. She wasn't sure why she had told her, except that this was one time she wanted to hear what her sister had to say. Unfortunately, her sister wasn't very sympathetic. In fact, Tamara thought the entire situation was hilarious.

"Girl, I told you what you had to do," she reiterated between chuckles.

"I'm not sleeping with him," Essence muttered hastily.

"Well you should," Tamara insisted. Her tone was playful but her meaning was not. "That man wants you and even though you try to deny it, you want him too." When her younger sister was slow at responding, she added. "Listen Sis, the only way you're going to find out how you truly feel about him is if you give him some. I guarantee it."

Essence snorted an answer. Leave it to her sister to think sex was the answer. She didn't know how her brother-in-law put up with her.

"Give it a chance; otherwise you're going to regret your decision."

Tamara hung up before Essence could tell her to mind her own business.

The dream started out the way it always did for Mark Saunders. Erotic and arousing. He was in bed with Essence, mouth to mouth, naked body connected to naked body. Her legs were wrapped around his waist. He was buried deep inside her…lost in her heat. His hand moved from the curve of her hip up to cup the swell of her breast, and his own body tightened as he heard her moan with satisfaction, felt her nipple harden beneath his fingers. He resumed pumping inside her in a smooth steady rhythm. Joy became pleasure, and pleasure became necessity, until they were lost in the overwhelming need to belong to each other.

Even while it was happening, he knew it was a dream. The kind you rewound again and again. Tangled in sheets, drenched in sweat, a strangled cry rose in his throat and then he sat up abruptly in bed.

*This isn't working,* he thought, as he swung his legs over the side of the bed and moved toward the bathroom. He had never before been interested enough in any woman to do more than offer her a quick roll in the sack. Yet, here was a woman who wanted nothing from him, while he was the one that wanted more. Hell, he wanted it all. She was unlike any woman he'd ever met. Essence was strong, intelligent, and independent. Too independent for her own good. Yet he respected her, admiring her strength. He also wanted her with an ache that was beyond anything he had ever experienced.

Thoughts of making love to her, really making love to her, made him brick hard, made him groan with frustration. He could take a cold shower to provide some relief, but it didn't help for long. Only one thing would alleviate the problem and she was not here.

Mark reached inside the shower stall and turned on the water. He had to be at Essence's in two hours. After a night of tossing and turning, a shower was in order. The last several days had been hell. He had thought if he spent a week building the sexual chemistry between them, it would have eventually crumbled her defenses and she would have agreed to marry him. If he had realized the torture he would be causing himself, he wouldn't have even bothered. No, that wasn't necessarily true, he thought as he stepped into the stall. He knew good and well that as long as his son was involved, he would have gone through with the plan anyway. On one occasion, he almost believed that his plan might be working. Or perhaps he was just fooling himself, he thought wryly, and sighed.

Reaching for the bar of soap, Mark lathered his washcloth and scrubbed it across his face, using the strong scent as an eye opener. With a little tyke, he needed to be wide-awake and on top of his game.

*Maybe, I'll grill steaks tonight.* She loved his cooking. It hadn't taken as long as he had envisioned for her to give in to his using her kitchen. Now if only everything else was just as easy. He scowled at the thought. Essence was one tough cookie to break. He had two and a half weeks left and he was no closer to convincing her to marry him than he had been when he had first arrived in Delaware.

❧

Essence stood onstage with her students as they sung Jingle Bells. With bells in their hands, they shook them to the beat of the music. She was proud of her class. Every year each classroom tried to outdo the other. This year, her class outdid themselves. They were each dressed in holiday colors. The twins wore Christmas hats. In art class, they had worked on making a sled and cardboard reindeers with Shane

Daniels dressed up in a cotton ball beard and red suit for their rendition of "Santa Claus is Coming to Town." She had convinced him to put his loud voice to use so that his *ho ho ho* could be heard across the gymnasium.

The audience laughed and later applauded as they filed back to their seats.

Essence moved to the back of the room where several of the other teachers were standing.

"Essence, your class was wonderful!" Tabitha exclaimed.

"Thanks, they did it all themselves," Essence beamed proudly.

She glanced up at the stage where the six graders were now putting on a skit.

"You have big plans for the holiday?"

As she nodded, she glanced down the aisle at her students to make sure they were behaving, then returned her attention. "Yes, my family always gets together at my parents' house."

"And what about that handsome man of yours? Are you planning to come back after the break wearing a rock on your finger?"

"I don't think so."

"Well, if you don't want him, I'll take him, cause he is definitely a catch," she giggled.

*If only it were that easy*, she groaned inwardly.

Yes, she had to agree he was definitely a catch, and if she was conniving, she would have used Tyler to trap him into marriage a long time ago, but that had never been the case.

Mark had been true to his word and he never mentioned marriage again…to her disappointment. She didn't know what she wanted anymore. If he asked her she was angry, and when he didn't she was angry. She was getting a headache and didn't know which direction to take. All she knew for certain was that Tyler needed his father and Mark needed him. The rest was complicated. For the sake of her son's future was she ready to risk her heart? And if she did, would Mark grow to love her? *Oh*, she groaned. If only she knew the answer was yes. She would run off and marry him tomorrow.

"Whatever Essence and I decide is between us."

Kelly rolled her eyes. "Sure it is. Just like your decision to leave for two years and forget about her. Just like your decision to just walk back into her life and continue as if nothing had happened."

Without commenting, Mark rose off the floral couch, frustrated and mad. He was running out of options and time. "She said no," he finally said.

Kelly kissed her nephew then lowered him to the living room floor. "Then make her say yes," she replied, frowning with concern.

Sighing audibly, he closed his eyes for a few seconds. "And how do you expect me to do that?"

He moved to stare out of a floor-to-ceiling window and marveled at the view. It was a winter wonderland. Blankets of white snow could be seen for blocks.

"I don't know, but you better figure it out before someone else knocks you out of the race."

He swung around, his face a mask of stone as he remembered finding Malcolm's arm around Essence. He couldn't explain it, but once again a wave of uneasiness swept over him. The feeling had been stronger than when he had discovered Carmen kissing another man.

"Why don't you let me watch Tyler while the two of you spend a night out on the town?"

He moved around a glass coffee table and returned to his seat. "Since when is my sister a romantic? I don't see the men beating down at your door."

She waved dismissively. "I've got issues."

"I agree," he replied, chuckling. His sister's personality was so dominate he felt sorry for any man that stuck around for long. Kelly chewed them up and spit them out. Men naturally flocked to his sister, drawn to her petite figure and beautiful doll-like features. She was one of those women that a man would go the extra mile to make her acquaintance, yet was ready to run for cover only a short time later. Kelly had yet to find a man that complemented her personality.

"Anyway, you're not here to discuss me," she countered, anxious to steer the conversation away from her own personal problems.

"True, but you still haven't told me why you've asked me over here."

"You're here because I was dying to see my nephew." She glanced over at Tyler who was sitting on her sage carpet playing with his building blocks.

She shifted on the couch, tucking her legs beneath her. "Now let's work on a plan."

He chuckled. "I thought I was the big brother?"

"Yes, but you suck at love."

"And you don't?" he gaped.

Grudgingly, she admitted, "I can give advice. I'm just not good at using it on my own love life."

Dark eyes narrowed on her for a moment. "Who said anything about love?"

"What else could it be?"

Mark wasn't ready to comment. He sighed. "I'm tired of fighting a losing battle. I'll just have to come see my son whenever I can."

"Are you crazy! How often do you think you'll be able to fly in from Texas? No where near enough."

"What else am I supposed do?"

"Fight, big head, fight!" She made a sound that was part snort. "Come on big brother, time is of the essence."

He breathed deeply as his eyes met Kelly's. "I'll take any suggestions."

She simply smirked and said, "I thought you'd never ask."

Hours after Mark had left, Kelly put the remainder of a pot roast in the refrigerator, then reached for a dish towel and wiped down the stove top.

Her brother was definitely a piece of work, she thought as she sprayed cleaner over a caked on spill. However, after talking extensively for the better part of four hours, she was certain there was hope for the couple after all. Because even though Mark hadn't realized it yet, he was madly in love with Essence Monroe.

Her lips curled unconsciously upward as she remembered the signs. The evidence had been quite obvious. She had always been able to read the gold tones of his eyes that usually shifted to bronze when he was worried or concerned about something that he had very little control over.

Kelly chuckled softly as she rinsed out the rag and draped it over the faucet of the sink. She was truly thankful that a woman had finally taught her big brother how to love again. After that witch Carmen had broken his heart, she didn't think this day would ever come. And since she was responsible for introducing Mark to Essence in the first place, she planned to take all the credit.

Essence had been the easy part. One look at her at the mall and Kelly had been certain her heart still belonged to her brother. It would only be a matter of time before the two of them, along with Tyler, became a family.

Humming to herself, Kelly switched off the light and strolled into the living room to catch the evening news. She reached for the remote control then pressed the power button and changed channels until she found a local station.

She took a seat on her couch and sank between several lime green pillows. She kicked off her house shoes and curled her legs beneath her. Laying her head on a pillow, she sighed with contentment. After a Christmas party with her students on Thursday, she had escorted them out to the buses and bid them goodbye. She looked forward to the next two weeks alone in her apartment or surrounded by her family. She was thankful for the love and support of her family because she couldn't seem to get that kind of love or commitment from any man. Instead, the men she had encountered turned out to be one disappointment after the next. When she admitted to her brother that she had issues, Kelly had hit it right on the nail.

She glanced away from the weather report and stared at an original Thomas Blackshear collectible setting on top of the television console. The piece had been a gift from her last boyfriend, Lance Lewis.

She had thought he loved her and he had told her numerous times that he respected her belief to save her virginity for her wedding night. Only he didn't really understand. He had hoped after months of wining and dining, she would have eventually invited him to her virginal bed. Finally, after six months of refusals he had deemed the situation impossible and tired from trying to change her mind. He had turned out to be like so many others, interested in her body first, everything else second.

Although she believed that there were good men out there who appreciated a woman with values, she just hadn't found one yet and had since given up looking. Good things came to those who waited and she was determined to stand for what she believed in with the hope that someday a man would walk in her life who would love her for who she truly was.

She glanced down at the screen in time to find that more snow was in the forecast. She was glad. She loved having fresh white snow on Christmas. It was something she had in common with her big sister Calaine.

She adored her older sister. They had been close since they first met over two years ago. Since then, she had visited Calaine and her husband David in Missouri on several occasions. In fact, she had been by her sister's side at the birth of their daughter. She couldn't wait for them to arrive. They would be staying with her parents during their visit before going to San Antonio to spend time with David's family.

She loved hearing the fascinating story about how the two had met and David's determination that the two of them were meant to be together almost ten years before the two were reunited. It reminded her of a crush she once had on her brother's best friend, Diamere.

Kelly had only been thirteen when she had first met him. He had been eighteen at the time and more handsome than Denzel. She sighed deeply as she remembered answering the front door to find the man standing on the other side. Diamere and Mark were attending Delaware State University and had been studying for midterms. She spent the entire evening finding excuses to go into her brother's room just to catch a glimpse of his friend.

After that, Diamere became a regular at their house and Kelly found herself taking extra care in her appearance. By the end of eighth grade, she had fallen in love with Diamere.

She remembered telling him she was saving herself for her husband and he told her that her virginity was one thing she should never let anyone take from her until she was ready.

She even remembered asking him to marry her.

She chuckled at the memory. She remembered counting the days until she would turn eighteen. Now that she would finally be considered a woman, she had hoped that Diamere would take her seriously. But by then he was engaged to Jada and had broken her heart. It wasn't until she left for college that she had finally gotten over her childhood crush and moved on with her life. She thought about Diamere from time to time and the only reason she was thinking about him now was because Mark had told her Diamere had decided not to re-enlist in the Air Force and had considered coming home to run the family restaurant chain.

Kelly hugged a pillow close to her chest, then released a peaceful sigh. Diamere had always been a fixture at her parents' home for the holiday. Her heart tingled at the possibility of seeing him for Christmas.

❧

Essence shut off the water and stepped out of the shower stall. She reached for a towel hanging on the rack next to the sink and quickly dried off. She was tired, more mentally than physically. Now that school was closed for the rest of the year, she planned to sleep late in the morning. That is, if Tyler decided to sleep late himself. He had been sound asleep since eight o'clock. Glancing down at the waterproof watch on her arm, she noticed it was barely ten.

Reaching for her flannel gown that was hanging on the back of the bathroom door, she pulled it over her head and moved toward the sink. She stared at her reflection in the mirror and all she could do was think how dumb the woman staring back at her had been.

When Mark had dropped Tyler off earlier this evening, they both knew that the need for Mark to be at her house early in the morning was over. School had ended for the year. Any further interaction with her son would be scheduled time. It saddened her because she had gotten used to them being in her house together feeling like…like a family.

She reached for her face cleanser and spread it across her face and neck then took a wet cloth and lathered it in. After she rinsed it off, she grabbed her toothbrush and paste.

She had discovered her heart wasn't in it anymore. She no longer wanted to deny the inevitable. She wanted him with an intensity that scared her.

After she returned her toothbrush to the holder, she moved into her room and climbed under the covers. The bed felt so cold and alone. How wonderful it would be if Mark were here, warming her bed and her soul. She ached for his presence, to feel his warm body pressed against her. Deep in her heart, she knew she could never settle for a loveless marriage. But what did that have to do with her own personal fulfillment? She had needs that hadn't been met in two years and she was ready to explode with longing. She wanted one man and one man only. She wanted Mark and could no longer deny it. She had come to the decision and the next time she saw him she was going to tell him. A smile curled on her lips while a warm feeling flowed through her blood.

*A sexual relationship.* That way Mark would be getting half of what he wanted, she would get hers, and Tyler, well, Tyler would have both of his parents. Mark was welcome to visit them from Maryland as often as he liked.

She hugged her legs to her chest. It sounded like a wonderful arrangement. What would Mark say?

She clicked off the lamp on her bedside table then lowered her head on the pillow and pulled her covers up to her neck. Now that she had made up her mind, sleep was going to come easier tonight.

It wasn't long before she was dreaming. Mark was showing her in the only way he knew how that she was everything to him. The phone rang, practically scaring her.

"Hello?"

"Essence?"

"Mark?" Tenderness filled her heart.

"Did I wake you?" he asked his deep powerful voice carrying easily through the phone.

She sat up in the bed and unconsciously ran her fingers through her hair. "No. I was up, um…reading." There was a long moment of silence. "Is there something I can do for you?"

"Yes, there is. I want to know if you'd have dinner with me tomorrow night?"

"I'd love to," she replied not bothering to hide the pleasure in her voice.

"Good," he said. "I'll call you in the morning."

"Okay."

"Sweet dreams, darling."

She was still cradling the phone long after she had said goodbye.

# CHAPTER ELEVEN

Essence moved to a small vanity in the corner of the room and took a seat in front of an oval mirror. She brushed her curls, then used pins to pull her hair up and away from her face. Satisfied, she reached for her foundation and within minutes, she had applied bronze eye shadow, a light dusting of rose-colored blush, and matching lipstick. Staring at her reflection, she noticed the moles on her upper lip and at the corner of her right eye. They were hereditary on her father's side of the family. When she was young, she tried unsuccessfully to conceal them. As she had grown older, she'd learned to accept them.

Reaching for her favorite perfume, Escada, she dabbed a little at her wrists and behind her ears, then moved across her bedroom.

Kelly had called during breakfast wanting to keep her nephew overnight. Essence had Tyler packed up and ready to go by noon. She was amazed how quickly Tyler had taken to his auntie. He had left without crying and had even waved his little hand as they pulled out the driveway. It brought tears to her eyes the way her son had grown attached to his paternal family. She could never deny him his heritage. *Never again.*

Since she had risen, the only thing Essence could think of was Mark. She had spent hours agonizing over what to wear, but nothing seemed right for such a special occasion.

It had taken several hours at the mall with Tamara, before she had decided on a simple bronze two-piece outfit, consisting of a knit skirt and matching tunic top that stretched provocatively over her body. She also found a pair of high-heeled chocolate suede boots that made her legs appear longer.

She stood in front of a full-length mirror, staring at her reflection. She pursed her lips. The skirt might be just a little too tight around the hips, she thought. "Oh, well, it's too late to change now." Mark was scheduled to arrive at any minute.

She reached for a small suede purse and moved into the kitchen. Looking inside the cabinet, she removed a bag of pretzels. In her excitement, she had eaten very little for breakfast and only a small salad while at the mall food court for lunch, which she had barely touched.

As soon as she had unloaded the dishwasher, the doorbell rang, sending her pulse into a gallop. She took a deep breath, then opened the door to him. She forced a calm expression when in actuality her stomach was balled up in a knot.

If she'd had any doubts about her appearance, they were quickly put to rest when she saw the flicker of approval in his golden eyes.

Happiness filled her heart. Just to see Mark standing on her doorstep wearing a warm lazy smile insured her that she had made the right choice. As her pulse fluttered, there was no denying her feelings. Any doubts about where the evening may lead were far and few. She was confident she had chosen the correct path.

"Hey baby."

The words glided off his tongue and landed on her breasts then hummed through her veins. She had to struggle for a greeting of her own.

"Hi, f" came out in a raspy whisper.

Mark looked impeccable in a smoke gray dinner suit and a long tweed coat. With his hands tucked into his trousers pockets, he appeared relaxed. All she could do was grip the door like grim death as her knees went weak. She smiled drinking him in and lost track of time until he quirked an eyebrow.

"As much as your beauty warms my soul, it's quite nippy out here."

"Oh, I'm sorry." With a blush, she stepped aside and allowed him in with a soft laugh that they shared. Essence closed the door and turned to him, eyes smiling up at him. Before she lost the nerve to do as she had planned, she stepped forward, placing a hand at the center of his chest. She rose on her tiptoes and kissed him. Mark lowered his head and when their lips met, she was certain there was an explosion, shocking her senses. Fireworks went off as vivid as on the Fourth of July. He kept his arms by his sides and allowed her to lead. Essence mated her tongue with his. Each kiss told them she was a woman and he was indeed a man. She could have continued the kiss, but she had plans and kissing was only the tip of the iceberg.

Pulling back slightly, she stared up at him then winked, breaking the moment.

"Wow!" was all Mark was able to say and for now that was more than enough.

Gold eyes narrowed dangerously, though they couldn't hide the glitter in his eyes. "Girl, you've got me dangling on a string tonight."

If only he was, she thought wistfully, but this was just part of the plan and she was determined to keep her side of it. "It's nice to know I have that kind of power," she whispered in agreement.

"And what exactly do you intend to do with it?" The softly seductive question sent shivers down her spine.

Essence's smile was seductive itself as she toyed with his lapel. "Well, now...that's for me to know and for you to find out," she purred, glancing up at him through her lashes.

Mark growled low in his throat. "Did anyone ever tell you you're a dreadful tease?"

Her smile broadened into a grin. "Hmm, actually I've heard that quite often, but no one ever seemed to mind." She brushed past him and sashayed into the kitchen, with him hot on her trail.

"Would you like a drink before we leave?" Her back was to him as she reached for a glass out the cabinet and moved toward the refrigerator for ice.

"No, I'm fine," Mark said. He leaned against the counter with his hands folded across his chest and slowly took in her appearance from head to toe. Essence glanced over at him in time to watch him assessing her.

"I take it I'm dressed appropriately for the evening?"

He allowed his gaze to roam over the discreet outfit she was wearing and nodded approvingly. "You look fabulous." His dimples deepened. "That color on you takes my breath away."

"Thank you. You're looking quite delectable yourself." Essence turned and leaned back against the refrigerator, folded her arms, and tipped her head to one side. She spied a single red rose peeking out the inside pocket of his coat. "Is that for someone special?"

Following the trail of her eyes, he reached into his pocket, removed the flower and presented it to her. "Yes, it is. Someone very, very special." A fire glowed in the depths of his eyes.

Mark continued to stare at the woman he planned to marry and his breath caught in his chest. Essence looked stunning from the curls piled high on her head, to the outfit that showed all her beautiful curves. A pair of diamond earrings sparkled at her lobes and an elegant diamond bracelet was clasped around her left wrist. She wore light make-up and his favorite red lipstick that added a gleam of fire to her hair.

"Flattery will get you everywhere," she replied, while batting her eyes innocently. Suddenly losing her thirst for anything but Mark, she lowered the glass to the counter.

"In that case, you look good in a pair of sweatpants," he confided gruffly. The two-piece outfit showed very little bare flesh, but brought havoc to his imagination. "In fact, you look so good tonight that I'm tempted to stay right here just so I can have you all to myself."

"Oh, no. I didn't get all dressed up for nothing."

He chuckled then shook his head. "It's going to be difficult to keep my eyes and hands off you, but I'll try."

"Good," she declared with satisfaction. "It's only fair. You've had the same affect on me since your return," she admitted honestly.

"What else have I been doing to you?" he asked in a tone that skittered along her nerves, setting them at attention.

"Captain, if you play your cards right, you just might find out," she replied in a flirty voice. Lifting her eyes to his, she was unable to resist adding, "I've been looking forward to this night all day."

"In that case, let's get a move on."

She agreed, seconds before he pulled her effortlessly into his arms, taking her lips in a long deep soul-searching kiss that she returned in equal measures, and which, when they finally broke apart, left them breathless but temporarily satisfied.

"Good Lord, I can't seem to get enough of you," he said thickly, resting his forehead against hers. Mark settled his hands on her hips, holding her to him so that she could feel the effect she had on him. Just as she had thought, he was hard as a brick.

Essence linked her hands around his neck and sighed. "I love hair on your face."

His eyebrow rose, surprised at her comment. Most of the women he had encountered said it irritated their face if he rubbed against them. "I wish I could wear a beard, but the military doesn't allow it unless you have a shaving profile."

"What's that?"

"It's a waiver." She still looked confused so he tried to explain.

"Have you ever seen a man whose face is all broken out?" Essence nodded. "Well, in cases like that, a soldier can get permission to wear a beard."

"Oh, then I guess I better enjoy it while I can."

"Yeah, you notice whenever I'm on leave for longer than a week, I allow it to grow freely." He returned her smile. "It's nice to see how I look with hair from time to time."

"It looks fabulous." She rubbed her cheek against his stubble. Mark took a deep breath, inhaling her fabulous scent. The smell caused a stirring in his loins. If they didn't leave now, they would be spending the evening in her bed.

"Let's get out of here."

She nodded in agreement. Essence reached in the closet for a long camel-colored wool coat that Mark helped her into. She locked up and headed down the steps where she found a silver Eldorado.

"It's my dad's," he commented when she glanced sideways in surprise.

"Very nice."

He nodded in agreement. "He just bought it last week. I thought I'd test it out tonight."

Opening the passenger side door, he helped her into the car, and shut the door as she pulled the seat belt across her chest.

Glancing over at him as he pulled out the driveway, she could not help but glance at his profile. Her pulse jumped. His mahogany face and chiseled features were mesmerizing. She had to pinch herself to keep from staring.

"Where are you taking me?" she asked.

He tore his eyes away from the road long enough to say, "It's a surprise."

She relaxed against the leather seat, watching the festive city whiz by as Mark turned onto the highway, heading toward Wilmington. Christmas lights were hung on almost every building and house they passed. With Christmas only three days away she was beginning to feel the spirit.

Mark reached over and pushed in a CD and the sounds of the R&B group Dru Hill's "Do You Believe" filled the interior making it unnecessary to talk. She was glad because sitting beside this virile man gave her a lot to think about. Giving into her feelings seemed to be the most natural thing to do. Anticipation bubbled up inside her. Tonight when Mark made a pass, she would be willing and ready.

They had crossed the toll bridge before he spoke again. "My mother has asked me to invite you to Christmas dinner."

She glanced over at him. "Would you like me to be there?"

Without looking away from the flow of traffic, he nodded and replied, "I would be honored to introduce you to my family."

"Then I would be honored to attend," she said gleefully. Essence used her hand to conceal a wide smile. Meeting his family was a positive step.

"Be prepared...they are a very large and affectionate group."

She nodded, knowing already what he meant. When she had met his mother for the first time at the mall, she had quickly pulled her into an affectionate embrace. Kelly was the same way the entire year they had taught together. A thought occurred to her. Was that the reason why Mark had a habit of touching her even when she asked him not to? If so, was his affection toward her a habit or was it impossible to deny himself the pleasure of having her in his arms? She swallowed and hoped it was the latter.

"My sister, Calaine, should be arriving early Christmas morning with her family."

"Isn't she the sister you just recently met?"

Mark nodded as he pulled off the highway. "Yes, and I can't wait to see her." He and his sister were introduced for the first time three months before he had received orders that he had been reassigned to a military intelligence unit in Germany. He found his sister to be a beautiful woman with a loving heart. She had quickly found a place in his heart when she had forgiven his mother for giving her up for adoption when she was only a few weeks old.

He pulled into the parking lot of a fancy little Italian restaurant and maneuvered into a parking space near the door. He left the car running long enough to reach across and clasped her fingers. Glancing over, their gazes fused. "Tonight is about you and me."

His words flowed through her like fine wine. The look in his eyes told her that dinner was only the beginning.

They moved inside the building where a man was standing behind a podium. "Good evening, Mr. Saunders. Two for dinner?"

"Yes, please."

Mark's hold on Essence's waist tightened as they followed the young man to a table for two in a far corner. A lit candle was at the center of the table draped with a white tablecloth. Soft violin music was heard in the background.

Mark seated her before sitting down opposite her. The *maitre d'* handed them each a menu then told them their waiter would be with them shortly.

While looking over the menu, an elegantly dressed man and woman came to the table. Introductions were made and Essence learned they were the owners. They welcomed her to their restaurant, asked Mark to tell his parents hello, then returned to the back of the establishment.

She glanced across the table at Mark and smiled. "Friends of your parents?"

Nodding, he gave her a dazzling smile. "Mr. Giovanni and my father were on the force together. After he retired, he and his wife, Carmela, opened this restaurant. That's their son Donny who greeted us at the door." He paused to chuckle. "I should have known Donny would run and tell them I was here with a female. I think they wanted to get a good look at you."

Essence dropped her lashes and blushed. "They seem like a nice family."

"They are." He lowered his menu and reached for her right hand from across the table. "Why don't I order a nice Italian wine and we share a toast?"

She stared at him through her lashes unaware of the seductive gesture. "What are we toasting to?"

"To us."

"That sounds wonderful." She tore her eyes away from his magnetic pull and looked around the crowded room. Every table was occupied. "This restaurant is wonderful. I had no idea it was here." It was virtually impossible to find a restaurant with less than an hour wait on the weekend.

He nodded in agreement. "*Giovanni's* offers two things I find invaluable…good food and a friendly atmosphere."

She had his undivided attention during their meal. They could have been the only two people in the room. The food was delicious. They both had a house salad with homemade Italian dressing and fresh baked bread. She chose the seafood pasta with a white sauce, while Mark chose the house special—spaghetti. Essence practically split her side when Mrs. Giovanni brought the food out personally and fed Mark several forkfuls until she was certain the sauce was to his satisfaction.

It was late when they finally left. Essence had no idea where the time had gone. She settled in the luxury vehicle with a sigh of satisfaction and allowed her thoughts to drift as Mark set the car in motion. Happiness was a warm bubble inside her and she felt that way simply by being with him.

When they pulled into the driveway, Mark climbed out and assisted her by opening the door.

Her heart raced as they mounted the steps to her home. She looked into his eyes and, even in the darkness, she could see the fire burning way down deep inside. Desire had been an unspoken emotion between them all evening. The silent companion had been quietly building up, only recognized in a look or a touch. Until now, it was just below the surface—ready to explode out of control. Essence's stomach tightened, starting up that familiar ache inside her. She wanted him desperately. At the same time her heart skipped. From the glazed look in his eyes, he was giving her a choice. If she wanted to end the night right now, he would kiss her goodnight and leave or she could invite him in.

She reached into the bottom of her purse for her keys and fumbled twice before she successfully opened the door. As soon as they stepped inside the house, Mark caught her shoulders and drew her toward him. His lips sought hers. Just like every other time, Essence was lost at once.

She had been yearning for this moment ever since she had made the decision to allow things to happen naturally. She wrapped her arms around his neck, arching so that her breasts pressed tightly against him through their coats. A gasp escaped her lips when Mark thrust his tongue inside, his hands slipping down her sides to grasp her waist. He inched forward, pressing her back against the door that stood ajar. When his mouth left hers to trail down her neck, she tipped her head slightly to the side, releasing a murmur of pleasure. Then she shuddered and brought his head back around so she could nip at his neck in return, enjoying the slight roughness of his chin against her lips and tongue.

"I love the way you taste," he murmured breathlessly, raising his head to kiss her lips again. He kissed her passionately, one hand dropping down over her stomach, then lower until it rested between her legs. There, he pressed gently, and his kisses became more teasing than satisfying. A growl of frustration slipped from her throat. Then, Mark withdrew his hands, and his lips, and gave her a quick peck on the nose.

"Thank you for dinner. I'll bring Tyler home tomorrow afternoon."

Eyes blinking open, Essence stared in amazement at his retreating back. Leaning her head against the door, she watched him climb back into the car and seconds later drive away.

Tamara's expression was one of disbelief. "I can't believe he played you like that."

Essence turned away from the counter carrying two cups of hot cocoa to the table and met her sister's amused features. She found very little humor in her present situation.

"I can't understand it. I invited him in and had every intention of asking him to stay the night when he turned and walked away. I don't know what is wrong with that man?" she huffed.

She had never been so angry in her life. She had bought a new outfit, allowed Kelly to keep Tyler overnight and had planned to spend an entire night in his arms. What did he want from her? He had made it very clear that she had to make the next move. So what happened? She thought her body language spoke for itself. Apparently, it hadn't.

Angry and too humiliated to sleep, she had climbed into her car and driven the fifteen-minute drive to her sister's sprawling two-story house. No sooner had she stepped into the house, she related the events of the evening. Just as she had expected, Tamara thought the entire situation was hilarious.

"I'll tell you what's wrong," Tamara said as she leaned across the kitchen table. "He's tired of playing games."

"Who's playing games?"

"You are," she laughed softly as she reached across the table to add a few marshmallows to her cocoa. "You have strung that poor man along since he got back, when you know good and well you want him."

Essence rolled her eyes to the recess lighting on the ceiling. "I never said I didn't want him. I just don't want to marry him."

"Then what's the problem?" Tamara's penetrating gaze caught and held her as she took a cautious sip.

A distressed look marred her face. "The problem is I'm so horny I don't know what I'm going to do." She flopped down at the table, leaned her forehead in the palm of her hand and groaned. She couldn't understand it. For two years, she went without even thinking about sex. She had been content with her celibate state because it had been her choice. Then Mark had to come along and disrupt her life. Now she couldn't sleep without dreaming of him. He made her ache. He made her want. He made her realize how long she had been without a man and as a result, she wanted him again as her lover. She was shocked at the intensity she felt to be naked and hot beneath him.

"I told you what you got to do—seduce him," Tamara reminded.

Essence emitted a groan. "What do you think I was trying to do?"

"Try harder. Girl the ball is in your court. You hold the trump card."

Her forehead bunched with confusion. "The trump card?"

She smirked. "Yeah, Tyler."

Essence gave her a dismissive wave. "Girl, whatever."

"What's really the problem? You said it yourself…Tyler needs his father. You love Mark and he wants to marry you." When Essence rolled her eyes, Tamara repeated, "So, what's the problem? It sounds like the perfect solution."

"He doesn't love me." Grief and despair tore at her heart.

"Girl, he will learn to love you if he hasn't already." Tamara spoke slowly as if sensing her doubts.

Essence tunneled her fingers through her hair, pushing thick curls off her forehead and behind her ear. "Nope, I think I'm going to end it. I can't deal with this emotional stress." She didn't know how much more she could take.

"Wait a minute! You're going to end it?" Tamara gaped from across the table.

Essence loved Mark in a way that she would never love another man, and the pain of knowing that, made her future that much more impossible.

Swallowing the sob that rose in her throat, she looked up and said, "Yes, I have to."

Reaching for her hot chocolate, Tamara took a sip. "I hope you know what you're doing?"

Essence glanced over at her and hoped that she looked more confident than she felt. She hoped she wasn't about to make a grave mistake that she would end up regretting later.

"I can't believe you're all bent out of shape over a woman," Diamere cackled. "Not with all these gorgeous honeys in this joint."

After Mark had gotten away from Essence as fast as he could, he had returned home to find that Diamere had called. Mark wasn't sure why he had agreed to go out and have a drink, except that he hadn't seen his homey in years. He and Diamere had grown up together and had been best friends since third grade. When he had joined the Army, Diamere had joined the Air Force. As a pilot, Captain Diamere Redmond enjoyed meeting women as he traveled all over the world. He was a ladies' man. Settling down was the farthest thing from his mind.

The barmaid brought them another round of beers. Her short, spandex dress did not go unnoticed.

"My, my, my, you look good enough to eat," Diamere cooed.

Her thick painted lips curled into an overly seductive smile as she took in his fair skin that magnified the inky blackness of his eyes. "Down boy." She tickled his chin and moved to the next table.

Even though the music was blasting from the speakers, it was unsuccessful at driving out his thoughts. Mark hadn't meant to leave Essence as abruptly as he had, but he knew that if he hadn't left when he did, there would have been no way to have stopped him from having her tonight. He wanted her with a burning ache and was ready to explode.

All through the night he had sensed her nervousness when, unable to resist, he'd done nothing more than reach out and touch her face or hand.

She should consider herself lucky, Mark decided as he tilted his head back and took several long swallows from the Heineken bottle. He'd wanted to touch her elsewhere, kiss her everywhere. Just yesterday, he'd battled to keep from coming up behind her while she stood in front of the stove and turn up the heat by slipping his hand inside her baggy sweatpants. But he'd decided to stick to his guns and wait for her to make the next move, even if it was killing him to do so. He had been dead serious when he told her he wasn't going to make love to her until she came to him. It needed to be her decision, not his, that brought her to his bed. She had to make up her mind that she was willing to enter into a relationship that might never be more than two people sharing in their child and intimacy.

He had to admit, tonight, Essence had been different. He could see it in her eyes when he had arrived. Something different had burned in their depths. When she had kissed him, it was as if she'd just struck a match and lit the wick on a candle. The slow burn had continued during the entire outing. He had been rock hard through dinner and it had persisted on the ride back to her house. *No*, was one word he couldn't bear to hear. Nor could he bear to play her game any longer. Something told him she had wanted him tonight, while another part told him she was still unsure. Oh, he was definitely frustrated, but until he heard her say it, until she made the first move, he was determined to keep their physical contact to a minimum.

"So when do I get to meet this hottie who has your boxers in a bind?" Diamere asked, interrupting his thoughts.

"She's coming to my parents' for dinner."

"Good, cause I'm planning to be there. I haven't seen your fine little sister in a while."

Mark's eyes bore a silent warning. "Don't even go there. My sister isn't interested in being added to your list of women."

It was no secret Diamere had the hots for Kelly, but Mark didn't have to worry. Kelly wouldn't give him the time of day.

"I still can't believe you're a daddy." He shook his head with utter disbelief.

Mark brought the bottle to his lips, then grinned. "Yeah, and you're about to become a daddy. So what are you going to do?"

Diamere took a sip from the bottle, then shrugged. "Ryan's threatening to sue for child support. I think I might have to marry her."

Mark choked on his beer. "You're kidding, right?"

He rubbed his clean-shaven chin. "You know what they say...it's cheaper to keep em."

Mark gave him a skeptical look. "Yeah...I guess."

A woman strolled by wearing too much perfume. Diamere's eyes followed her across the room.

Mark laughed. "Are you sure you want to give all this up for marriage?"

"Nope...but I will. Besides, we're not here to talk about me. We're supposed to be discussing you. So what are *you* going to do?"

"I don't know, man. I've never had to work this hard before. It's challenging and frustrating."

"Yeah, but is she worth all that?"

Thinking about Essence's smile, he nodded. "Oh, yes, she's worth it. However, she is going to have to make the next move." *Even if it kills me.*

# CHAPTER TWELVE

Essence awakened the next morning after a restless night of tossing and turning. She slipped into her favorite lavender sweatpants and purple T-shirt and padded into the kitchen only to discover that she was out of coffee. Mumbling under her breath she settled for a cup of warm milk while she watched the news. The weatherman forecasted ice and freezing rain. By the time she burned the bacon and overcooked her eggs, it was clear to assume it was not going to be a good day.

She was angry. Angry because Mark was playing games. Angry at herself for allowing him to do so.

"Stupid," she mumbled under her breath as she pulled the vacuum cleaner out the hall closet and dragged it into the living room. "You haven't learned a thing in two years," she scolded. Removing a two-toned beige rug from the floor, she shook the dust onto the carpet then laid it aside. She reached for a box of gingerbread cookie scented carpet fresh and sprinkled it around the room then moved into the kitchen and grabbed a rag and a bottle of furniture polish from under the sink. While she polished the marble inlaid tables, she thought about what Tamara had suggested the night before.

After last night, seducing Mark was out of the question. Essence refused to run after him. She had never run after a man before and she was not about to begin now. If anyone should be doing the chasing, it should be him. After all, Mark had left her after making it clear he didn't want a commitment, only to return two years later to find out that she gave birth to his son and now had the audacity to offer her a loveless marriage. Her lips puckered with annoyance. What kind of fool did he take her for? Well, she wasn't having it. If anyone was playing games, it was him.

She moved behind the vacuum cleaner and switched it on, taking her frustrations out as she pushed and pulled the machine around the room. Essence was surprised she hadn't dislocated a shoulder blade in the process.

Hearing something, she shut off the power and listened long enough to realize it was the doorbell. Stepping over the cord, she walked to the door and opened it.

"Hi Malcolm," she said warmly, pleased to see him. "What are you doing here?"

He wiped his feet off on the mat, then stepped inside. "Do I have to have a reason to see you?"

He pulled her against his damp coat and did something he had never done before. He leaned over and kissed her full on the mouth, prying her lips apart and slipped his tongue inside.

*Good Lord! What had gotten into him?*

When she finally managed to pull away, she turned and quickly shut the door. Facing him again, Essence noticed faint uneasiness gnawing away from his usual confident demeanor. "Is something wrong?" she asked.

Malcolm continued to stare down in her eyes. "No, I've simply missed you, that's all." He exchanged a smile with her. "I'm leaving in the morning and wanted to try one last time and see if I could convince you to come with me."

Malcolm had been asking her repeatedly for almost a month to drive with him to South Carolina for the holiday. Each time she had given him the same answer.

Slowly, she shook her head. "I've already told you I couldn't. I have family coming for the holiday."

Malcolm smirked. "A brother won't know unless he asks." His smile wavered slightly. "Come, have a seat. I want to talk to you."

She saw the seriousness of his gaze and hesitated slightly. "What is it?"

He winked. "It's a surprise."

Malcolm took her hand and led her into the living room where they took a seat on the couch. He pulled her down beside him. After they each had shifted comfortably on the cushions, Malcolm reached over and placed her hands in his lap.

The silence was killing her. "What is it, Malcolm? Did something happen?"

His nose was red from the wind and his hands cold. His dark satin eyes were intense as they came down to study her. Essence noticed a strange eager look flash in his eyes and she knew then without a doubt what he was about to say. *Oh no!*

"Malcolm, listen...I—"

He raised a finger to her lips and silenced her. "Don't say anything yet. Let me speak first." He lowered his hand and placed it on top of hers, cupping her hands between his.

"I don't want to leave before I have a chance to tell you how I feel." Again he stopped her before she could interrupt. "I love you Essence, and if you'll let me, I want to spend the rest of my life making you and Tyler happy." In the blink of an eye, he slipped a ring on her finger before she could protest. "It belonged to my grandmother."

Essence merely stared, stunned and speechless, until her lashes eventually dropped to hide her eyes. She wished that Malcolm hadn't chose today of all days. Tears glistened her eyes. Why couldn't it have been Mark slipping a ring on her finger and confessing his love?

She opened her eyes to gaze down at the ring on her finger then closed them again. It was beautiful, but she felt no desire to stare down and admire the diamond for an endless amount of time, the way a woman would when she was in love. Instead, she felt a strong desire to cry because she felt nothing—absolutely nothing—for him.

She finally raised her head and glanced at Malcolm. He must have mistaken her tears for joy, for he leaned forward and reclaimed her lips. When he pulled back, excitement sparkled in his eyes. "Sweetheart, I know we'll be good together. I promise to do everything in my power to make you the happiest woman in the world," he vowed with intense pleasure.

*Say something!* This was her opportunity to set him straight before things went too far. "Malcolm, this is really nice but—"

"Please, don't say anything until I get back," he insisted.

Essence knew she should have tried to shake some sense into him and insisted that he listen to reason but, unfortunately, she was too stunned to argue.

Another objection bubbled in her throat, and Malcolm planted a swift kiss to her lips to keep her from voicing them.

Finally, he rose to his feet. "The weather forecast calls for freezing rain this evening, so I'd better get a move on."

Essence moved with him to the door, anxious to get rid of him as quickly as possible. Mark was due to arrive at any minute and she needed time to think. Besides, with the animosity that vibrated between the two the last time they were both in the same room, she knew she needed to send him quickly on his way and get his grandmother's ring off her finger.

She swung the door open. Malcolm draped an arm around her waist and his lips swooped down to capture hers. His kiss was urgent and exploratory, and lingered longer than she deemed necessary. And just as she found the guts to push him away, she heard tapping on the storm door glass that caused her to jump away from Malcolm.

"Mark!" she gasped. As their eyes met, shock ran through her.

With Tyler asleep in his arms, he opened the glass door and stepped into the house.

"It looks like I arrived just in time," he said. Essence saw a cold fury settle into his features as he looked from her to Malcolm.

She took a deep breath and forced a smile. "Malcolm was just leaving."

Mark tore his eyes away and looked at the man to his left who was smiling smugly. "Then I advise him to get a move on."

Essence heard the challenge in his voice and quickly spoke out. "Yes, yes, the…uh, snow is getting quite heavy."

Malcolm's teeth gleamed straight and white, either oblivious or clearly ignoring the tension surrounding them. "Now that I've given Essence her Christmas present, I will be on my way."

Her heart thumped. *No, please don't say it,* she groaned inwardly. But Malcolm showed no signs of relenting. In fact, he seemed to enjoy her struggle to regain her composure. He squeezed her closer, then glanced at Mark.

"Let me be the first to tell you…Essence and I are officially engaged."

*Oh, no he didn't.* She was speechless as Mark's eyes shifted down to her hand where Malcolm's ring fit snugly on her finger. Mark glanced up, his dark gaze locking onto hers with the intensity of a bull preparing to charge. She struggled to pull air past the knot in her throat.

"Congratulations. You're a lucky man."

Mark wore a sickly sweet smile that caused the pit of her stomach to churn. Even though his comment was directed at Malcolm, his gaze was glued to hers. Eyes locked, he glared at her until Essence couldn't take anymore. She looked away. Seconds later she felt a breeze as he brushed past her and moved with Tyler down the hall.

Tears were burning at the brims of her eyes when she wiggled away from Malcolm's hold. She faced him angry enough to scratch his eyes out. "Why did you tell him that?" she asked through clenched teeth, not wanting Mark to overhear their conversation.

Malcolm was surprised at her rough tone. Realizing that he had acted hastily, he offered her an apologetic smile. "I'm sorry. I got a little carried away. But you haven't said no. So as far as I am concerned we are engaged until you tell me otherwise."

*I did try to tell you no, only you weren't listening!* No amount of time would change her mind, but Essence didn't have the courage to tell him that just yet, especially not while Mark was somewhere in her house possibly listening. She was already hurting. No point in ruining Malcolm's holiday. The least she could do since she was already wearing his ring was to wait until he returned to break the news. Her problems had suddenly grown worse. Not only was she going to end her relationship with Mark, she also had to break Malcolm's heart. *Why me?*

Malcolm leaned over and his lips brushed hers as he spoke again. "I need to go. Are we still on for New Year's Eve?"

She had almost forgotten he had asked her to attend his company's annual holiday party. "Sure." It wasn't as if she had anything else to do.

"Good. Merry Christmas. I'll call you when I arrive at my parents."

She nodded, and as the snow continued to fall, she stood inside the door and watched as Malcolm pulled his silver Lexus away from her house.

Sighing with despair, she shut the door and strolled into the kitchen. Before she prepared dinner, she needed to try and get the ring off her hand.

She glanced down at the beautiful marquis setting. It was a beautiful ring; unfortunately, it had been given to her by the wrong man.

With another sigh, she reached down and tried to remove it from her finger but it wouldn't budge. *Now, how had he been able to get the ring on without a problem?* She tried tugging once more then gave up. She'd remove it while she washed the dishes.

Moving toward the sink, she filled it with warm soapy water. After washing her breakfast dishes, the ring wiggled. She finally freed it from her finger and placed it on the ledge of the window.

She released a shaky breath as she wiped down the counter top. She should have stepped up and corrected Malcolm, but she hadn't. Now Mark was angry and she wasn't ready to face him yet. *Maybe it's a good thing.* She had planned to end things anyway. Malcolm had given her an excuse. Maybe being engaged was the way to end things once and for all; further discouraging any confidence Mark might have that he would eventually succeed at changing her mind.

While nibbling nervously on her bottom lip, she reached for the ring and slipped it back on her finger. She would continue to wear it for now.

Hearing something beating on the window over the sink, she glanced up to find that the snow had changed to sleeting rain. The weather was definitely getting bad. Her brow bunched with worry. She hoped Malcolm had a safe drive south.

Strolling over to the counter, she decided to make a pot of tea. She reached for a tea bag in a canister by the stove, then moved to fill the pot with water.

Leaning against the counter, she forced herself to think of something other than the two marriage proposals she'd received in one week. "Dinner, think about dinner," she said aloud. She decided to make beef and broccoli stir-fry. She already had a strip steak thawed in the refrigerator. She quickly busied herself with making dinner and pushed her problems aside.

By the time she had the broccoli nice and tender, she heard Tyler waddling down the hallway. She turned around in time to scoop him up into her arms and gave him a loving hug.

"How's my baby?" she asked.

"Ma Ma," he said, then wrapped his short arms around her neck.

"Let's see if we have any cookies."

She moved over to the cookie jar and raised the lid. Tyler reached in and removed a chocolate chip cookie then quickly brought it to his mouth.

She lowered him to the floor and had her back to the door when she heard Mark move into the room. Her pulse skittered to attention. He remained silent but a spot at the back of her neck warmed where she was certain his eyes penetrated. Without turning around she took a deep breath and suggested, "The weather is getting pretty bad. You're welcomed to stay if you'd like."

There was a noticeable pause before she finally heard him say, "Thank you."

"I've started dinner."

"Good. I'm starving."

Silence enveloped them again. Growing increasingly uncomfortable, she finally swung around. Her confidence lessened at the sight of his pained expression. Mark stood in the doorway with his arms crossed, the rich outlines of his shoulders strained against his sweatshirt. His jaw thrust forward in a stubborn line, his eyes watching her.

The pit of her stomach churned. She had some explaining to do and fast.

"Mark...I..." she began.

He dropped his arms to his side. "No need to explain." He reached for Tyler. Essence watched as they moved into the living room. Her mind was in despair. It wasn't until she heard the television that she returned her attention to the stove.

Dinner was a strained affair. She couldn't remember what she'd eaten. She had no idea if they even talked at all. She was glad when Tyler became cranky because it took the focus away from her.

There were so many things she needed to say and yet she hadn't the foggiest idea how to get started. Mark was equally quiet, even though his eyes, cold and unresponsive, kept watching her. When Mark offered to put Tyler to bed, she quickly escaped to her room.

She sat on the end of her bed with her hands folded in her lap for the longest as she suddenly realized that once Tyler fell asleep, the two of them would be all alone. *What were you thinking, inviting him to spend the night!* Even though he would be in the guest room across the hall, they would still be in the same house. It was clearly not a good day. Rising from the bed, she moved to take a shower.

She couldn't have been under the spray of water longer than five minutes when she realized she wasn't alone.

Before she had even wiped the water away from her eyes, she knew he was there. Through the mist clinging to the sliding shower door, Essence saw Mark leaning against the bathroom entry. *Where the heck is his sweatshirt?* Obviously, he had already made himself at home. His arms were folded over his naked chest with one hip cocked against the frame. His shoes were gone and his feet were bare. The expression on his face told her he enjoyed watching her bathe. He looked relaxed as if he was sitting in front of the television. She was not the least bit relaxed, nor had she been since he appeared on her doorstep.

Essence had shut the door to her bedroom but had left the door to her adjoining bathroom wide open so the mirror wouldn't fog up.

Or so she'd told herself. In the back of her mind, she knew that as soon as Tyler had drifted off to sleep, Mark would come looking for her. Now she hoped that he would boldly remove his clothes and join her under the spray of hot water.

Instead, Mark just stood there and stared while she continued to slowly lather her body. He followed the motion of her hands as they slid across her body. She imagined that it was his hand in place of the washcloth.

For the first time, showering was purely a sensual experience. With every stroke across her moist skin, she imagined his big strong hands touching her there. With every pass over her breasts, she remembered his soft caress. With every random beat of her heart, a consuming heat radiated through her body. Essence's senses spun with possibilities. When she considered the direction the evening might lead to, she couldn't deny the spark of excitement at the prospect.

*Obviously nowhere*, she soon realized after she finished washing and Mark still hadn't budged an inch. Maybe he didn't like what he saw. She wanted him to find her desirable. *But he's seen me before.* Realization washed over her as she remembered Mark hadn't seen her since she'd given birth to Tyler. He might not appreciate the faint stretch marks around her waist, the slight roundness of her belly or the fullness of her hips.

Something was definitely stopping him.

After concluding that he wasn't going to do anything but gawk, Essence turned her back to him long enough to wash her hair. By then, her quickened pulse had subsided and she turned off the faucet. She stepped out of the shower onto a woven mat outside the stall, then grabbed a bulky white towel hanging on the rack to her left and slowly dried herself off. Although she kept her eyes focused on the carpet, she was quite aware that Mark continued to study her but she didn't dare look at him…not yet. She waited until she was completely dried, had slipped into her robe, and had tied it at her waist.

Though she felt self-conscious, Essence appeared calm as she raised her eyes. She met his gaze, dark and intense and, oh, so seductive. He stood motionless as if awaiting some sort of response. Essence supposed she should have said something but came up shorthanded.

Mark continued to silently regard her, the tension as thick as the vapor that had risen from the shower. She had no idea what he was waiting for, but she suspected it might be some kind of signal from her—something that would indicate she wanted him to act on the electricity generating between them. Despite her best intentions, and even though she shouldn't, she still wanted him to make the first move.

But the shouldn'ts and couldn'ts never seemed to matter much when he was around. They didn't matter now as he kept his eyes fastened on her flushed face. She only knew that she wanted him with an urgency that discounted logic.

The last remnants of Essence's common sense melted away along with any chance of breathing normal. She was driven by her own passion. As if it had a mind of its own, the top of her robe fell open in brazen invitation.

Without speaking, and without removing his gaze from hers, Mark pushed away from the door and slowly strode toward her. Essence gasped then her pulse took off in a fierce gallop. She stepped back until she was touching the cool wall. Mark kept coming until their bodies touched. Lowering his mouth to hers, he gave her the kiss she'd been craving since he had slipped into her room. Keenly aware of his goal as he kissed her, Essence had a hard time drawing air during his daring exploration.

In the distant recesses of her consciousness, Essence knew it would be wise to halt what he was about to do. But her mind was weak and shaky, and her body limp. She didn't have the willpower to utter a single protest.

Mark took her face and held it gently as he touched a finger to her cheek and searched her face. "You can still say no."

Opening her eyes, she studied his tense expression; discovering his mouth was only inches from hers. "Do you want me to say no?" she whispered.

He drew in a deep breath then let it out. "Not on your life. But I want you to fully understand that once I start I may be unable to stop."

She felt his uneven breath on her cheek. "Then what are you waiting on?"

His lips quivered with uncertainty. "Why are you letting this happen?"

Essence gave him an innocent smile as she nodded with consent. "Why are you asking so many questions when you could be kissing me?"

"Because I want you to want this as much as I do." He waited what felt like an eternity for a reply. "Do you want me, Essence?"

A tiny tip of her tongue slid across to wet her lips before she nodded.

His senses spun by the scent of her freshly showered body. An overwhelming need to possess her curled in his gut. "I need to hear you say it."

The sparks shooting from her eyes were hard to miss, but that was not enough. He needed to hear those words. He'd been dead serious when he told himself that he wasn't going to make love to her until she came to him. It had to be a conscious decision, not his, that brought her to him.

Her breasts rose and fell gently with each shaky breath she drew. "I want you Mark. I've always wanted you."

He didn't need another invitation. He'd been waiting for this for what seemed like his entire life. To hell with his conscience, he'd merely been using it as an excuse to keep his emotions intact. Right now that reasoning had very little significant value. His desire for her overrode everything else. What mattered most was being with the woman standing before him.

He pressed her firmly into the wall with his body and covered her lips with his mouth, kissing her with all the passion and hunger that had been building since he had entered the room. The soft suction of her breasts pressed into his chest and he drove his hips into action. The hitch in her breathing told him she was fully aware of his erection.

He reached between them, his fingers quick and sure as he opened her robe completely exposing her breasts.

"This robe...is ...driving me ...crazy," he growled between hungry kisses, shuddering when the soft warmth of her right breast brushed again the back of his knuckles.

"Then take it off," she managed to say, sounding breathless and bothered. She then bent her knee and pressed against his other hand as he worked against the fold to caress her bare thigh.

"I plan to do just that." He untied the belt with one hand and continued his exploration with the other.

"It's...uh..." She bit her lip and cried out when his hand seared down her abdomen and found the heat of her.

"This...robe..." hardly recognized his voice as he worked it over her shoulders, "is coming off." The robe fell in a heap on the rose-carpeted floor.

With a great deal of effort, Mark flattened his palms against the wall and stiff-armed pushed it away. He wanted to see her. He wanted to see the damage he'd done to her lips that were swollen, wet and parted for him. He wanted to see the sexual haze in her eyes as she watched him with anticipation. She looked ravaged and willing and so ripe he groaned with the rush of desire that knotted his groin. What he had believed to be merely a moment of physical desire had somehow ripped at his soul. No longer was his interest just for the sake of his child. He wanted Essence. All of her.

"You are so unbelievably beautiful," he murmured and looked his fill. Her breasts were full and round, the weight of them heavy and firm. Her aureoles were chocolate, her nipples delicate velvet peaks.

"Touch me," she whispered boldly.

Those two words damn near drove him over the edge. He reached out traced a finger around her erect nipple and felt a tremor race through her.

"Like this?"

Eyes closed, she moaned softly as he rolled her nipple between his finger and his thumb.

"Tell me what else you want," he demanded even as a finger traveled down her abdomen then circling at the inside of her thighs.

She clutched his shoulders to keep from falling. "Your mouth. I want your mouth," she murmured. Before Essence could catch her breath, Mark hauled her into his arms and framed her face in his palms, holding her in place to accept what he was so willingly to give—a kiss that threatened to dissolve where she now stood. It was a meeting of lips and tongues that greatly affected her balance.

Mark dragged her against him, then leaned her back and lowered his mouth to her breast. Nothing tasted like her. Nothing. He'd never forgotten the feel of her in his mouth and didn't know how he had lived this long without grazing his teeth along the silk of her skin.

He had planned to seduce her slowly. He had planned to lay her down and love her in the comfort of her bed. But she did things to his plans. Things he didn't seem to have control over. Trying to move to the other room would take time, time he didn't have to waste.

*Time is of the essence.*

Before he knew it, he had reached for his belt buckle. With his mouth at her throat, he somehow managed to get it unfastened.

Searching for an anchor, Essence braced one hand at his waist. She needed to feel every part of him, every lovely inch of him. She reached between them to jerk open his fly. When he didn't stop her, she slipped her hand inside his briefs. His hands dropped to her shoulders and he squeezed them tightly when she touched him with firm inquisitive strokes. Just imagining him inside her made her dizzy, and delirious.

After Mark groaned, Essence suspected he would scoop her up and carry her to her bed, yet he continued to touch her again in much the same way she now touched him, kissing her with unrestrained passion. She was completely and utterly devoid of will. A tiny pinch of apprehension tried to rear its head, but Essence pushed it out of her mind determined to concentrate solely on her goal—to break Mark down, one touch at a time.

Mark murmured a few sexual words. His body's reaction needed no interpretation. He was as achingly hard as he'd ever been in his life, as desperate for her as he'd never been for any woman. Her smooth, solid caress overrode his resistance, drove him to the brink, and sliced his good sense to shreds.

And he couldn't do a damn thing to stop it.

With his mind caught in a carnal haze and his body screaming for relief, Mark lowered her down onto the bathroom floor. There was no way he could make it to the bedroom. He wanted her and he wanted her now.

He rose to his feet and anxiously removed his jeans and briefs. All the while, his eyes were glued to her, drinking in the slimness of her waist and the darker tangle of hair at the juncture of her thighs.

Watching him remove his boxers made her breath come out in shallow breaths as she studied every inch of him. The old Essence would have protested, questioned her wisdom, his intent or, at the least, have looked away. But this newer version couldn't resist Mark Saunders. When he was completely nude before her, her legs fell apart trembling with desire. She watched as he prepared to protect her. Mark tore the package open with his teeth and rolled the condom on. She was surprised that he even had the presence of mind to think about her protection.

"Are you ready?" he asked, sinking down on the carpeted floor, positioning himself between her thighs. Her nod was all he needed. Without another stolen moment, he thrust into Essence's body. The extreme pleasure he felt at that moment came out in a rough sigh as he battled to hold on to his composure at least for a while longer. He worked his hands into the damp curls spiraling at her shoulders and kept his eyes fixed firmly on hers, searching for any resistance or any sign that he had read her wrong. He was pleased to see that she couldn't disguise her body's reaction. He felt her walls tighten snugly around him.

Determined to hold off his climax for as long as he could, Mark leaned down and took a chocolate nipple into his mouth. She whimpered and tilted her head back, her eyes closed, her lips trembling. Mark sensed she was on the verge of an orgasm. He wasn't very far behind. She wrapped her legs around his waist and he slid his hard pulsing flesh in and out of the wet area between her thighs as they rode the storm together.

Beyond that point, Mark stopped thinking of anything but the raw passion that blocked everything from his brain as a climax ripped through Essence. He plunged deeper into her body, until his body convulsed uncontrollably.

He wilted against her chest and his breath came out in ragged gasps to match hers. Mark held her tightly, reveling in the clean rain shower scent emanating from her silky hair and soft skin, the taste of her still lingering on his tongue and lips. He experienced every brisk beat of her heart against his chest and each lingering pulsation where they were still joined. But as the sensation began to subside, awareness struck him like a fist in the face.

Essence Monroe was more than he'd remembered her to be as a lover, even in his most untamed dreams. Regardless of what she'd done to his body, done to his mind, it couldn't compare to the havoc she was creating in his heart. She had set free something in him that he'd never expected, something far removed from physical gratification and he knew he would never be the same from this point forward.

Never in his thirty years had he wanted a woman as a badly as he wanted her. He had taken her on the bathroom floor for there was no way he could have made it to her bed. His needs had grown beyond his control. She drove him to the brink of obsession, and had dismantled his heart. He loved her.

The truth of it struck him hard. The vibration swept through his soul and rocked the center of resolve.

*She's engaged to someone else.*

He jerked and quickly rose.

"What's wrong?" she asked.

Mark reached for his pants while trying to ignore her pained expression. "I'm sorry," he murmured. He then turned and walked away.

He returned to the guest room and lay across the bed. What had he just done?

He loved her. It was no use denying it any longer.

He tipped his head back and stared up at the ceiling. Right now, his thoughts centered on Essence, on the fact that she was down the hall, alone, confused and he was in the guestroom hurting like hell from wanting her. He needed to be inside her again with an urgency as unfamiliar as having a woman in his heart.

Since Carmen, he'd never found a woman who'd encouraged the kind of feelings that led to love. He never even considered settling in a committed role. That is…until he met Essence.

With Essence, he wanted the emotional love that a husband felt for his wife. The kind of love a man felt for his son. Maybe that's why having her in his life had scared him so much. He had quickly hopped on a plane that had sent him thousands of miles away. And as much as he hated to admit it his feelings for her did alarm him on a very basic level. He'd mistakenly thought he could control his emotions. He really believed that he could handle having her without the emotional attachment that came with it. Only it didn't turn out as he had expected. Emotions like he'd never imagined had taken over and he wasn't sure yet how he was going to handle it. Essence had broken the wall guarding his heart and now he had to decide what to do about it.

Essence was breathing fire! *Who does Mark think he's playing with?*

Angrily, she ran a brush through her dismantled hair as she stared at her image in the mirror. Her lips were bruised and her cheeks flush, telltale signs burned in the depths of her eyes.

Their coming together had been everything she had remembered but before she even had the chance to realize what had happened, Mark jumped up and high-tailed it out of there.

"Well, we'll see about that," she murmured. Essence tied her robe tightly around her waist, waltzed through her room then stomped across the hall. She stepped into the guestroom to find Mark lying flat on his back with his hands behind his head.

"How dare you!" she bellowed.

"Not now, Essence," Mark warned in a low dangerous voice.

"Yes now!" Her nostrils flared as she took a deep breath, her breasts rose and fell rapidly. She moved toward the bed and glared down at him. Heat seared through her. He was still naked. Rumpled hair, stubbled chin, thick thighs and muscular calves tangled in the twists of linens. Against her will, her eyes swept over his broad chest and down his flat stomach to the tumbled sheets covering the hardened flesh, which had brought her so much pleasure. It was distracting as hell.

She tried not to think about what was underneath and quickly raised her narrowed eyes back to his face. "I want an answer Mark, and I want it now!"

"Woman, if you don't give me a minute to think, I swear—"

"A minute…a minute! How dare you make love to me like a savage beast and then—" Before she could finish, Mark pulled her down onto the bed beside him then rolled on top of her.

Mark tugged her chin up until their eyes met. "Did I hurt you?" he asked. Essence was quiet and he tightened his hold. "Essence, answer me!"

"No," she finally said.

He softened his hold then continued to stare down at her. She closed her eyes so he wouldn't see the pain he had caused her.

"Before I explain my actions, you need to answer one question."

She swallowed the despair then answered. "What is it?"

Tilting his dimpled chin, he gave her a sidelong glance. "Are you planning to marry Malcolm?"

"No."

"Then before I bury myself deep inside of you again, I want his ring off your finger."

Her heart soared. Mark planned to make love to her again! "Alright," she whispered.

"Now!" he commanded.

She circled her arms around his broad back and fumbled with the ring, surprisingly it came off. Reaching to her right, she rested it on the nightstand. "Satisfied?"

"Yes," he answered with a look that said this was no joking matter. Essence, in turn, pressed her lips tightly together and waited.

"This is very difficult for me to say," he began, "but here goes." He made sure he had her full attention before he started again. "Essence, you have gotten to me. I thought I could keep from getting emotionally involved, that things could be strictly an arrangement with no emotional attachment. But that is no longer the case. You touched me deeply. At first I thought it was because of Tyler, but I now know it's more than that," he said with a tremulous whisper. "What I feel for you is like nothing I've ever felt before." What he admitted was true. He was confused. He didn't know how to describe it. All he knew was that it was the first time he'd experienced an emotion so deep. "What happened in your bathroom scared me shitless. I've never felt such an overwhelming need to have someone like I had to have you. I want to make this work. I want a *real* relationship." He lowered his head until their mouths were only inches apart. "I've never been a patient man. But because I'm leaving soon and time is of the essence, I plan to do everything in my power to not only win your trust but to capture your heart."

Her chest felt like it was going to explode. Essence had been holding her breath since he had begun. She suddenly parted her lips and released a big gush of air. Her chest rose and fell heavily as she asked, "I thought you wanted a marriage in name only?"

"I do…I did…I don't know how else to say it except that I want you in my life *permanently*. I'm willing to do whatever it takes to make it work. Will you give us a chance?"

Essence didn't know what to think. All she knew for certain was that she loved him. Part of her wanted to wrap her arms tightly around his neck and shower his face with kisses, while part of her was still scared. What if he changed his mind along the way and decided he wasn't capable of loving her?

While nibbling on her lower lip, she toyed with the possibility of taking a chance and quickly decided that she wanted to know; even if it was temporary and even if, in the end, he changed his mind and broke her heart. *For Tyler's sake.*

After her prolonged silence, Mark continued. "Since my return there hasn't been a single night I haven't lay awake wishing you were in my bed, with me lying on top, buried deep inside of you," he confessed in a deep husky voice. "I want you in my life, Essence. I want an honest relationship with no games and no limitations."

Her heartbeat increased with each word. He stared at her with a seductive look in his gaze. She loved him and was willing to give him all of her. There was no point in fighting a losing battle when her heart wasn't in it. She was willing to risk her heart to be with the man she loved. She loved him and that was all that mattered. The corner of her mouth tipped. "I've lain awake many nights wanting the same. I've been so lonely and wished you were here holding me." Intense waves of sexual longing washed over her. She shivered. "I'm willing to try."

"Are you cold?" Mark asked.

"No…" Essence whispered unable to say anymore.

He covered their bodies with a heavy blanket and drew her closer. Essence felt the hard evidence of his desire. Pulling back, she smiled up at him loving everything she saw.

She loved him.

Mark framed her face with his hands, rough and warm, searching her eyes for a long, heart stopping moment, passion dancing in their depths until he finally settled his mouth over hers. She parted her lips taking him in, savoring his kiss, his powerful embrace. Her body melted against Mark.

"It's not over yet," he said, running his hand down the long curve of her back and drawing her closer to his erection. "We've only just begun."

She looked up, her eyes shining, laughter sparking their depths. "So, I see," she said and gave a sudden thrust of her hips toward him. He moaned with pleasure.

They lay there kissing for the longest time. Consumed by a magic she had never felt before, Essence surrendered herself totally. Moaning softly, she gave in to the sweet sensation aroused by Mark's hands as they skimmed lightly inside her robe. The warmth of his hands touching her breasts, created a burning sensation inside her chest. His palms moved slowly down capturing the curve of her, cupping and caressing her buttocks, bringing her closer to the fit of him.

When he spoke, his voice was raw with need. "Essence, once was not enough. I have to have you again. I have to have you now."

"Tonight, I'm yours," she moaned.

Before she could say more, Mark's lips found hers again. Her body arched as if to become one with his. His hands found the belt to her robe. She sucked in her breath and shivered with pleasure as he peeled the robe away for the second time.

His touch set her body on fire as she writhed sensuously. Essence held her breath as he reached out and caressed one nipple and then the next with the back of his hand.

"You are so beautiful," he whispered. His breath warmed her cheek. "I won't be satisfied until you are panting and quivering beneath me."

Her heart swelled with a furious passion. His fingers sent a sensual chill tingling her spine down to the wet area between her thighs. His stubble chin caused her jaw to tingle. Mark created a new ecstasy with each touch. He tenderly sucked the buds of her breasts until they beaded like pearls.

He kissed her again. Their mouths fused, their tongues danced as he stroked her tender breasts with his gifted fingers. Her stomach fluttered, filling her with warmth and pleasure.

She couldn't keep from watching as his tongue claimed every inch of her flesh. Even when he finally reached his destination and settled his mouth between her trembling thighs, he licked and she became hot and instantly wet. The silence was broken by her small gasps of delight…gasps that turned to broken cries as he suckled the wet pink petals of flesh, teasing them open, stroking them with desire to bring her as much pleasure as he could. The intense sensation made her almost pull away from Mark's sinful torment. Grasping her hips, he tried to hold her still, but couldn't. She could only drop her chin to her chest and buck against his mouth. Watching the erotic scene unfold before her sent an earth-shattering climax tearing through Essence.

Mark released her hips and slowly traveled up her abdomen, nipping her with his tongue along the way.

She purred his name, "Mark…"

His lips moved from her breasts to an area behind her ear. "Yes?"

Essence moaned. "We have to…"

His lips found the sensitive hollow of her throat. Her unasked question hovered in the air.

"Don't worry baby," he responded with a whisper. "I have protection."

He stopped his assault long enough to get suited up before she burst with the need for him to be inside her. He positioned himself and urged her legs wide apart.

"Open your eyes," he commanded and guided himself to the sweet wet opening that invited him in with the sensuous buck of her hips. "I want to see your eyes when I come inside."

Her hips rose to meet him, her back arched in invitation. He studied the emotions flickering in the depths of her eyes as he slipped into her hot nectar.

Essence wrapped her legs around him and held on, abandoning herself to the urgent need to become one with Mark, to know his power when buried completely inside her. He thrust deeply, burying himself into her moist softness, and established a rhythm that left them moaning and gasping for their next breath.

She kissed his shoulder, his neck while inhaling the sensual fragrance of his skin. "Oh, baby," she rasped near his ear. And then she brought his mouth down on hers, cutting off everything but the incredible rapture.

His hips rocked in an in-and-out motion. With each strong, deep thrust Essence thought she was going to lose her mind. His breathing came fast and hard in the blinding throes of a passion she shared. One final thrust an orgasm ripped through her as she rocked against him. She screamed his name at the top of her lungs.

With a shout of exhilaration, Mark filled her with his love. He held her, covering her with kisses. She could not speak. Even long after their breathing had returned to its normal rate, she could only nestle into him, absorbing his warmth. Mark held her as if he would hold her forever. Drifting in the afterglow, words seemed unnecessary.

# CHAPTER THIRTEEN

Through a profusion of woods, a classic white farmhouse came into view. The setting was ideal: an eleven-acre piece of land including two streams and a walking trail running through it.

Mark turned his vehicle up a long winding drive to the house.

"Ganny," Tyler squealed from the rear of the car.

Essence eased around in her seat to meet his smiling face. "Yes, sweetheart, we're at grandma's house."

"Ganny," he giggled.

She glanced over at Mark and shared a smile before he turned off the car.

For Essence, the last forty plus hours had passed in a blur. She was so happy that she felt sure she wore a permanent smile on her face. Their passion for each other had not diminished. In fact, it had seemed to deepen so that the more they made love, the stronger their need for each other had become. Mark had taken her to a height of passion she had never experienced before. Her body still hummed from the after-shocks of their lovemaking.

Nevertheless, even though Mark had confessed that he wanted a real relationship with no pretenses, Essence wasn't wearing blinders or fooling herself into believing everything was going to magically work itself out. Over breakfast, Essence resolved to enjoy each day as they came. Even though she knew the end of his visit was less than two weeks away, for now all that mattered was that she loved him.

She climbed out of the car. The sky was white and it had begun to snow again. If the weather continued through the night, they would definitely have a winter wonderland on Christmas morning.

Mark reached into the back and unstrapped Tyler from his chair. With a smile, he pulled his hat down around his ears, then lifted him into his arms.

"Well Champ," he whispered close to his ear, "wish me luck."

Carrying a coconut cake in her hand, Essence came around and stood beside them. Mark glanced down at her, then coiled his free arm around her waist and led them up the stairs to the front door. Essence shifted the cake to her other hand and rung the doorbell. The front door opened. They were greeted by her sister and brother-in-law.

"Merry Christmas," Tamara cheered. Stepping aside, she ushered them into the cozy foyer.

Once they were inside, she shut the door and leaned over to hug her sister. "Is that him?" she whispered near her ear. Essence's silence was answer enough.

She draped a loose arm around his waist and made the introductions. "Mark, this is my sister Tamara and her husband, Paul Silver."

Twin dimples creased Mark's cheeks as he stared down at the woman who resembled the mother of his child. With flawless brown skin and identical vibrant eyes, it was apparent they were sisters. "I see beauty runs in the family."

Tamara let out a quaint chuckle. "Aren't you a charmer?" She stepped forward and engulfed him in a warm embrace before Mark dropped a kiss to her right cheek.

Tamara was dazzled by his killer smile. Stepping back, she took in the handsome man, standing by her sister's side with a possessive hand on her shoulder. It was obvious where Tyler got his good looks. After seeing the gentleness of his jewel-like eyes she was certain Mark would some day become her brother-in-law.

When they pulled apart, Paul extended his hand and Mark shook it. They exchanged polite greetings while Tamara took her nephew from his arms and smothered him with kisses.

"Take your coats off and stay awhile. Almost everyone is here," Paul said before he moved to answer the doorbell again.

Tamara helped Tyler out of his snowsuit while Mark assisted Essence in slipping the coat from her body before shrugging out of his own. Essence led him to a large coat closet at the end of the hallway. Shifting the cake to her left arm, she grasped his hand and led him through the house with a trail of introductions.

The front of the house was filled with voices and laughter. Several little children were racing down the hall. An infant's cries were coming from upstairs. Teenagers were standing in front of the stereo, changing the Christmas music to something a little more upbeat, while the adults had already found a comfortable place to sit.

There was a chorus of greetings as Essence led him down the wide foyer toward the kitchen. She stopped along the way and gave Mark a tour of the place she had once called home.

He admired the house that was a prime example of nineteenth century Pennsylvania. Stone was used on the front of the house as well as on the wood-burning fireplace in the living room. Nine-foot ceilings conveyed an element of grandeur. Graceful curved stairs climbed a wall in the foyer in nod to traditional elegance. Stepping through the archway openings, he moved through a large dining room to the kitchen where a long farm table was covered with dishes.

There were two large turkeys—one baked, one fried—a spiral ham, a large pan of macaroni and cheese, collard greens, sweet potatoes, corn casserole and several other dishes covered in foil that he couldn't identify.

As soon as Essence put the cake on the counter, Tamara clutched her sister's arm and pulled her into the food pantry.

"Girl, he's gorgeous!" she exclaimed.

"Yes, he is," Essence agreed in a quiet voice.

"Well?" Tamara asked.

"Well what?" she asked, pretending as if she had no idea what her sister was referring to.

Tamara's gaze remained locked with hers. "Have you agreed to marry him?"

Essence pretended to give the question some thought before she shook her head and answered, "No."

"Don't tell me you're still angry with him? Why the hell not?"

She sent a scolding glance in her big sister's direction. "You know why and I will not have this conversation again."

Essence noticed the slight smile tugging at her sister's mouth before she asked, "What about the sex?"

She shrugged at her question. There was no way she was going to tell her sister she had been Mark's love toy since two nights prior. "Not yet, but now that he is staying with—"

"*Whoa!* Back up a minute." The words had claimed Tamara's immediate attention. "Did you just say Mark is staying with you?"

Essence blushed openly. "Yeah, but only because he wants to be there to see Tyler on Christmas."

"Uh-huh." Tamara gave her a wide knowing smile. "Hey, he's halfway there. It's just a matter of time before the two of you will be rolling around in the sheets."

Essence rolled her eyes heavenward then scooted past her sister before she asked any further embarrassing questions.

She found Mark standing near the sink talking to her sixteen-year-old cousin, Pamila. It was obvious by her body language that she was flirting.

"Sorry Cuz, but I need to steal this one away." With her right arm curled possessively around his waist, she led him in search of her parents.

Essence arched a sweeping eyebrow at him. "You looked like you needed rescuing."

Mark chuckled softy, the sound rumbling in his wide chest. "I appreciate it."

She found her parents in the living room sitting beside an eight foot Christmas tree decorated with ornaments that had accumulated over a thirty-year span.

Flashing a grin, Essence leaned over and first kissed her mother then her father. She reached for Mark's hand again and pulled him beside her. "Mom, Dad, I'd like you to meet Mark Saunders. Mark, my parents Julia and Jarvis Monroe."

Mark leaned over with his hand extended. Julia accepted it without hesitation. "It's a pleasure to finally meet you both," he said cordially.

"Welcome, Mark." Julia rose and planted a warm kiss to his cheek. "I hope we see a lot more of you."

"Indeed. I plan to be around for a long time." He flashed her a warm smile and slowly took in the elegantly dressed woman's friendly brown eyes. There was no doubt the silver-gray haired woman was Essence's mother. The two shared the same small upturned nose and smooth brown skin.

Clearing his throat, Jarvis replied in a gruff voice, "Finally, we meet." He rose and gave Mark a firm handshake as his jaw twitched with irritation.

"Sir, I wish it could have been sooner," Mark said by way of an apology.

While Julia was instantly drawn by his charm, her father was hesitant as any father would be with his daughter.

Jarvis released his hand and rubbed it over his nearly baldhead several times. "I'd like to have a word with you later, in private."

Mark could tell that Mr. Monroe had been a handsome man. He was tall, almost at eye level, with thin salt and pepper hair. Fine lines were around hazel eyes that crinkled even more with his stern expression. "That will be fine, sir."

Essence didn't like the idea of the two discussing her, but knowing her father, there wasn't much she could do about it. She moved beside her father and curved an arm around his protruding stomach. When he lowered his head to kiss her tenderly on the top of her head, she murmured, "Behave."

His expression softened as he pulled her close—a possessiveness any father would have for his daughter.

A great aunt entered the room. Essence introduced Mark, then took his hand and led him away from her father's watchful eye.

"I don't think he likes me too much," Mark murmured.

She squeezed his hand in assurance. "He's a pastor. He not only likes you, but as a messenger of God, he actually loves you."

Mark paused briefly, then smiled. "Thanks for the encouraging words. I'll definitely need it when he and I talk later."

She draped an arm around his waist and pulled him along.

Mark lost track of the names as he met aunts, uncles, and dozens of cousins. The only persons who appeared to be missing were her paternal grandparents. They had returned to their summer home in Panama until the spring. Essence informed him that her maternal grandparents had both passed away while she was in college.

While sipping homemade eggnog, Mark spotted Tyler being passed around from one family member to the next as he was being smothered with kisses.

Tamara's husband and several male cousins were involved in a football debate. Mark fit right in as if he had always been a part of her life.

While he was being entertained, Essence helped her mother set the table for the meal.

"Tyler looks just like his father," Julia commented.

Knowing where this conversation was heading, Essence was determined to remain cool and unaffected in front of her mother. She removed a pan of cornbread from the oven before answering, "Yes he does."

"I really like him. Have the two of you made any plans about the future?"

Essence glanced uneasily at Julia, who was assessing her from across the kitchen. "Other than sharing in the raising of our son, no."

She gave her daughter a sympathetic smile. "He's a nice man. I had hoped that maybe the two of you…" she purposely allowed her voice to trail off.

She was tempted to tell her mother about what had transpired between her and Mark the past couple of days. However, she was afraid that if she made too much of it, she would somehow jinx any possibility the two of them may have. "No Momma. I'm content with the way things are." She crossed the room and took a seat at the table.

Julia frowned as she rounded the table and pulled out the chair beside her. "I thought maybe you had changed your mind."

Her statement surprised Essence, especially since her mother knew how stubborn she could be. "Why would you think that?"

A smile twitched her lips. "I have eyes Essence. Anybody can see the way he looks at you."

"What look?" she asked quietly.

"The same one your father gave me when we first met." Her smile was bittersweet. "That same one he's been giving me ever since."

"Mom, Mark isn't that kind of guy. He's made it quite clear on more than one occasion that he isn't looking for love."

Julia was a diehard romantic and refused to believe a word of it. "Well, I think he'd make a wonderful husband."

Essence let out her breath slowly. "Mom, please."

Her mother reached across the table and took both her hands into her own. "Life has a way of surprising you and so do people if you give them a chance. Don't close yourself off to the possibility that Mark will someday come to love you, too."

A frown drew her eyebrows together. It was a nice thought but she wasn't about to hold her breath—again. "I doubt it."

Julia's gaze swept her face and she carefully examined her features. She could see something in her eyes that told her that her daughter was so much like her. When she gave her heart to a man, it was for eternity. "You love him, don't you?"

Essence folded her arms on the table and leaned forward. She didn't have to think about if she loved Mark. She already knew that she did and was no longer afraid to admit it. That is, to everyone but him.

Essence had known she was still in love with Mark the instant he walked back into her life. She'd tried to ignore it, but it kept coming…he kept coming. It wasn't just that he was a great help or that Tyler adored him, but that he was so willing to do right by both of them. *She and Tyler.* Essence knew her heart was at stake, his feelings for their child lying in the path. But what about his feelings for her? She understood all too clearly that Mark wanted her in his bed, but did he want her in his life? *Really* in his life? It would change so much for both of them, but Essence couldn't see the future. She didn't want to anticipate failure. Since Tyler's birth, she had tried to be practical. She'd tried to do what was best for herself and her son. Now a decision had to be made.

Tyler needed his father.

Essence needed to be loved.

"What's there not to love?" she finally said. "He's gorgeous, intelligent, and a wonderful father."

Julia eased back in her chair. "Have you told him how you feel?"

"Good Lord, no!"

"I think you should." Julia had picked up on the sexual exchange between the two.

Her daughter lifted twin brows. "Why would I want to do that?"

A slight smile curved Julia's mouth. "Because he loves you too."

The frown on her face deepened as she lifted her chin a notch. "No he doesn't."

Julia's eyes were wide and shimmering in the light. "And why not?"

Essence rubbed both her hands across her face then took a deep gulp of air. "Because he's said so," she answered simply, truthfully.

She looked to her mother to see amusement dancing in her eyes.

"Men don't always know what they want or truly feel. That's why God created women."

Essence placed her hand over her mouth to keep from laughing aloud.

"I'm serious. Your father is no exception. When I met Jarvis Monroe he was so handsome and the gentlest man I'd ever known." She folded her arms beneath her breasts and grinned at her youngest child. "Your father swept me off my feet, wining and dining me. Then when I told him I loved him, he told me that he wasn't looking for love, but only a woman to run the house and fix him a few square meals. I was tempted to tell him where he could go with his caveman belief. But I thought long and hard about it and realized I loved him too much to lose him. I prayed that eventually he would come around. And sure enough after a month of my good home cooking, love and devotion, that man finally admitted that he couldn't live his life without me."

Essence smiled at her, filled with emotion. "How come you never told me that story before?"

Her mother squeezed her hand. "You never needed to hear it until now."

She couldn't believe her mother had been willing to risk her heart at such a high price. Was she also willing do the same for the sake of Tyler, knowing that Mark might not ever come to love her? There was a comfortable silence before she spoke again. "Why are you trying to marry me off?"

"Because I know he's your soulmate even if you haven't realized it yet."

They drove down the highway in silence, until Essence finally asked, "What did you and my dad talk about?"

Mark glanced away from the road long enough to meet her curious eyes. Essence had been relatively quiet for most of the ride. However, he knew that after spending close to an hour with her father in his study, she would eventually ask him about it. "It was man talk."

Her heart skipped a beat as she gazed over at him. "What kind of man talk?"

His smile was dazzling. "Private stuff."

She could just imagine what her father had wanted to talk to him about. "He asked you what your intentions were, didn't he?"

"Yep and I told him."

Essence fell back against the seat and groaned. "Please don't tell me you told him I refused your marriage proposal!"

"Okay, I won't tell you."

She nervously gnawed on her bottom lip. "But you did, didn't you?"

Mark saw the worried look in her eyes. Feeling the need to touch her, he reached down for her hand and brought her palm to his lips. "No, but I did tell him that we've discussed marriage and hadn't come to an understanding yet."

*Oh no.* That was just as bad. A slight frown lined her forehead. Her father was sure to call her before the week was over.

She forced her eyes away from him and tried relaxing against the leather seat. However the sexual tension that had been surrounding them all day made that close to impossible. The air sizzled.

It was Christmas Eve. She tried not to think about the other night. Her body stirred all the way down to her toes when she thought about what had happened between them. First, she deemed it a mistake, now she wasn't so sure.

A mixture of desire and longing tried overpowering her senses, but she refused to let it.

By the time they arrived at her house, heavy snow was falling. It was a good thing they arrived home before the roads had become hazardous.

When they finally pulled onto the driveway, Tyler was sound asleep. Mark put him in bed, while Essence put the leftovers away in the refrigerator. She moved into the living room and turned on television. She tuned in to "It's a Wonderful Life."

She was nervous with anticipation. Tyler was sleep after a long day going from one relative to the other. Chances were he would be out for the night. That left just her and Mark, *alone.*

"I love that movie," Mark said when he strolled into the room.

She glanced over her shoulder at the sound of his voice. "I haven't watched it in years." She returned her attention to Jimmy Stewart for several seconds then back at Mark who had moved to take a seat beside her.

"Are you ready to play Santa?" she asked.

He became instantly excited. "Yes I am," he said, flashing her a heart-melting smile. "Why don't we put on something a little more comfortable before we start lugging toys out the closet?"

"Alright." Quickly nodding, she escaped.

They each went to their room. Essence changed into her gown, slipped a satin robe over it and tied it tightly around the waist. When she moved into the living room, a lump formed in her throat. Mark had slipped on a comfortable pair of flannel pajamas. There was a fire, roaring in the fireplace.

"How about some hot chocolate?" she asked.

"Sounds great."

She moved quickly into the kitchen, quite aware of the rapid beating of her heart. She reached for the teakettle, filled it and placed it on the stove.

Tonight anything could happen and she prayed that it did. She was ready. Last night had been invigorating. Hot passionate sex she had felt clear down to her soul.

Within seconds, she popped two mugs with water in the microwave and put two minutes on the timer. She then leaned against the counter, trying to get her emotions under control. Sexual tension had sizzled. She felt it and knew he had too.

Five minutes later, Essence moved into the living room, carrying a tray with two piping hot mugs and a plate of Christmas cookies her niece had baked. She lowered it onto the coffee table and took a seat beside him on the floor. She handed him a mug and when their fingers touched, tiny jolts of electricity were felt down to her toes. She looked up in time to witness that he had felt it also. She reached for her own cup, then pretended to watch the movie. She took several sips while fully aware he was watching her.

Mark sipped his cocoa as he studied her. The flames of the fire reflected in her hair. The sight of her shook him. She was wearing one of those gowns that the hem touched her thighs, leaving her long shapely legs exposed. She looked sweet, soft and fragile. Her body rocked him with a hard jolt of desire.

"Ready to get started?"

When Mark's shoulder nudged hers, hard and warm, she glanced up from the screen and met his gaze. The husky tone of his voice made her feel warm inside. Mark set his mug down on the tray and moved to the spare room. She quickly took another sip, appreciating the warm liquid as it worked its way down past the knot in her throat.

Mark returned, lugging a large bag.

She flashed narrowed eyes at him. "Those aren't the toys I bought."

"No…they are the ones I bought. Yours are over there." He pointed to a smaller bag beside the couch.

Even though she rolled her eyes upward, Essence couldn't resist a smile. "Our little boy is going to be spoiled."

He shrugged. "This is his first real Christmas. I want to make it special."

"Just your being here makes it special."

"Thanks."

"Tyler is already crazy about his daddy."

He shot her a curious glance. "Really?"

Such surprised pleasure filled his voice that she smiled. "Yes, really."

While they watched the movie, they set up the train and wrapped several of his toys. They didn't talk much. Conversation was unnecessary. Putting the toys together wasn't about talking, but about sharing the love of a special little boy.

When the movie was over, Essence excused herself and dashed down the hall to the bathroom, when she returned Mark was holding a long box.

"What's that?" she asked softly.

"Why don't you open it and see."

She reached for the box. Leaning against the couch, she sat with her legs folded then slowly ripped open the paper. Inside was a gold ring with a single ruby birthstone. "It's beautiful," she gasped.

"It's a mother's ring. Look, there's an inscription on the inside of the band."

She turned it over and read, "Tyler, July 23, 2002."

A faint glimmer of emotion shone in her eyes. "Oh, Mark, thank you so much, but I-I didn't get you anything."

"Yes, you have." His voice was just as intense as his expression when he said, "You've done a fabulous job of raising our son. I couldn't wish for a better gift than him."

She blushed openly then reached for her mug. "Your being in his life now is what matters most. You've made quite an impression on him."

"And what about his mother?" He reached out and gently traced his index finger along her cheek. "Have I made an impression on her too?"

His blatant question and bold caress set off an immediate ache within her. She forced herself to stay composed even though her hands trembled. He sat very close now. Even with the fireplace and the television as her only light, she could still make out the desire luminous in his eyes.

And she knew they were finished talking. She couldn't turn away even if she had wanted to.

Mark took her mug, placed it next to his on a side table, then took both of her hands in his. His eyes fixed on hers; an aching hunger danced around them.

He touched one of his long, sensual fingers to her jaw and cupped her face with his palm. His eyes glittered with longing as he lowered his head.

When his lips touched hers, Essence sighed and lifted her mouth to meet his. When her lips parted for him, his tongue slid gently into her sweet haven. He pulled her hard against him and deepened the kiss. Essence moaned and pressed her body to his. Tentatively, she ran her hands across his dark curls, testing the texture, and loving the way the hairs tickled her palms.

Mark cupped her buttocks and groaned against her with such a low needful sound that she felt herself contract and go wet.

"You know what I want, don't you, Essence?"

He had drawn back to look at her flushed face. Her lids lifted slowly. Desire flickered, flared and raged through her. She nodded and moistened her lips.

"I want to make love to you. I want to taste every inch of you starting right here." Mark nipped her earlobe.

Essence drew in a shuddery breath, then exhaled on a sigh. He stroked his palm across her smooth cheek and she nuzzled against it.

"You want that, too?" he asked.

She met his serious gaze. "Yes." She wanted it so badly, she was willing to bypass all the preliminaries and get directly down to business. It was a need so powerful, she barely had control. However, when Mark lowered his head and touched his lips to hers again, she suddenly remembered that good things come to those who wait.

He overwhelmed her with his soft, experienced kisses. Essence thought she'd turn into a blazing inferno if he slid across her teeth with his tongue again. Sure enough, he did and she nearly combusted on the spot.

Without breaking the kiss, he picked her up in his arms. Her own were locked around his neck as he carried her to the bedroom. He managed to jerk back the covers then lay her down and lowered himself beside her.

Essence arched her back and held him close. "Oh…Mark."

He caught the fabric of her gown in his teeth and tugged it over her breasts. "I need to taste you, Essence."

She sighed with pleasure as he cupped her breasts, circling them then thumbing her nipples. Sparks blazed from his calloused hands straight to her heart. Essence closed her eyes and let her head fall back as she savored the sensation he evoked.

"You can touch me, too." He pulled his shirts from his pants and yanked the snaps apart. Within seconds, the shirt lay on the floor.

She gazed at him in admiration. Mark had a marvelous chest. Fine dark hairs dusted his clearly defined pectorals and abdomen. Essence reached for him, then drew back. Sensing her reluctance, Mark caught her hand and rested it against his breast. On her own accord, her fingers moved, flexing over his taut male nipples.

His lids drifted closed and then he inhaled deeply. "Oh, yeah. That's it."

She stroked both palms across his chest in a slow, circular motion, then lowered them to skim his belly and ribcage. Shudders of sensation rippled through him and she, too, had to take a deep breath to maintain control.

Mark reached out and captured her hands, then pinned them over her head as he moved to capture a nipple in his mouth, suckling until she squirmed on the bed. He then transferred his attention to her other breast. Her breath came in short pants and she nearly cried. When his lips left her breasts to travel down her abdomen, she thought she would die from wanting him. Without her even realizing it, her gown was gone and she lay before him in nothing but what the good Lord had given her.

Mark gently eased her thighs apart. He tasted his way past her knees, her thighs to the part screaming for his attention. She knew what he planned to do. He had done it many times before. Nevertheless, nothing could prepare her for the lightning strike of his tongue. She reached out and slapped a hand over her mouth.

He nipped her thigh. "Don't. I want to hear you scream."

"I won't," she defied just as she arched her soft mound to move against his lips.

"Yes, you will and you'll love it." He sucked the point of her desire into his mouth and set her off. A raging river traveled through her bloodstream and she promptly proved his words.

"That's it, sweetheart, lets see if you can do that again."

She did, several times.

Although the heat in his groin raged full force, Mark gave himself over to the pleasure of pleasing her, to giving her what she wanted. His needs weren't important. Only hers. Her smell and soft pleas drove his desire onward until suddenly tasting her sweet nectar on his tongue wasn't enough. He wanted…needed…to give her everything he had to give in the most intimate way.

Essence opened her eyes to find him standing above her. His gaze poured over her like melted chocolate. Mark made her feel desirable…sexy…needed. Watching him was more exciting than she could bear. He stood before her naked, ravaging what little sanity she had left. Her mouth watered. Her skin tingled. Anticipation of what he was planning to do left her panting.

Naked. Mark knelt on the bed and rolled on a condom. Hungrily, she reached for him. Opening her legs wider, she wrapped them around his waist and urged him on. Thus far, he'd been gentle, but she no longer needed gentle.

"Easy darling." He nibbled her ear and pressed his lips against her throat. "We have all night."

"Now!" she demanded in frustrated desire.

Mark chuckled. "Yes, ma'am." With one deep thrust, he drove so deep inside her he thought he would drown from the sensation. Essence arched off the bed at the erotic pleasure. He eased her back down, filling her again and again. Essence matched his tempo, then picked up the rhythm until she couldn't move fast enough to satisfy her need. Her pulse pounded. Her blood raced. When her legs finally gave out and fell widely apart, Mark plunged deeper and raced toward completion. Essence's entire body contracted then exploded, and Mark followed.

Mark rolled to his side and pressed her close to his chest. He nuzzled the back of her neck while one palm skated down her abdomen then up to cup her breast. He whispered into her ear, "Woman, you are dangerous."

His voice curled around her, low and intense. Essence fell asleep with a smile on her lips.

# CHAPTER FOURTEEN

Again and again, all through the night and into the morning, Mark made love to Essence. He wanted to express all the feelings and desire he'd been holding onto since the day he had left.

And it still wasn't enough.

He wanted more. He needed more. Desperation had driven him, consumed him. Essence was a fever burning inside of him that rose to temperatures so high, it made him wild and out of control. He took a deep breath. Even after their intense mating, he felt something that was stronger than sex. An inner peace that he hadn't felt in years. Essence had accomplished something that no other woman had in his entire lifetime. She made him feel whole. As he stared down at her lovely face, Mark realized that since his break up with Carmen he had placed every woman he'd encountered in the same manipulative category. He had stopped trusting and hid his heart behind a steel door, determined to never fall into the trap again. Deep down, he never thought he could find happiness and had been too afraid to try.

Until Essence came along.

He stroked his fingers along the side of her face, consumed by her beauty. He never thought he could have an emotional and physical attachment to a woman. Essence was different, unique and special. Feeling a stirring in his chest, Mark pulled her against the length of his body and even closer to his heart.

Essence dreamed that someone was kissing her. She opened her right eye and then her left to find that it wasn't a dream after all. Mark lay next to her, showering her forehead with soft wet kisses.

"Good morning," he said, grinning.

She rolled her head to face him and smiled. "The same to you." She lowered her lids and opened them again. "How long have you been up?"

"Long enough to watch you drool all over your pillow," he teased lightly

She shot up off her pillow. "I don't drool!"

Mark's brow rose. "Okay…whatever you say."

Appalled, Essence playfully swung at his chest. Mark filled the air with hearty laughter as he blocked each punch. He overpowered her, then rolled her gently onto her back and pinned both arms above her head.

"Just kidding, sweetheart," he whispered as he kissed the side of her neck. "I enjoy watching you sleep." He kissed the other side. "You looked so beautiful I couldn't take my eyes off you." His mouth traveled around and captured her lips.

She felt a stirring. His thickening manhood throbbed against the inside of her thighs, causing the blood to pump faster through her veins. *Goodness*, she wanted him again.

"Mmm, you taste good," he moaned as his lips traveled from her mouth down her neck to her collarbone and finally to her right nipple. He skimmed his teeth and his tongue over the chocolate peak. She almost came off the bed when she heard Tyler's voice coming through the baby monitor.

"Uh oh, Tyler's awake," she whispered.

"I thought that cooing was you," he murmured as he continued to tease her nipple.

"Oh my God! Mark?"

He raised his head and gazed down at her. "What, sweetheart?"

"It's Christmas."

His face lit up with realization. "I guess it is. Let's go get Tyler."

They sprung out of bed. Essence slipped on her robe and Mark slipped back into his pajama bottoms. They giggled like little children as they moved across the hall. Mark scooped Tyler into his arms and traveled to the living room.

"Let me put some coffee on before we begin," Essence suggested.

"That sounds great. I'm going to run out to my car and get my camera."

He put Tyler in his playpen and moved to the corner of the living room. He slipped his shoes on his feet, then reached for his coat and dashed out to his car.

It was snowing again and he found himself grinning from ear-to-ear. There was nothing better than a white Christmas. By the time he joined them in the living room, the sound of Christmas carols rang through the house.

Essence plugged in the tree then turned to face him. "Ready?" she asked, eyes burning with excitement.

"More than you'll ever know." He shrugged out of his coat and scooped Tyler from his playpen. Carrying him over in front of the tree, he took a seat on the floor. "Merry Christmas, Champ."

Essence took a seat beside him and watched as Tyler moved and grabbed a large red Fisher Price telephone.

Essence giggled as she watched him mimic how she cradled the phone between her shoulder and ear. Mark joined in the laughter and snapped several shots. They watched in amazement as Tyler moved from one gift to the next. After Mark had used up half the film, he lowered the camera, reached over and laced his fingers with hers.

He turned to Essence and said, "Thank you so much."

Her lashes fluttered. "For what?"

He exhaled a long sigh of contentment. "For making this the best

Christmas ever."

"I'm glad you're here to share this moment with me."

"I hope I get the opportunity to share many more," he whispered close to her ear.

Feelings of love overflowed her heart. Who was she fooling? No matter how much she tried to deny it. She wanted the same. She loved this man. He had her heart and her soul. Spending the rest of her life with a man that loved her was the only gift she wanted for Christmas.

With that in mind, she got up and crawled over to the tree. Reaching all the way to the back, she pulled out a long box and handed it to Mark.

"What is it?"

"What does it look like? Last night while you were sleeping, I thought of the perfect gift. Now open it." She returned to her seat beside him and waited for him to open his gift.

Shaking his head, he dropped his lids briefly then raised them again. "I told you last night you didn't have to get me anything. Just letting me to be here is Christmas enough."

"Don't be silly."

Mark finally removed the wrapping and opened the box. Inside was a 10"x13" collage of eight different studio photographs taken of Tyler since he took his first breath.

For a long moment, he stared down at his gift. When he finally looked at her, his eyes were brimming with something Essence never expected to see—vulnerability. It wasn't until that very moment that Essence realized that she held onto his future. She had the key and the choice that would affect the rest of his life. She saw uncertainty and even fear. At that very moment, she wanted to reassure him that he had nothing to worry about, that his future was secure. But she couldn't just yet. She felt she needed to wait until she had made the decision to marry him.

"Thank you so much," he finally said.

"You're welcome."

He pulled her onto his lap. "You know I'm dying to thank you properly."

She flashed a smile. "At ease, soldier."

"I think it's a little late for that," he chuckled lightly. He pulled her tightly against him so she could feel exactly what he was talking about.

"Oh, boy, what are we going to do about that?" she teased.

"I have some suggestions." He wagged his eyebrows suggestively.

The gleam in his eyes left little doubt of his meaning. She giggled as he ran a trail of kisses down her cheek and neck.

Wanting to join in the fun, Tyler walked over to his mother and also kissed her on the cheek.

"Thank you, sweetie." She kissed him back, then Tyler dropped down on all four and crawled over to a set of building blocks.

"I've got something for you, too," Mark whispered. Reaching behind him, he pulled out a long velvet box.

Essence shook her head in protest. "You have already given me a gift."

"And now I'm giving you another."

Before she even opened it, she knew the box held another piece of jewelry. Inside was a gold chain with a small key, dangling from the middle. She removed it from the box and took a closer look. The eye of the key was a diamond.

"Thanks." Her lips brushed against his as she spoke.

Mark nodded and stared at her in an intense silence. Essence watched the play of emotions of his face before he finally said, "You know, don't you?"

"Know what?" she asked with a significant lifting of her brow.

"That you hold the key to my heart."

The underlying sensuality of his words captivated her. She was touched, yet she wondered if he meant her or was he referring to Tyler. She decided to leave well enough alone for now and focus on having an unforgettable Christmas instead.

A half-hour later, Essence was playing with Tyler while Mark went to the kitchen to fix them something to eat.

She sat with her legs crossed on the floor. Tyler sat beside her, laughing gleefully as they played with his cars. It was a sight Mark would never grow tired of seeing—Essence and his son together. The two of them filled a deep need within him. Until today, he'd never truly realized how lonely his life had been.

He no longer wanted to deny his love for her and truly realized he wanted her in his life forever. Even if Tyler hadn't been born, he'd have still wanted her. He never thought he'd be capable of that kind of love, but watching the two of them together and experiencing the rush of warmth flowing through his chest, he now knew otherwise.

Mark made fluffy omelets and pancakes. He somehow managed to pull Tyler away from his presents long enough to eat a few bites. Afterwards, he sent Essence to her room to relax while he cleaned the kitchen.

As he loaded the dishwasher, he smiled just thinking about her ability to arouse a sexual hunger in him that was mind-boggling. Now he just had to convince her to marry him. He frowned. Convincing her wasn't going to be easy. Essence thought the only reason why he wanted to marry her, was Tyler. He didn't blame her, since he had been the one who told her he was incapable of loving another woman. So if he told her he loved her, now, chances were she would think he was lying.

Actions spoke louder than words. He would just have to find a way to show her.

Moving into the living room, he found Tyler sound asleep in his playpen. Reaching for a small blanket, he laid it across him and tucked it around his shoulders.

Mark stepped into the bedroom and heard running water. He smiled and quickly discarded his clothes. He moved into the bathroom where Essence was taking a shower, and opened the door and climbed in, closing the door behind him.

She turned around and smiled. "I was hoping you weren't waiting on an invitation."

"Not on your life," he murmured only seconds before capturing a nipple between his lips.

"Well, look who's finally here."

Essence leaned forward so Mrs. Saunders could kiss her on the cheek. "Thanks for inviting me," she said as they moved apart. She stepped into the house, and Mark strolled in behind her, carrying Tyler.

"No need to thank me. Whether you know it or not, you and that little tyke are part of this family."

Essence was grateful for her kind words.

It looked like they were the last to arrive. Cars were lined on both sides of the street and in the driveway. The house appeared to be filled to capacity.

She knew before she walked in that everyone wanted to see Tyler. Sure enough, before his coat was even off, he was being passed around. She expected him to cry around a bunch of strangers, but instead he seemed to enjoy being the center of attention. *What a ham*, she thought with a smile.

Mrs. Saunders took her coat and Mark placed a hand at her elbow and escorted her to the living room. He introduced her to one family member after the next and as fast as they were coming, she knew there was no way she was going to be able to retain any of their names. The Saunders' family appeared to be twice as large as the Monroe's and very close. Her face ached from smiling and saying, "nice to meet you" at least four dozen times.

Taking her hand, Mark led her into the kitchen where Essence finally found a familiar face. "Kelly."

Kelly turned away from the woman standing at the sink next to her with a toddler on her hip. Her face lit up with recognition.

"Essence, I was wondering if you were going to make it." She moved over and embraced her in a hug.

"Why did you think that?" Mark asked.

"Because by now I would have thought she had gotten tired of you." She punched her brother in the side.

The woman with the baby stepped forward. "You can't speak."

Mark glanced down, then gasped. "Well I'll be damned. I almost didn't recognize you with all that hair." When he had last seen his sister, her hair was short and tapered. He leaned down and gave the beautiful woman a kiss and a hug. "When did you get here?"

"Just this morning."

"Essence," he announced, handling the introductions. "This is my big sister, Calaine and this must be my gorgeous little niece, Dominique."

She extended her hand. "Pleasure to meet you."

Calaine clasped her slender hand. "Thank you. I've heard so much about you."

"I hope it was all good."

"Don't worry, it was." Calaine shifted her gaze to her brother. "So Mark, I hear I have a nephew."

He beamed with pride. "He's somewhere around here. Why don't you let me hold my niece and we can go find him?"

She nodded. "Good, then we can find David."

Mark glanced at Essence. "You coming?"

She politely shook her head. "No, you go ahead. I'm going to stay and help Kelly."

Mark hesitated.

Kelly pushed him toward the door. "Go on, big brother. I promise not to embarrass you."

When they left, Essence moved over to the island. "What can I do to help?"

"How about you finish stuffing those deviled eggs for me?"

"Sure thing." She rolled up the sleeves of her silk turtleneck and moved to wash her hands at the sink.

"So how have things been?"

Essence glanced over her shoulder. "Are you referring to your brother?"

She smirked. "Of course."

"Better than I had expected," she answered honestly. She moved to the end of the counter and reached for a paper towel.

"Does that mean you have agreed to marry him?" Kelly asked.

Her head snapped around again with a stunned expression.

Kelly gave her a sheepish grin. "Mark told me."

Essence took a seat at the table and reached for the plate of eggs. "No, I have not decided to marry him."

"Why not?"

She spooned a dab of the yolk mixture into the egg white before responding, "Because he wants to marry for all the wrong reasons and I think that will be a big mistake."

"I guess that means he has never told you he loves you?" When Essence simply nodded, Kelly didn't look the slightest bit surprised.

"My brother…he really worries me," she mumbled as she reached for the bowl of frosting and began icing a German chocolate cake. "It's been really hard for him after Carmen."

"What do you mean?"

"I mean she really did a number on him. Didn't I tell you this story before?"

Essence shook her head as she reached for another egg.

"Well, he was so in love with that slut, but all she was interested in was a man in uniform. I knew her *kind* the minute I met her, but I couldn't tell Mark. Eventually she left him for someone in the Air Force. It almost killed him when she terminated the pregnancy."

# CHAPTER FIFTEEN

Essence gasped. "She was pregnant?"

"Yep, she didn't tell him until after it was over and only then to rub it in his face."

She shook her head. No wonder it was so hard for him to love. Mark had been burned badly. Worse than she had in her past.

Someone called Kelly into the dining room and she left Essence alone to finish filling the last of the eggs. As she sprinkled paprika over the eggs, she finally realized why Tyler was so important to Mark. *He doesn't want to lose another child.* Mark was probably willing to do whatever he had to keep his son in his life. Including marrying her or even worse, telling her he loved her. Why did that thought make her feel so bad? Would he really stoop that low?

"What are you thinking about?"

Mark had stepped into the kitchen followed by his mother and two sisters interrupting her thoughts.

Essence forced a smile as she glanced over her shoulder at them. "Nothing important."

Coming up behind her, he wrapped his arms loosely around her waist and kissed her just below her ear.

"None of that around my food," Kelly joked. She had been helping her mother cook since last night.

"I agree," Dorlinda said as she reached for her apron. "Why don't the two of you go and mingle while I get everything on the table."

"Alright." Mark took Essence's hand and led her back to the front of the house where everyone else had congregated.

Essence was glad that she had worn loose fitting pants. After dinner and a sample of all the different cakes and pies there was no way she could have sucked in her stomach.

The family gathered around the tree for gift exchange. Each adult was required to buy a twenty-five dollar gift for someone of the same sex. Names were drawn and gifts were then exchanged. Essence had purchased a Waldenbooks gift card that Calaine received. Essence received a lovely Christmas pendant from Mark's great aunt.

Tyler was having the time of his life crawling around on the floor with two of his cousins.

He received several more toys from several of his relatives, not to mention all of the gifts he received from his grandparents. She had to shake her head. The boy was going to be spoiled.

"Hey baby girl," came a deep voice from behind.

As Kelly glanced over her shoulder at the man standing in the corner of the room, surprise parted her lips. Immediately, she identified a pair of jet black eyes that had captured her heart many years ago. Over the past few years their paths had barely crossed.

A smile crept to her face as she turned on her heels and moved in his direction. Her gaze moved slowly over his features. She hadn't changed much in three years, while Diamere had changed drastically. Gone was his Jeri Curl and in its place was a short, tapered cut. His dark eyes were mysterious, reminding her of a dark winter night. The deep lines of his square face were due to a combination of maturity and hard determination she was certain his career in the Air Force had caused. A pair of gray wool slacks and a black turtle-necked sweater emphasized his well-proportioned six-foot two-inch frame. Diamere was in phenomenal shape.

A bright smile indicated that he was also glad to see her. "Hello, Diamere."

Kelly inhaled sharply, feeling the hard strength of Diamere as he snaked an arm around her tiny waist. Diamere hugged her, the top of her head coming just under his chin. Her eyelids fluttered close and she took a deep breath. She inhaled sharply, overpowered by the masculine scent of his body, then let the air out slowly. Wrapping her arms tightly around him, she was met by a series of tremors from being in his warm embrace. It surprised the hell out of her. Especially since she had gotten over him years ago.

Diamere pulled back slightly so that he could see her face, then asked, "Where's your husband?"

His comment was the splash of water she needed to douse his affect over her. Pulling out of his embrace, Kelly wrinkled her little nose and replied, "You know good and well I'm not married. What about yourself? Have you ever bothered sticking around long enough to break someone's heart?"

Diamere laughed; the sound low and sensual as it bubbled from deep within his chest. Sobering he replied, "I see you still know how to give a brother a hard time."

"You better believe it," she smirked.

"True, but can't you give us a break from time to time?" he asked, grinning broadly.

Kelly shrugged her slender shoulders beneath a red cashmere sweater. "Men like a good challenge."

Humor crinkled his eyes and magnificent mouth. "I guess I can't argue that point."

Her soft brown eyes filled with amusement. "Good, because you would lose."

Tilting his head at an angle, Diamere stared down at her youthful smiling face. He had spent the last few minutes standing across the room trying to get his thoughts under control. Kelly had had that type of affect on him since the summer she had turned eighteen when he discovered his feelings of brotherly love had suddenly changed. In the blink of an eye, she had changed from a little girl and had turned into a stunning young lady. He had never forgotten her large eyes or smooth coloring. He had also never forgotten the entrancing sensuality of her mouth. Mark would have killed him if he had known what he had been thinking, but there were some feelings one just couldn't do anything about. He wanted to keep thinking of her as the sweet kid he had always known, but instead his thoughts turned to what it would be like to truly hold her in his arms and join their bodies as one. He wasn't sure what might have happened had he not left for basic training when he did. When he had returned, Kelly was already away in college.

"I've heard you're thinking about coming home," she prompted, breaking through his thoughts. The smile had vanished from his face and she didn't have a clue as to what he was thinking. From the way he was staring at her, she thought maybe he was checking her out.

Her comment elicited a nod. "I'm doing more than thinking about it. I've already put in my papers for an early retirement. My father hasn't been well and I think it's time I came home."

A warm fuzzy feeling swept over her at the idea that he would be back in Delaware. It was an emotion she hadn't felt in years. She didn't still have feelings for him, did she? Inwardly, she told herself it was a huge mistake. To read something in what he was saying was pointless. His handsome face had simply made it difficult to think clearly.

"That's wonderful," she managed to reply calmly. "I'm sure your parents will be so glad to have you home."

Diamere liked the way her short new haircut flattered her high cheekbones. Leaning closer, his head was only inches from hers when he crooned, "And what about you Kelly, will you be glad to have me home, too?"

Kelly wanted to kiss him, to put her mouth against that cocky smile, those curved lips. His warm breath washed over her nose like a seductive whisper. Meeting his direct gaze the black eyes deepened. He held her captive as he stared at her unblinking. Could Diamere possibly be flirting with her? *Nah, couldn't be.* As much as she wished it were true, she knew better than to even consider such foolishness. She had discovered a long time ago that Diamere would never look at her as anyone but Mark's little sister.

Somehow, she reined her thoughts in and answered, "It's always great to have friends around."

"We're ready to head into the family room," Mr. Saunders called.

Several rose, faces shining with excitement. Mark reached for Essence's hand. "Come on."

"Where are we going?" she asked as she laced her fingers with his.

Mark looked down and met her questioning stare. "It's time for our traditional karaoke Christmas."

"Karaoke?" she gaped.

"Yep, and I can't wait to hear you sing."

She shook her head, a smile playing at her lips as they moved into the room. Several rows of folding chairs had been set up like a movie theatre in front of the big screen television.

Mr. and Ms. Saunders stood at the front of the room with the microphone in their hand. They started with Peaches and Herb's, "Reunited."

Next, Calaine's husband moved to the front. Essence found David to be a very attractive man, but it was nothing compared to his voice. He sang Boys to Men's rendition of "Silent Night." He had a beautiful voice that vibrated through her body and brought tears to her eyes.

Mark whispered near her ear. "Do you want to try it?"

"No way. I'm too embarrassed to stand up there in front of your family and sing."

"It's all in fun. Half the people in here, including me, can't even carry a tune."

She shook her head. "There's no way I'm going to make a fool of myself."

Mark rose from the couch. "Suit yourself." He moved up to the front and his cousin Dana handed him the microphone. Essence covered her mouth hiding her laughter. She couldn't believe he was going to sing. Several of his family members cheered him on as he took a moment to choose his song. He whispered to his cousin his choice and waited for her to stick in the appropriate CD.

The music began and Mark cleared his throat to ready himself for when the words appeared on the screen. As he stared out at her, he sung "This Christmas" by the Whispers.

He had a lovely singing voice. He sung with just enough passion to make her feel all warm inside. She was so caught up in the deep sound of his singing voice; she didn't realize the lone tear streaming down her face until it traveled under her chin. Essence swiped it away never looking away from the intensity of his eyes.

Mark returned to his seat and kissed her flush on the mouth. She heard catcalling, oohs, and aahs from his family.

On the drive home, Tyler was sound asleep in his chair. Essence moved over next to Mark and laid her head on his shoulder.

"I had a wonderful time with your family."

"I'm glad. They really like you."

Later that evening after they put Tyler to bed, the two moved to her room to change into their pajamas. After a long day, they decided to lie in bed and watch a new DVD. Halfway through the movie, Mark pulled her snugly in his arms and kissed her so deeply, she responded instantly. What choice did she have? Her mind was consumed by him. Her body craved him. Already her most sensitive area was throbbing in response to his kiss. She had no choice but to moan with desire, and welcome Mark back home.

Mark rolled her over onto her back. He slid her panties down past her ankles then tossed them onto the floor. Straddling her, he kissed first her abdomen, and then lower still. He pushed her thighs open, then began to lick. His tongue was slick and demanding. She immediately became hot and wet, and within minutes, she bucked against his mouth. He continued to taste until she was on the verge of exploding.

"Mark," she whispered.

"Yes, baby, tell me what you want." His breath was cool, tingling the hairs around her core.

"I want you," she moaned.

"That's good, cause I've got something for you." Mark quickly unbuttoned the fly of his pajama bottom and rolled on protection. He then spread her thighs wide and entered her in one fluid motion.

Essence gasped. It felt so good having him inside her again she couldn't hold still. She wanted all of him inside her. She met each of his powerful thrusts as he pumped his body into hers. As she felt herself on the verge of exploding, Mark commanded her to wrap her legs firmly around his waist and she held on as his thrusts increased. A few seconds later an orgasm ripped through her body. He pushed harder and deeper and, shortly after, his body tensed and he convulsed in her arms.

**225**

He lay draped over her and sighing with satisfaction.

They didn't speak, still catching their breaths, yet he palmed her spine, her buttocks, in a slow motion. She was mystified by the sexual power he had over her. When they were like this, he made her feel that together they could get through anything.

She wanted to tell him what she was feeling, but was still too scared to say anything yet. She loved him and knew there was no way she could continue to say no. Her heart was no longer in it. She wished she didn't love him so deeply, though she had already known her heart was on the line the day Mark walked back into her life. She loved him and if he asked her to marry him again, this time, her answer would be yes. She just wished he loved her.

"Diamere, thanks for bringing me home," Kelly said as they pulled in front of her house.

"It was my pleasure," he replied, although he wasn't so sure bringing her home had been such a good idea.

Diamere had stayed behind long after the rest of the family had bid their goodbyes and departed. While Kelly washed dishes and he dried, they caught up on the last several years. He had always known she would be a schoolteacher. It had been a dream of hers since the fifth grade. He also knew that he had never had a teacher that looked like her when he was in elementary school.

Glancing over at her delicate profile, he groaned inwardly. If he had known she had left her car at home and ridden over with one of her cousins, he would probably have left when everyone else had. Instead, she had asked him for a ride and, since her apartment was along the way to his parents' house, he had agreed.

He climbed out of his Avalon, then walked around and opened the passenger door for her. When Kelly stuck her leg out the car, Diamere swallowed hard and forced his eyes away from her shapely calves. Bringing her home had definitely not been a smart move on his part. The sooner he saw Kelly safely into the building and drove away, the better off he would be.

It would be quite some time before he returned to Delaware. He wasn't scheduled to get out the military for another ten months. By then, he and Ryan would be married and his child born. His responsibilities as a father and husband would dissipate the attraction he had for Kelly.

The past several hours had been nothing in comparison to the trip they had shared in the car to her place. He tried to keep the conversation casual and his body from responding. The attempt proved to be hopeless. His loins stirred from the slightest smile. He fought the kick of desire that tightened his gut and hardened his body. It was a good thing his sweater was long enough to cover his arousal.

As he followed her into the building, Diamere watched the sway of her lush hips. *This is going to be difficult,* he thought to himself.

A short while later he was walking her up to her second floor apartment. "I probably won't get the chance to see you before I leave for Colorado. So I want to say it was good seeing you again."

"It was good seeing you too, Diamere," Kelly said when they reached her apartment. She fumbled with her key ring as she tried several attempts at opening the door.

"Here, let me do that for you." As he reached down for the keys, his long fingers brushed against hers and sent off another round of tremors.

He opened the door and she glanced up at him. "Thanks."

Diamere met her smile and was suddenly tongue-tied. She was so beautiful that she stole his breath. He wanted to reach out and stroke her cheek. And her lush mouth…he wanted to feel those lips pressed firmly against his. Instead, he folded his large arms across his chest to prevent the impulse to touch her.

"You want to come in?" she asked in a voice as soft as butter.

Diamere knew he should have said *no* and been on his way, but he just wasn't ready yet to leave her. Her smile was warm, generous and made his insides tighten and his stomach muscles clench. "Sure, maybe for a few minutes."

Closing the door behind him, he then followed her into the living room with the scent of her familiar perfume leading the way. Kelly removed her coat. He shrugged out of his own and gave it to her then watched as she moved to the closet. The short navy blue skirt emphasized her narrow waist and shapely hips. He had always been a leg and butt man. Kelly may be a small woman, but she definitely had a generous helping of both.

He tore his eyes away from her curvaceous figure and tried to concentrate on his surroundings. The contemporary-styled room was femininely decorated in sage and beige with soft floral pastels as accent colors. "Your place is nice."

"Thank you," she replied as she turned to face him again. "Why don't you have a seat?"

Diamere nodded and took a seat on the couch. Kelly lowered in the chair across from him, slipping off her shoes and curling her feet on the couch beneath her.

"Would you like something to drink?" she asked, pointing toward a small oak bar in the corner.

Diamere shook his head. "No thanks."

There was then a long moment of silence before Kelly said, "I'll be right back. The remote to the television is over on the end table." She then scrambled off the couch and jogged quickly toward the back of her apartment.

*What are you doing?* a voice asked. Diamere wasn't sure. All he knew was that he needed to get away from Kelly as quickly as possible. Little Kel had grown into a beautiful and desirable woman, and he had not expected the surge of pleasure or the heat that coiled in his belly. Being around her, he discovered, was becoming quite dangerous. Something had thickened in the air between them. It was soft and warm and made it almost impossible to think straight.

"You avoided my question earlier. How come you've never married?"

Diamere flinched at the sound of her voice. He hadn't even noticed she had returned to the room. She had changed into a pair of stretch pants and an oversized T-shirt.

Shifting slightly on the couch, he answered, "I haven't met the right one yet."

Kelly chuckled as she flopped down in a chair. "I don't think you would know the right one if she was smack in your face."

"True," he admitted. But that no longer mattered. Right or wrong, he was going to ask Ryan to marry him as soon as he got back to Colorado. "What about you?" he asked, hoping to shift the conversation from him.

Kelly shrugged nonchalant. "I date occasionally, but I'm only twenty-four. I've still got plenty of time to think about a family."

A muscle pulsed at his cheek. "A family? You're planning to have kids?"

Her expression said she found his question quite peculiar. "Sure. Why wouldn't I?"

"I don't know. It's strange to hear you thinking about having kids when you're still a kid yourself." He lied. But he couldn't let it be known that he felt a stab of jealousy at the thought of her pregnant with someone else's child.

"Wake up, Diamere. I'm all grown up. I can drive, vote and even drink," she murmured sarcastically.

He already knew that. Even if he didn't want to admit it, one sweeping glance of her body told him otherwise.

"I'm surprised you haven't fathered any children along the way."

Diamere blinked twice. Kelly had just given him the opener he needed.

"Actually, I've been dating someone for a quite while. She told me last week that she's pregnant."

"You're having a baby?" Her disappointment with him was apparent.

"It appears so."

Jealousy gripped her hard and quick. She forced herself to hide it. "Congratulations. I hope you're going to do right by her."

He shrugged nonchalantly. "If you're talking about marriage, I don't know yet."

Kelly's anger flared. "What do you mean?"

"I mean I don't know what I want to do. I'm not ready for marriage."

She stiffened and glared over at him. "You obviously don't know anything about protection either. And you called me, a kid."

"Kelly, I really don't need to hear this."

"Then you better leave." She rose and moved toward the closet to retrieve his coat.

He jumped up in front of her. "Kelly, look, I'm sorry. I just—"

"Don't worry about it."

Standing toe to toe, he could feel the warmth of her body and his loins began to fill. Diamere's gaze dropped from the fire in Kelly's eyes to her mouth, sensuous and very feminine. A mouth made for a man to enjoy. Lips he wanted so desperately.

He leaned closer, whispered against her temple as he lowered his head. "I've tried my damnedest not to touch you, but I can't. I've wanted to do this all evening," he murmured barely touching his mouth to hers, drowning in the feel of her.

He pulled her into his arms and brushed his lips over hers. As she kissed him back, Diamere discovered a flavor so rich, he hungered for more. It was gentle at first, then that wasn't enough. Her mouth parted beneath his, allowing him to take what he wanted. He began mating sensuously with hers. She clung to his shoulders and responded to him, sending his body spinning to a state of oblivion. Kelly returned each kiss with enough passion that made him forget every reason why he shouldn't be doing this. He couldn't stop now even if he wanted to. Instead, he sought more.

He pulled her closer and deepened the kiss. Every stroke of her tongue ignited deeper passion. Her lips were sweet, ripe and held for him the joy of discovery.

His hand boldly moved down her body to the curvaceous swell of her soft behind, bringing her snugly against his erection.

He wished to God she'd step away before he did something they both might regret later. Kissing her wasn't enough. He wanted to taste her all over. He wanted to join their bodies together.

He was about to lower her onto the couch when the sound of a car's horn brought him back to his senses. He breathed in deeply, trying to regain his control. He rubbed his hand over his face and wondered what the hell had just happened.

He lifted his head and it was a moment before she opened her eyes. He felt a tightness in his chest as he peered down at her. He had expected her expression to be unreadable, but it was obvious she had been just as moved by the kiss as he had.

"I'm sorry," he said as he tried to get his breathing back on track.

She nodded, tried to take a step back, but Diamere reached out to stop her.

"I don't know what I was thinking," he groaned, his voice muffled by the torment he felt. He couldn't believe he had just kissed her that way. He glanced down at her and when he did, he found her watching him with an intensity that stole his breath away.

"There is nothing to be sorry about." Stepping away from his hold, she moistened her kiss-swollen lips. "I wanted it to," she confessed.

Diamere inhaled deeply. He hadn't expected this to happen, at least not to this degree. Though he couldn't rationalize it, it seemed he had always known that it would be good with her. He just never expected it to be so intense. Now he was stuck in a state of arousal. His lips had been hard and greedy. His desire for her had come on to him fast and furious. Part of him wanted to get as far away from her as possible, while the other half imagined carrying her to bed. Realization crept in filling him with alarm. He felt more than physical attraction to the woman gazing up innocently at him. His feelings for Kelly Saunders came dangerously close to love.

Feeling his resistance slipping, he tilted his head back and kissed her again. He placed a hand at the curve of her hip. Unable to rationalize a reason not to, he slipped inside her parted lips and the kiss deepened. As the kiss intensified, so did the desire to join their bodies as one. He heard a desperate sound escape her lips and he continued to kiss her, tasting her repeatedly.

Moments later, breathing deeply, he tore his mouth from hers and looked down into the desire blazing in her eyes.

He sighed as he took a step back reaffirming the decision he just reached. "We need to quit while we are ahead."

Her ragged breath echoed around the room. "I was actually enjoying it."

"So was I, but that doesn't make it right. I didn't come here to take advantage of you."

Her expression cooled. "Advantage? You didn't do anything that I didn't allow you to do."

He knew he had to grow firm, regardless of what he felt. "Nevertheless, it was a mistake. You are like a sister to me and I don't want to jeopardize that."

"Alright," she replied after a long pregnant silence. Kelly stepped back, still aroused, battling the part of her body that refused to behave—her heart.

She thought she would have drowned beneath the deep, lingering feel of his mouth. Diamere had kissed her in a way she had only read about. She knew she should have stopped him, but as he deepened the kiss, a sweep of desire washed over her. Nevertheless, he was right. They could never be anything more than friends.

Frustration gripped her. He was still rejecting her after all these years. She wasn't going to cry. There was no way she could ever let him know how she felt about him. Drawing a deep breath, she crossed her arms beneath her breasts and tossed her head. "You're right. Your kisses can't change the fact that you have a girlfriend who's pregnant."

"No they can not." He saw what looked like pain in her eyes. *Now look what you have done.*

"Thank you so much for bringing me home. I guess I'd better get some sleep."

He didn't blame her for trying to get rid of him. If he were in her shoes, he would have done the same.

He nodded. "Good-bye, Kelly."

Without giving her a chance to respond, he retrieved his coat and walked out of her life once again.

# CHAPTER SIXTEEN

For Essence, the next few days passed in a blur. She was so happy, she felt sure she wore a permanent smile on her face. Their passion for one another had not diminished. In fact, their desire seemed to deepen. She was having so much fun she pushed the future aside and enjoyed each day as they came, even though she knew the time would eventually come for Mark to return to active duty.

Friday evening they returned to the house after going out to an authentic Mexican restaurant with Calaine and David. It was their last night. They were leaving for San Antonio in the morning. As they pulled into her garage, Mark suggested that they go away for the weekend.

"Go where?" she asked, eyes sparkling at the possibility.

"To Philadelphia. I want some time alone with you."

She saw the seriousness in his expression and knew the weekend would mean a lot to him. "Yes, I'd love too. When do we leave?"

"As soon as I make all the arrangements."

The following afternoon they arrived in Philadelphia. Mark booked them at the Radisson Plaza, which was rich in tradition and allowed easy access to the city's commercial district. It was an elite hotel with prestigious accommodations. No two rooms were alike. They featured upgraded guest amenities as well as terry cloth robes and feather beds.

"Wow, I can definitely get used to this," Essence said after they carried their bags into the suite.

"So could I," Mark added. He would give anything to have her all to himself from this day forth.

Essence lowered her bags and took a quick tour of their accommodations. There was a kitchenette, a living room with a pullout couch. A bedroom with a king size bed, and a balcony with a magnificent view of downtown.

Essence smiled at his handsome face. "What would you like to do first?"

"I can think of several things." He pulled her against him and seared her lips with a kiss. When they finally came up for air, he smiled down at her and said, "Why don't we get out of this room before I ravish you? Let's make reservations for dinner and take a tour of the city?"

"That would be wonderful."

They caught a cab to Chestnut Street where they hired a private horse-drawn carriage for an hour-long tour of the city. Although she had lived in southern Pennsylvania most of her life, Essence had yet to experience Philadelphia's history aboard a stylish coach. While sitting snuggly against Mark wrapped in a thick wool blanket, she journeyed back in time during the enchanting carriage ride that whisked them through the tree-lined streets of Philadelphia's National Historical Park, Society Hill and Old City.

When they returned to their room, Essence took one look at the large Jacuzzi tub and decided if they planned to make dinner, it would be safer to take a shower. Nevertheless, they ended up staying under the water longer than intended. Essence thought she was going to explode as Mark found several different ways to make her reach a climax. She was on the brink of exploding when he wrapped her legs around his hips and entered her slowly.

Leaning her against the shower wall Mark pumped fiercely inside of her, afraid he could never get enough of her. After Essence collapsed in his arms, he came shortly after her then carried her into the room where he laid her gently across the bed and kissed the water from her breasts.

"Mmmm, you've got to stop or we will never make it to dinner," she crooned.

"When I have you, food is the furthest thing from my mind."

"I wish I could say the same, only I haven't eaten since lunch and I am starving."

Mark gave a reluctant groan. "Alright, Ms. Monroe, if it's food you want, then it is food you're going to get. We will continue this when we return."

She changed into a pair of black dress slacks and a gray turtleneck. Mark reemerged in the room dressed in navy blue pleated slacks and a royal blue sweater.

"You look handsome."

"And you don't look bad yourself." He took her hand and kissed her lightly on the lips, escorting her out the room and down into the lobby.

They had reservations at The Prime Rib located in the hotel lobby. Voted the "Best of Philly," the sophisticated restaurant featured a thirty-two-ounce prime rib as well as fresh seafood. They had shrimp cocktail for an appetizer. Each ordered prime rib, a baked potato, and steamed vegetables, along with a house salad and fresh baked bread. For dessert they each had a slice of a New York cheesecake that was to die for.

Essence sighed and snuggled against Mark as the deejay played a slow ballad. After dinner they had gone to the hotel lounge for drinks and dancing. Mark was a fabulous dancer. In the past hour, they'd done everything but the electric slide and she was having a ball.

"I haven't danced this much since I was seventeen," she'd told him. "I'd forgotten how much I loved it."

"A shame. You're a natural."

And he'd been right. All the moves had come back to her and the steps she didn't know she'd learned quickly from Mark's strong lead, laughing as he whipped her around in a two-step. She found his sensual moves sexy with his loose-hipped style and Essence hadn't missed the blatant perusals by a couple of single women in the room. She had the childish urge to pin a sign on his back that said, "he's mine."

Most of the night they had the small dance floor of the hotel lounge practically to themselves. Only one or two other couples joined them occasionally. The other patrons had drinks at the bar or in a dark corner of the room, and they soon thinned out, leaving them alone except for the deejay and the bartender.

"Getting tired?" he asked.

"A little, but I don't want the evening to end. I'm having a wonderful time. Besides, we haven't heard a line dance yet."

He grinned. "I doubt if this guy has the cha-cha slide, but I'll ask. You want something else to drink while I check?"

She nodded.

He seated her at the table, held up two fingers to the bartender, then went to speak with the deejay. Mark returned a few minute later with news. "We're out of luck, but he thinks he might have another slow jam you might like."

As it turned out, he played Luther Vandross' "Dance with my Father." Mark led her onto the dance floor one more time and held her snugly to his chest. Essence closed her eyes, wishing the moment would never end. However, when the song ended, she was suddenly anxious to be alone with Mark again.

As soon as they closed the door to their room, they quickly removed their clothes. Mark suited up then swept Essence into his arms and strode to the bed.

"I've been waiting for this all night," he whispered.

"So have I," she said, opening to him, reaching for him.

Kneeling between her legs, he lifted her hips and licked. Essence almost came off the bed.

"You're wet. Hot and wet. God, I could eat you up."

"I want you inside of me. Now! Hurry."

Coming to her swiftly, he covered her mouth with his and plunged deeply, his tongue driving as hard and deep as his shaft.

"Hold me, Essence. Move with me."

"Oh, Mark…" she whispered, as she brushed her breasts against his body hair, back and forth with a delicious sensuality that spiked his hunger for her until it was all-consuming.

He thrust even deeper inside her. "Tell me you want me," he demanded. "Tell me, Essence!"

She locked her legs around his waist and whispered, "I want you more than I can say. I want—Oh, Mark, now! Please now!"

Mark was more than ready. Seized by their bodies' rhythm, he drowned in rapture. Mark chanted her name, then he heard her cries mingle with his.

His forehead fell to her shoulder. His throat heaving, his heart trying to force its way out of his chest, he clung to her as if he were drowning.

She asked softly, "Mark, are you all right?"

He was quiet for a full minute before he finally answered, "No. But if you marry me I will be."

This time, Essence accepted his proposal. Now all she needed was his love.

It was close to midnight when Diamere pulled up in front of the building. Leaning over the seat, he glanced up at the second floor window.

"Damn," he scowled. Something told him Kelly would be home.

He had been trying to reach her since that night he had left her apartment, hard and aching with desire. He had called her home, phoned her parents, he had even tried the cell phone number they had given him and each attempt had been unsuccessful. His last call had been less than a minute ago and she hadn't bothered to pick up. Kelly was avoiding him.

He couldn't blame her. He had made a major mess of things. Sitting in his car with his engine idling softly, he couldn't figure out how he had gotten himself in this mess.

"You really should just leave it alone," he muttered.

However, he couldn't. Every time he closed his eyes, he could still see her full moist lips and her innocent expression. They haunted his thoughts. But it was the unfamiliar tightness in his chest that he could not ignore. Why Kelly of all people? Never had a kiss been as sweet before. No way should she make his blood heat. The attraction was too strong. And he didn't like it one bit. Mark's little sister was off limits to him. She deserved a lot better than a fool like him.

That was neither here nor there. Regardless of what he was feeling, he had allowed his lust to get in the way, and took advantage of a vulnerable opportunity.

Now he needed to apologize.

*But what good is that going to do?* He had a strong suspicion that it was only going to make matters worst. He should just go. Instead, he killed the engine and pushed redial on his phone. When her answering machine came on, he ended the call and climbed out of the car.

"Enough with the games," he murmured as he shut the door.

He entered the building and walked up the flight of stairs. Moving to her door, he heard faint music coming from her apartment. He drew in a ragged breath then knocked.

"Who is it?"

"Kel, it's Diamere."

"What do you want?" she snapped.

"I need to talk to you." There was a long moment of silence. "Kel, you either let me in or I'm going to tell your brother what happened."

The door opened and she stuck her head out. "No you won't."

Diamere drew a deep breath. He realized with one look how much he still wanted her. "Why wouldn't I?"

"Boy puhleeze, with a reputation like you have, Mark would kick your butt."

Diamere could tell she was trying to resist a grin.

"You're right, he would," he replied with a silly grin on his face. Diamere knew he should turn around and leave, but instead he stood there and stared at her standing in the slit of the door.

Kelly opened the door wide. She was wearing a long sleeve yellow shirt that emphasized her beautiful breasts. Hanging from her hips was a pair of flannel boxers that showed off her slim hips and slender legs. Diamere swallowed. Her feet were bare. To him, nothing was sexier than a woman with pretty feet. He tuned out the voice in his brain whispering to him step forward and kiss her senseless.

She leaned against the doorjamb. "Are you just going to stand there or are you going to come inside so we can talk?"

He knew staying in the hallway was safer, but after hearing a door down the hall open, he realized it was better to discuss their business in private.

He stepped into the room, catching a whiff of her soft perfume as he passed. He didn't bother to take a seat. He waited for her to close the door and turned to face him before he said, "I came to apologize for the other night."

Kelly glanced down at the floor then up again, looking slightly uneasy. "No need. We're two consenting adults. You didn't do anything that I didn't allow you to do."

Clearing his throat, he could feel himself scowling at the thought that he still wanted to kiss her. The lipstick on her lips drew attention to their fullness. Forcefully, he shifted his eyes away from her mouth. "Regardless, I was wrong," he began. "We have been friends for too long and I don't want to jeopardize that."

She studied his face and the regret that she read there upset her even more. She ignored the pounding in her heart at the mere sight of him and asked, not because of curiosity but because she needed to know, "Why did you kiss me?"

Diamere gave her an incredulous look. "Who wouldn't want to kiss you? You've grown into a beautiful and desirable woman. If I'd known you were going to look this good, I would have taken your schoolgirl crush seriously."

She stiffened and squared her shoulders. "I got over you years ago."

"Are you sure about that?"

"Positive." *Then why are your palms shaking and your heart skipping?*

He was quiet, then nodded. "I'm leaving in the morning."

Although she had been ignoring his calls, knowing that he was leaving caused a lump to form in her throat.

Diamere had no idea what she was thinking but her face told him that she still had feelings for him. Why did that please him?

He didn't like the sadness he saw in her big brown eyes. It was because of him the sparkle had gone. He couldn't leave knowing he had made her angry and sad all at the same time. That was why he had come over to make amends. So why then was he contemplating kissing her again?

"I hope everything works out for you in Colorado." She finally said.

"Do you really mean that?"

She gave him a stiff nod. "Of course. I wish only happiness for you."

"Then if you want to make me happy, you should be able to understand why I need to kiss you again."

Her eyes grew round in surprise. She backed away but Diamere stepped forward and took hold of her by the shoulders, connecting his hips with hers.

"Please, don't," she whispered, but there was little force behind her words.

The look in her eyes told him she didn't really mean it. He tipped her face up gently and the look in her eyes told him that she wanted it too. In fact she licked her lips anticipating his touch.

Lowering his head, he pressed his mouth to hers and revealed his fierce hunger for her. The kiss seemed to go on forever. A kiss, he thought dimly, that she was more than returning.

Her arms were around his neck, silently encouraging him. Kelly's firm breasts were pressed to his rock hard chest. In passionate gratitude he felt her open to the thrust of his tongue, matching each stroke with skilled moves of her own. Kelly wanted him as badly as he wanted her.

Diamere buried his hands in her hair, his lips sweeping the curve of her cheekbones. As he did so the fragrance of her skin filled his nostrils. He then unbuttoned her shirt and pushed it off one shoulder, kissing her collarbone and the gentle hollow of her throat. Then he found the firm rise of her breasts; his heart thudding against his ribcage, Diamere cupped its weight, the softness warm and in his hand. He teased her nipple to hardness. Kelly moaned his name, her palms splayed against his chest, her fingers playing with his body hair in a way that inflamed him. He kissed her again, straining her to him, knowing there was nowhere on earth he would rather be than in her bed.

His kiss was everything she wanted. Her body ached for her to invite him into her room and let him make love to her. Is that why she had held on to her virginity for long, because she had been saving it for him? Diamere Redmond. The man she had intended to marry. Only this was all wrong. What they were doing was wrong. She and Diamere would never be. He was intending to marry someone else, and she refused to be a pawn. She pulled away quickly.

When he opened his eyes and stared down at her, her expression was cool and guarded.

"Damn, Kel. I didn't mean to do that."

"Why can't you just admit that you are attracted to me?"

Several seconds passed before Diamere finally said, "Alright. I'm attracted to you."

Kelly smirked, pleased by his confession. "Good. Now that that's settled you better go home and get some sleep."

"Why can't I sleep here?"

She frowned at the suggestion. "Because it's not a good idea and once you give it some thought you will realize the same." She paused to release a deep breath. "Come on into the kitchen and I'll make us both a cup of hot chocolate."

# *CHAPTER SEVENTEEN*

Mark opened his eyes. "Hi."

Essence affected a mysterious smile. "Hi yourself, Captain."

He squeezed her thigh. "I'm almost afraid to hear what you have to say."

"I'm not talking myself out of anything, Mark." *Because I am deeply in love with you.* She spent most of the night wondering if she had made the right decision about marrying him. Then she thought of their son and was certain that she had.

"Then what are you thinking" he whispered softly. "I can see those gears grinding in your head."

Attractive lines deepened around her lovely brown eyes. "No, you can't."

"Yes, I can. You're still trying to talk yourself out of marrying me."

"No. I'm trying to figure out why you would want to give up your freedom for us."

He gave her a look that said the reason was obvious. "I love Tyler."

"Oh, that I have no doubt. But what about you and me, Mark?"

He sighed. "You know how I feel about you."

"I know how your libido feels, but what about you?"

Mark struggled with his words. He wasn't sure if she was ready to hear what he had to say and whether or not she would believe him. He'd spent half the night trying to gather his feelings into one neat package and failed. "I...I don't know how to say it," he said truthfully.

She sucked her teeth.

Shifting his head slightly on the pillow, he stared at her. "Can you tell me how you feel about me?"

She gazed at him as she pondered his question. There was no way she could let him know how she truly felt, not when he was unable to do the same.

"No, I can't. My feelings are jumbled and Lord knows I've tried to piece them together since your return." She pushed out of his arms and sat up in the bed. "I care about you a great deal Mark and I know it's not just because of Tyler. I have adjusted to providing a home for Tyler without you." She looked at him. "But you haven't. You came back to a ready-made family."

He leaned over and pressed a kiss to her nose. "Yeah, *my* ready-made family."

"Come on, it's not that easy."

"No, it isn't. It was a shock finding out that I had a son. But all I had to do was take one look at my little boy and I was lost. And his mother does crazy things to me."

"I'll never know if you care for me because of him or for myself."

"You'll have to trust my word."

She couldn't quite bring herself to do that. Not just yet. If he shouted to the heavens that he loved her, she wouldn't believe him anyway. There was still a huge part of her that didn't trust a man to tell the truth and mean it. She thought her last fiancé was a decent man until he betrayed her. Granted, they hadn't been in a tough situation like the one she was in with Mark. There were no claims of undying love to sway her. Despite his desire to commit himself to her and their child, was he ready for what she wanted from him?

When she remained silent, staring at him with an odd look in her eyes, Mark's tender side came out. "I know I didn't do right by you all these months, but I want to make that up to you. I know we can make this work.

"And what if it doesn't work?" The words exploded from her mouth.

"It will work."

"Why, because I'm the mother of your child?"

"No, because you're the woman I want."

For a moment, Essence felt as if an arrow landed straight in her heart. She couldn't explain it, but she believed him…and smiled.

Mark returned it, then his expression sobered. "I promise to make you happy, Essence."

She stared, wanting to trust his words. Needing to believe him.

"You'll let me know when you trust me, right?" he said, and she blinked.

How could this man read her like that? It was irritating and a little comforting. "Yes, I will." At least he'd accepted the fact that right now she was borderline.

Mark captured her lips in a long erotic kiss, and she became a victim of pure sensuality. She came apart in his arms, her fingers slid across his buttocks, her body pressed firmly against his. She inched up, running her tongue over the seam of his mouth before she kissed him.

He groaned, trapping her in his arms.

"We're amazing together, aren't we?" she whispered.

He shifted them to the side, running his hand over the curve of her hip. "True that…true that," he murmured against her mouth.

From his position, her bare breasts were too much of a temptation. He tipped his head and took a nipple deep into his mouth.

Her sharp indrawn breath filled the room, followed by a low throaty moan. It was hard not to be vocal when Mark touched her like this. He cupped her breasts, kneading them as he sucked. The pull sent spirals of sweet sensation out to her fingertips. Her toes curled.

*Only him*, she thought, scrubbing her hands over his chest and then lower. The muscles of his stomach flinched and she smiled to herself. He nuzzled between her breasts and Essence shifted lower, leaving hot grinding kisses in her wake. His breathing labored, his grip on her tightened.

"Essence."

She met his fevered gaze, stroking his stomach, her hand gliding over his skin then slowly closing her fingers around his arousal. He was already hard. She arched a brow.

Humor invaded him. "It's your fault."

Then she bent and licked. He howled and she took him in between her lips.

"Aaah!" Mark was helpless, sinking fast and furiously into the sensation rushing and churning inside him. His body reeled in ten directions all at once. His hands fisted in the sheets. His blood shimmered in his veins and rushed to collect where she touched. She tasted and he felt himself on the verge of losing control. He grasped her arms and dragged her on top of him. "We better do something about that," he growled, "*Now.*"

"I thought I was." Essence smiled as she rolled on a condom then straddled his hips. He didn't give her a second to breathe, pushing into her and bucking. She laughed and spread her hands over his chest, riding him, rocking hard and watching his face. He rose up, pulling her legs around him then quickened their motion. Gazes met and locked as their bodies beat a frantic rhythm. Sweat trickled, damp flesh melted. She gripped his shoulders as he pushed and pushed.

"You are so hot," he said against her mouth.

"And you feel good," she moaned. Essence then told him what his touch did to her, what he felt like inside her, thick and pulsing. Mark tossed her on her back and thrust harder and faster as she begged for more.

"Essence," Mark chanted over and over. Then they both came; glorious spasms roared through them leaving their pulses pounding.

Sapped of energy, Mark shifted to his side and collapsed.

Later that morning they had breakfast at the Capriccio's Café, a local favorite that offered a variety of international coffees, muffins and breakfast sandwiches.

By the afternoon, they headed to an African-American museum that had thousands of objects and images, ranging from fine and folk art, to memorabilia and costumes. The Museum was committed to telling the story of African-American family life, the Civil Rights movement, arts and entertainment. Essence was pleased that they had arrived in time to experience a tribal folk dance.

Afterwards they went to the Franklin Mills Mall. Caught up in the seductive mood of the afternoon, Essence and Mark walked in and out of several department stores, shopping and browsing then topped off the evening when Mark steered her to every jewelry store in the mall in search of the perfect ring.

Essence was stunned and landed on cloud nine when Mark insisted on buying her a two-carat diamond solitaire surrounded by ruby gems. While the ring was being sized, they went and had an Italian dinner. It was after eight when they finally returned to the hotel, bags in their hands and a sparkling new diamond on Essence's finger.

Mark suggested they celebrate in the Jacuzzi.

"You sure you like it?" he asked, seeing her staring down at her hand.

Her eyes sparkling like the jewel on her finger. "I love it."

He poured them both a glass of champagne to toast their engagement. "Here's to a lifetime of happiness."

She cast her eyes downward, blushing as Mark leaned over and kissed her tenderly on the lips.

Happiness was exactly what Essence expected. Now all she needed was his love. She knew as long as she had her faith in God that would also come. She took a sip, then asked, "So tell me what it's like to be an officer's wife?"

"The same as being a doctor's wife. Dress beautifully for social events and keep your husband satisfied." He wagged his eyebrows suggestively.

"Be serious, Mark. I want to know what military life is like."

"Well, you've got a lot to learn. We'll live on a military post."

"I thought it was a base."

"Base is Air Force. Post is Army."

Essence nodded in understanding. She had already learned something new.

"You'll buy groceries at the commissary."

Her brow quirked. "Why can't I shop at a regular grocery store?"

He reached up and ran a forefinger down the length of her nose. "You can shop wherever you want. But believe me, once you see the prices, you won't want to shop anywhere else."

She nodded again.

"Everything you'll need will be on post: movie theatre, a gym, drugstore and department store which is called the PX, a post office, etc."

"Wow, a little city in itself."

"Right. As soon as we get back I want to take Tyler and get his ID card and put him on my health insurance. Then as soon as we are married you'll get yours."

She smiled, unable to contain her excitement.

"Have you thought of a date?"

There was a heartbeat of a second before she replied. "How about the spring?"

A rush of excitement washed over him. It was finally happening. "Don't make me wait too long. I don't want to be without you any longer than I have to. I promise to make you very happy." He leaned over and gave her a wet lingering kiss.

Then he felt her fingers encircle him, stroking the taut length of his penis. As his face convulsed, he muttered, "Keep that up and you're in trouble."

"Another promise?" she crooned as she put her glass aside.

"Yeah, it's a promise…" he couldn't hold back a growl, "…and I'm going to keep it."

His gaze held a promise of more to come. He lowered his glass to the side of the tub, then with a twinkle in his eyes, he picked up a bar of soap and lathered his hands. Slowly, he massaged her breasts in a slow circular motion with lingering tenderness. Sliding his hand over her hot damp skin, he feathered his thumbs lightly over the sensitive peaks. Her body was so relaxed that she had to brace her palms on the sides of the tub to keep herself from sliding into the water.

Mark's hands moved lower blazing a warm trail, washing her belly, then her thighs with gentle care. "Even after giving birth to our son, you're still beautiful."

Then he moved his hand exactly where she wanted it, his gaze holding hers while he fondled her. Essence squirmed against him then rewarded him with a gasp of delight. He slipped a finger inside of her and she met each stroke. She grit her teeth against the incredible sensation as warm water splashed against her breasts. A second later an orgasm ripped through her, shattering the last of her control. In a fever of impatience, she reached for the condom sitting on the side of the tub and rolled it on. She then brought her legs over so that she straddled

**251**

him, her breasts moist against his chest, her aching center meeting his hardness. Groaning out her name, he caught her hips and pushed into her slick wet body until all of his length was buried deep inside. She sucked in her breath in exquisite ecstasy. Closing her eyes, she struggled to hold on to her release.

She splayed her fingers on his chest. Then she rode him, her hips moving in a slow up- and-down motion.

As she moved, he trailed his hands from her shoulders to her buttocks. She established a rhythm that left both of them gasping for their breath. She rode him so hard the water sloshed around them. But he didn't want her to slow down. With her knees braced on either side of his body, her breasts gently bouncing, he took her by the waist, and pushed harder and harder. Her contractions squeezed him and pushed him over the edge until her body convulsed and she dropped against his chest.

When it was over, she laid weak in his arms. His mouth drifted along her neck and shoulders, tasting and leaving a trail of hot kisses. After a few long moments, he lifted her from the water holding her upright while he wrapped her in a soft towel. He then lifted her up into his arms and walked to the bed laying her down gently. The linens felt cool against her moist flesh. He settled himself beside her, bringing her close to the heat of his body.

Drowsy and contented she cuddled to him in the darkness, her head tucked onto his broad shoulder. His arm lay heavy and possessive over her stomach. As if in a dream she felt his mouth against her brow, his lips gradually searing a downward path until he parted her legs for the most intimate kiss of all. He caressed her with his tongue slow and gentle until she was ready to cry from the beauty of it all.

She tossed her head from side to side, trembling beneath his touch. She called his name repeatedly as the tension gathered in her body.

Then suddenly her body was taken over with the need for release. She cried out in pleasure as he held her close. The frantic hammering of her heart was reflected in his own.

Feeling as though he held the whole world in his arms, Mark murmured, "Essence, you're incredible."

She opened her eyes and smiled. "Yes, I am."

As they drifted toward sleep, Mark held her within the strong circle of his arms as if he could not bear for the night to end.

# CHAPTER EIGHTEEN

The following morning they ordered room service and another course of love making before they prepared to check out. Neither of them wanted to see the day end.

They arrived at his parents' home just in time for Sunday dinner. The aroma of pot roast and roasted potatoes met them at the door.

"Mom, something smells great," Mark commented as they stepped into the kitchen.

"Ma Ma!" Tyler squirmed until his grandpa lowered him onto the floor then scrambled into Essence's outstretched arms.

"Hello, sweetheart. Mommy missed you so much." She squeezed him tight and planted kisses all over his face.

"How was your weekend?" Dorlinda asked.

"Fabulous," Mark said, grinning from ear-to-ear.

Mark looked at Essence and when she winked, he reached for her free hand and squeezed it. "Mom…Dad, Essence and I are engaged."

"Well it's about time! Congratulations." She wiped her hands on a towel and moved over to hug both of them. "Let me see that ring." Essence gave Tyler to his father then held out her hand and proudly displayed the sparkling diamond.

"Oh, my! I'm glad to see that my son isn't cheap," she joked.

"I'm happy for both of you." George rose from his chair. Extending both hands, he grasped his future daughter-in-law by the shoulders and pressed his lips to her cheek. "Welcome to the family."

Essence blushed furiously. "Thank you so much."

While they ate, the women discussed having a spring wedding that

Dorlinda felt would be fabulous in her backyard. Thinking of her flower garden and large gazebo, Mark and Essence agreed.

They had hot apple dumplings and homemade vanilla ice cream for dessert. By the time they were each sipping a cup of French Roast coffee, Essence eyelids had begun to droop.

"I think my lovely fiancé is ready for bed," Mark teased.

Essence looked at him with half-lowered eyelids and gave him a silly grin. "I guess I didn't get as much rest as I had thought this week-end."

"I wonder why" George murmured against the rim of his mug. The other three couldn't resist laughing.

Mark removed Tyler's bib and lowered him onto the floor.

Dorlinda rose and carried her plate into the kitchen. "Oh, Mark, I almost forgot. Diamere called."

"I thought he left on Saturday."

"No. His father wasn't feeling well so he decided to wait until tomorrow. He wants to speak with you before he leaves."

"Alright. Let me go give my man a call." He carried his plate into the kitchen, then moved to his father's study down the hall.

Despite her future mother-in-law's protest, Essence helped clear the table while Tyler raced across the room. When she heard something crash in the other room, she moved into the hallway to find Tyler had knocked the phone off the hook. She reached down, picked up the receiver and heard Mark's laughter. Curiosity got the better of her and she put the phone to her ear.

"You're right man, it's definitely cheaper to keep her. Child support payments are no joke!" Mark said.

Diamere chuckled. "True that…true that. You're doing the right thing by getting married. If I have to marry my baby's momma then I will 'cause I refuse to give a woman half of my hard earned money!"

Essence swallowed hard. *Cheaper to keep her.* Is that all she was to him? Was that why he wanted to marry her so bad? She shook her head. She couldn't have possibly heard him correctly.

"Have you told her you've been reassigned to Texas?" Diamere asked.

Mark breathed heavily into the receiver. "Nah, I thought I would break it to her tonight."

Essence couldn't bear to listen to anymore and quietly hung up the phone. She stepped back as the room closed in on her. She shook her head. Her mind was playing tricks on her. Only it wasn't. The truth was out the bag and she was stunned. Mark had played her; he played her well.

She was quiet all the way home, still in a daze from the entire incident.

While Mark unloaded their bags from the car, Essence took Tyler inside and got him dressed for bed. She then carried him into the living room and placed him in his playpen. She turned the television to the Cartoon Network, then went into her bedroom to find Mark taking off his shoes.

"Did you forget to tell me something?" she asked in a rusty voice.

He glanced up at her, brow tight with confusion. "Tell you what?"

Although she was consumed with hurt and anger, her tone was neutral, lacking emotion. "Does the word *Texas* ring a bell?"

Mark winced, realizing that he'd been caught. She'd either heard him talking to Diamere or his mother had slipped and told. "I'm sorry. I was going to tell you."

"How…how long have you known?"

He hesitated, then said, "For almost a week."

Essence tossed her hands in the air, then released a rush of air from her pursed lips. She wanted to scream and shout, but couldn't. She should have been surprised but she wasn't.

He rose and reached for her, but she jerked away. Panic swelled up inside him. "I'm sorry, baby, for not telling you. I was scared if I told you, you wouldn't give me…us a chance."

"So you decided to lie to me!" she snapped, feeling tears swelling up inside her. "When were you going to tell me? Right before you had to leave? After we were married?" she laughed out loud when what she really wanted to do was cry. Her love for him made her feel even worse.

Mark ran a hand over his hair. "I was going to tell you tonight. I was waiting—"

Essence held up a hand silencing him. "You should have told me when you first found out!" she exploded. "You should have told me before you proposed to me."

After a brief tense moment he threw his hands up in surrender and answered, "You're right and I am sorry."

She braced her hands on her hips then shook her head vigorously. "You want to know why it will never work for us? That is…besides the fact that it's *cheaper to keep her,* but because we don't have trust or love. Without those two things, marriage is doomed from the start." She felt like such a fool.

"That's not true." He needed her to calm down and give him a moment to explain.

"Yes it is." Her voice cracked. Her heart was breaking. She loved this man and he had used her. He had gained her trust, and convinced her to marry him. It had all been one big lie!

Fury raged within. She removed the ring from her finger and tossed it at him. It fell at his feet. "I can't marry you."

Mark couldn't stand to see her like this. He knew she was about to cry. He could hear it in her voice. He could see it in her eyes. And it was because of him. He placed a hand on her shoulder, but she shrugged it away. "Baby, please listen. This is one big misunderstanding."

She took several steps back angry that even after all that he had done, her body was still responding to his touch.

The tears were now streaming down her cheeks. "The only thing I don't understand is why you're still here. Now pack your things and get the hell out of my house." She gave him a look that told him nothing he could say or do would make a difference. She swiped the tears away then ran down the hall to her room. When she came out, Mark was gone.

"I need another drink," Mark said grimly.

"Man, at that rate, I'm going to need to call you a cab."

Mark glanced over at Diamere sitting in the barstool beside him. "I could care less."

Diamere cast a curious glance at his childhood friend. "We've been here for over an hour and you still haven't told me what's bothering you."

He raised the glass to lips. "Who says anything is bothering me?"

"Man who are you trying to fool? This is Diamere you're talking to." He eyed him with a smile.

Mark gave him a nonchalant shrug in an attempt to throw off what he was really feeling.

Diamere reached for his longneck bottle and took a swig. "If anyone should be down in the dumps, it should be me. I'm the one with twins on the way and no choice but to get married."

"This is all your fault. If you hadn't called to tell me Ryan was having twins, none of this would have happened." Essence had it all wrong. When Diamere had mentioned he was having twins and couldn't afford not to marry her, Mark had joked that it was cheaper to keep her. Essence had heard the comment he'd made and thought it had been directed at her.

"My bad. I'll talk to Essence for you if you want."

"Nah, this is my problem, not yours," he murmured.

Diamere glanced at his gloomy expression and felt bad. Somebody deserved to be happy. Just because he was miserable didn't mean his boy had to be. The rug had been pulled from beneath his feet when Ryan called to tell him that she was pregnant with not one but two babies. He wanted to run and hide, but it was his duty to take care of his responsibilities. However, instead of thinking about them his mind and body was still on Kelly. They had parted as friends, but he wished he could have left as her lover. "Have you spoken to your sister lately?"

"Not since I've returned. Why?"

"Just asking."

Mark looked away from the glass of dark liquor long enough to bestow upon Diamere a long penetrating stare. "Make sure that's all it is. Ryan and those twins are the only people you should be thinking about."

"Would you lighten up? I have too much respect for your sister."

"Good. Otherwise I might have to break your leg."

Diamere forced a chuckle, then took a long swig of his beer. If Mark knew what he was thinking he would have broken *both* of his legs. His mind was telling him one thing when his heart was telling him something altogether different. He wanted to drop by and see her one last time but he knew that would be a big mistake. The best thing for him to do was to forget about Kelly, jump in his car in the morning, and get back to Denver as fast as he could.

"I really messed up this time. I doubt Essence will give me another chance." Mark knew this was different. This wasn't just an ordinary fight. He had betrayed their trust. She had put her faith in them and he blew it.

Diamere whistled softly between his teeth. "I'm sure you can convince her otherwise."

"I don't know." He slammed his hand against the bar.

"Are you in love?"

He glanced at his friend, but said nothing. It was much deeper than that. Somewhere along the way, Essence had become a part of him. Part of the air he breathed, his smile, his every emotion. Hell, yeah, he loved her.

"More than life itself." Only she didn't love him. That much was obvious and he couldn't blame anyone but himself. He had her love once and he had tossed it aside. Now he would do anything to have those feelings again.

"So what are you going to do?"

He raised his hand and signaled for the bartender. "I have no idea." He gripped the glass tightly. What he had with Essence was real. It wasn't something you could find in a Cracker Jack box. It was rare and only happened once. She was like a diamond—forever.

Some way, somehow, he had to find a way to fix this. "I do know one thing, I'm not leaving until my ring is back on her finger."

# *CHAPTER NINETEEN*

After sitting up for most of the evening kicking herself for being so stupid, Essence cried until her well ran dry. After tossing and turning, she finally fell asleep around two, only to be awakened by the phone at seven. Ignoring it, she stuck her head under the pillow hoping whoever it was would just leave her alone. Instead, they called back again. Without opening her eyes or moving her head from her pillow, Essence stretched out her arm and reached for the receiver.

"Hello?"

"Essence, girl how could you?" she heard Tamara shriek.

*Oh Lord,* she moaned. *Mark must have told her sister about their break up.* That was just what she needed this early in the morning. "I'm grown Tamara," she murmured. "I can do whatever I please."

"But you're making a big mistake!"

"I'm not marrying Mark," she said barely above a whisper.

"So you've decided to marry Malcolm instead?"

Essence rolled onto her back and groaned. "I'm not marrying him either."

"Then why is there an announcement in this morning's paper?"

"What!" Her eyelids flew open. "What paper?"

"*The Delaware News Journal.*"

Essence sat upright in the bed. "How could that have happened?"

Tamara snorted rudely. "Well let me guess. It probably had something to do with the fact that Malcolm proposed and you accepted his grandma's ring," she replied sarcastically.

She kicked the covers off with a huff. Why did she always have to tell her sister everything? "But I didn't say yes."

"You didn't say no either."

She sighed. Tamara was right. She had made a mess of things. "I was going to tell him when he got back in town."

"Well, he's due back today. Wait until Mom sees this. You know she and Dad read the paper every morning. Goodness, Essence, you shouldn't have taken his ring in the first place. How hard was it to say no?"

*Harder than you'll ever know.* She pressed a palm to her forehead. What else could possibly go wrong? Her entire world was spinning out of control. "What does it say?"

"Let see. It says Mr. and Mrs. Cole would like to announce the engagement of their son Malcolm and his fiancé, Essence Monroe. The couple plan to wed in the fall in South Carolina."

"I can't believe this! How could I have been so stupid," Essence murmured under her breath. Instead of sparing his feelings, she had given Malcolm false hope. Instead of him keeping his mouth shut until she had given him an answer, he went home and blabbed everything to his parents. And it was all her fault.

She groaned and prayed that Mark didn't see it.

Mark got up early and dropped by IHOP for breakfast. He parked in the lot, strolled inside the restaurant, and was immediately escorted to a small table in the corner.

He ordered pancakes and sausage, then sipped his coffee while he waited.

He had forty-eight hours left before he was to leave for Texas. Essence was mad at him and he still hadn't come up with a way to get her to believe that he truly loved her. Maybe confessing his feelings *was* the only way. Either she would believe him or she wouldn't. It was a chance he would have to take.

A couple sitting at the table to his right rose from their chairs. Looking down in the chair, he saw that they had left behind the morning paper. He reached over and grabbed it. Thumbing through it, Mark hoped to maybe find a place to take Essence tonight for New Year's Eve.

His waitress arrived with his food and as he reached for the syrup, his hand froze. He was too late.

Essence and Malcolm's engagement was official.

After Essence hung up the phone she loaded Tyler in the car and made a trip to the convenience store on the corner for a newspaper. She quickly turned to the social section and looked down at the announcement.

All she could think about was what Mark would say.

She loved him. Part of her wanted to hate him, while the other half still loved him. He had lied to her and had proposed under false pretenses, yet deep down inside she still wanted to be his wife.

When she returned home there was a message from Mark. He had wanted to know if she'd drop Tyler by Kelly's apartment this evening so that the three of them could spend New Year's Eve together. After listening to the message three times, Essence erased it. She stood there for the longest time. He hadn't mentioned the announcement.

Either Mark hadn't seen it or he really didn't care.

Essence paused in front of the mirror to check the fit of her scarlet velvet gown, a complement to her thick auburn curls swept up in a chignon. The dress displayed an abundance of cleavage, while the slim skirt was just below her knees. She had intended to decline Malcolm's invitation to his corporate New Year's Eve party, but after listening to Mark's message she decided that, with nothing better to do, maybe it wasn't a bad idea after all.

She would have given anything to go back to what they had had over the weekend. Everything had been so perfect and she and Mark had been so happy.

Finding everything in order, she put on an artificial smile.

"You look nice."

She swung around to find Mark standing outside Kelly's bathroom door. She had arrived an hour ago and had hoped to leave before he had arrived. Silently, she prayed for the courage not to fall into his arms. "Thank you," she finally said.

Glancing up at the towering figure, her heartbeat accelerated. But as soon as she remembered his "cheaper to keep her" comment, she became angry once more.

Mark placed his hand on her shoulder and stepped forward. "Listen Essence, can we talk?"

She felt herself being swept up again. She swayed forward then quickly stepped away. "Now is not a good time. I have somewhere to be." Quickly, she stepped around him. "Let me check on Tyler. He's been running an elevated temp but I think he's only teething."

She moved down the hall and Mark followed her to Kelly's guestroom where Tyler was lying in the middle of the bed. The moonlight was beaming in from the window, so there was no reason to switch on the light. She stroked his brow and found him slightly cooler. Turning, she faced Mark. "I gave him some liquid Tylenol an hour ago, so he should be fine for awhile. If he gets fussy, try giving him a Popsicle. They're soothing to his gums. I put a box in the freezer."

Mark simply nodded. He stood in front of the door saying nothing. Essence sensing the uneasiness, knew it was time to go. She headed toward the door while trying to figure how she was going to get pass him. "Uh, Mark, please call my cell phone if you need me."

Mark pushed the door shut. "I need you now."

Mark crossed to Essence determinedly, caught her about the waist and drew her against his chest. She tried to bring her arm up, but he had pinned them quickly to her side. When she opened her mouth to protest, he covered her mouth with his own, taking full advantage of the moment.

She didn't struggle, although it took several minutes of thorough kissing and fondling before she actually began to kiss him back. A moment or so more later and she became as liquid fire in his arms, moaning into his mouth. That was when he stopped. Taken by surprise, she sagged against the wall and watched blankly as he straightened.

"I just thought I would give you something to think about while you're spending the evening with your fiancé," he said with a wink, then opened the door and slipped out quickly.

A growl of rage slipped from her throat. Essence heard Mark chuckled as he went to join his sister in the kitchen.

Essence washed her hands and dried them on a plush holiday towel. Before heading toward the door, she rechecked her make-up and found everything in place.

She had already been at the New Year's Eve party for over an hour, yet there was still three hours before midnight. Her plan was to sample the food, sip a little champagne, then wait an appropriate amount of time before she faked a headache and asked Malcolm to take her home.

She moved through the foyer of the mansion into the ballroom that blazed with the light of a dozen crystal chandeliers. Glass encased candles gleamed against the deep burgundy velvet draperies. Priceless paintings hung on the walls.

She worked her way through a crowd that seemed to have expanded up the sweeping staircase to the second floor.

She stopped a strolling waiter and reached for a flute of white zinfandel. Sipping the cool liquid, her eyes traveled around the room. Essence wasn't in the mood to party, but had tried to make the most of a painful situation.

While she was in the ladies room, Malcolm headed to the buffet table to indulge in hors d'oeuvres. She now found him standing near a large French window talking to someone he had introduced her to earlier who worked in the governor's office.

Essence let out a breath, closed her eyes and waited for her world to settle. She wasn't as in control as she'd like. Her hand was shaking and her knees were wobbling. Even though she had not expected control to bring a change of heart, she had hoped to find a way to tuck her emotions away to avoid deepening the heartache she was experiencing.

She and Mark would have to come to some terms for the sake of Tyler. There was no way they could keep tiptoeing around each other.

Glancing toward the entryway, Essence spotted Tamara and Paul coming through the door. As soon as a greeter took her sister's mink coat, she traveled across the room.

Tamara's eyes sparkled with excitement. "You didn't tell me you were coming."

Essence smiled. "I didn't know either until this afternoon."

Tamara admired her new dress. "You look nice."

"You clean up well yourself." Essence smirked as she took in the long green satin gown.

"Thanks. I had to lose five pounds in order to get in it," she said with a chuckle. As soon as the laughter died, she asked, "Have the two of you talked yet?"

Essence wondered how long it was going to take before Tamara asked. "If you're talking about Malcolm, yes we talked. I gave him his ring back."

"Good for you, only I wasn't talking about Malcolm."

She knew who Tamara was asking about. Essence had hoped to avoid the conversation. She shook her head with dismay. "No, but he saw the announcement."

"Well, I think you need to tell him the truth," Tamara said after a long                    moment.
Essence bit her lip then took a deep breath. "Like he did?" She gave a painful laugh. "I told you from the beginning I was not going to marry a man who was marrying out of honor."

"Sis, you've got to sit down and talk to this man. Have you even told him that you love him?"

She shook her head.

"Then you've got to tell him. You might found he feels the same way."

Essence grunted rudely at the ridiculous notion. Before Tamara could pry any further, Essence found Malcolm and Paul heading their way. He looked quite handsome in a black tuxedo. If only she had a fairy godmother. She would ask for two wishes, to get over Mark and to direct all her feelings toward Malcolm.

Malcolm held out his hand. "May I have the honor of this dance?"

Essence didn't want to dance. She wanted to go home with her son and Mark, but she knew that wasn't going to happen. Forcing a smile, she said, "Of course," and took his hand and followed Tamara and her husband onto the dance floor. She loved the Isley Brothers. The slow song playing was one of her favorites.

Essence tried to concentrate on dancing with Malcolm, the festive voices and laughter, but couldn't drag her mind away from her problems with Mark.

"When are you going to tell me that you love him?"

She couldn't lie to him. Malcolm had been so understanding when she had told him she couldn't marry him and had given him back his ring. She told him she did not love him and it would be unfair to him. He deserved to be loved in return. Only she didn't dare mention her feelings for Mark.

"How could you tell?" she asked kindly.

"It's written all over your face." He let out a huff of laughter that wasn't really a laugh.

"Is it that obvious?"

At his prolonged silence, she pulled back and looked up into his face. She saw a hurt that she would no have expected to see from Malcolm.

"Unfortunately for me, yes." He finally said.

She smiled sadly. "I'm sorry, Malcolm."

He managed to conceal his emotions again. "No need to apologize. We have no control over who we fall in love with. The heart knows what the heart wants."

He was such a good man and she hated hurting his feelings. He was being so noble about the entire thing. He was letting go without a fight.

"Despite how I feel about him, he doesn't love me," she confessed.

"Then he had me fooled. I would have sworn he acted like a jealous husband."

She rested her cheek on his shoulder. "Yeah, he fooled me too."

At the beginning of the next song, her cell phone vibrated. Essence reached inside a beaded evening bag and removed the small flip phone. The call ended quickly. She looked to Malcolm, an expression of alarm on her face.

"That was Mark. Tyler's fever has gotten worse, and he's taking him to the emergency room."

"Let me take you."

She glanced up at him, touched by his tenderness. "Thank you, Malcolm."

Essence went in search of Tamara and told her what was going on. Taking her arm, Malcolm guided Essence to his car.

During the entire ride, she silently scolded herself for leaving Tyler. He had been cranky all afternoon. She thought he was teething and that he would be all right until his appointment with the pediatrician next week. Knowing he had a fever, she should have stayed with him.

Arriving at the hospital, Malcolm pulled into the circle drive behind an ambulance and put the car in park. "You don't need me in there, but if things change, call me. I'm just a cell phone away."

Essence leaned over and kissed his cheek. "Thank you so much." She opened the car and moved through the automatic doors.

Malcolm sat there for the longest time watching the girl of his dreams walk out of his life.

By the time Essence reached the emergency room, Tyler was being discharged.

"He has an ear infection," Mark said as he looked down at her distraught face. He knew exactly how she felt. He had been the same way on the ride over to the hospital.

She gathered Tyler into her arms and kissed him repeatedly. "Mommy's baby is sick?"

Tyler's bottom lip quivered. He lowered his head onto her shoulder.

"He's going to be fine," Mark said even though Tyler's face said he was far from fine.

"The doctor gave me a prescription for the infection and said to use Tylenol for the fever." They walked out to the car and he didn't ask her what had happened to her date.

Essence sat in the back seat with Tyler on the way to a twenty-four hour pharmacy, then they quickly got him home and in Essence's bed.

She escaped to the bathroom. When she returned Mark and Tyler were under the covers with Tyler's head on his chest as he read him The Three Little Pigs. She laughed right along with Tyler when Mark used a deep gruff voice to say, "And I'll blow your house down."

Mark sat on one side of Tyler and she climbed in and sat on the other. While Mark read another story, Essence stroked Tyler's forehead until he was fast asleep.

Mark closed the book, then slid slowly from under the covers. Essence signaled him to follow her out the room. As soon as she shut the door, Mark released a large gulp of air.

"I don't think I've ever been so worried in my life," he said in a tired voice.

Essence nodded. The seriousness of his expression aroused her fears all over again. "I've been with him sixteen months and I always worry. It's part of being a parent. When they hurt, you hurt too."

He nodded, then there was an awkward silence.

"Would you like some hot chocolate?" she asked.

Mark shook his head. "No. I think I'm going to try and get a little rest while he's sleep."

Essence nodded and watched him disappear in the other room. She stood there for several seconds at a lost as to what to do next. With a ragged sigh, she turned and went to her own room, took a quick shower then changed into her pajamas.

Climbing under the cool covers, she shivered. The bed just wasn't the same without him.

She didn't know what to do anymore. One minute she was mad at him for proposing under false pretenses and the next minute it didn't seem as important as it had been before. Mark was leaving the day after tomorrow and the thought of losing him again tore at her heart. Could she be wrong? Should she give them a chance with the hope that maybe, just maybe, love would come in time? Or should she hold her ground and wait for true love to eventually come her way? "There will never be another man like him. Mark is my one and only true love," she whispered.

Could he possible learn to love her for her and not as the mother of his child?

Her parents had taught her to face her problems head on. And this was, without a doubt, one of the biggest problems she'd ever faced. Maybe Tamara was right. Maybe she needed to throw caution in the wind and face her biggest fear.

"There was only one way to find out," she murmured as she rose.

On bare feet, she tiptoed down the hallway. The guestroom door was shut. Biting her lip, she slowly turned the handle and eased the door open.

Mark was sitting on the edge of his bed, his back to her, his head buried in his hands. He'd stripped to his black trousers the line of his spine was a long curve of defeat.

She couldn't bear to see him like that.

Essence slipped through the doorway and closed it behind her. As the door shut, Mark's head jerked up. He looked over his shoulder, saw her standing there and pushed himself to his feet. "Essence," he said hoarsely, "Is something wrong with Tyler?"

God, he loved his son. If only he felt that strongly about her. She shook her head. "No, he's still sound asleep."

Mark lowered back to his seat, grabbed a pillow and jab the center with his fist. "Then why are you here?"

"I had to come," she gulped. "We need to talk. I need to know...I need to know how you really feel about me."

He had showered and was clean-shaven for the first time since his arrival, a clear indicator that his time was coming to an end. His jaws were tight and there were dark shadows underneath his eyes.

Essence found she was holding her breath with her pulse racing in her chest. The rest of her life depended on what happened next. Praying desperately that he wouldn't shut her out, she waited for him to speak.

Mark rose again and walked over to her. Taking her hand, he guided her to the bed. He sat down and pulled her beside him.

In an angry voice, Mark asked, "Are you planning to marry Malcolm?"

She shook her head. "I gave him back his ring tonight. It's over between us."

At the shaky sound of her voice, Mark shifted on the bed so that he could look her in the face. She wore a simple Mickey Mouse nightshirt. Her hair was damp and pulled away from her face. Her eyes glistened with a mixture of stubbornness and insecurity. Both made him want her even more. He wanted to pull her in his arms and kiss her senseless, then lay her down in the bed and show her how he really felt. *Get yourself together.* Words were what she deserved now. Unfortunately, if he didn't put some distance between them, he wouldn't be able to express himself verbally.

Mark slid over near the edge, then reached for her hand and held it firmly between both of his. "I still want to marry you," he said huskily.

Essence wanted so badly to say yes, but he still hadn't told her how he felt about her. "But that's not enough." Essence said carefully. "I know you feel it's important for Tyler to have a family."

"He deserves to have a father."

"And I deserve to have a husband who wants me for me not because it is cheaper to keep her," she retorted sharply.

Mark chuckled softly. "The next time you decide to eavesdrop on my calls, listen to more than the tail end of the conversation."

She looked appalled. "I wasn't eavesdropping. Tyler knocked over the phone."

"If you had given me a chance to explain, you would have heard Diamere say his girlfriend was having twins and that he'd rather marry her than pay child support."

She nibbled on her lower lip. "But I heard you tell him it was cheaper to keep her. Is that how you feel about me?" she asked.

Mark reached over and caressed her cheek. "No. I want to marry you because I know it will work between us."

She shook her head. "But if two people don't love each other, then their marriage is doomed from the start. I can't do it Mark, I just can't."

Mark swallowed. "You don't love me," he said in an unreadable voice. "Is that what you're saying?"

Essence tilted her chin. "You don't love me, so why should it matter to you how I feel?"

He shook his head and finally put his pride aside. "Essence, I never knew how important family was until I met Tyler. I know in the beginning, I had no intention of showing you how I truly felt. I know I said I wasn't into commitments, but I never realized how lonely my life was. After Carmen, I thought I had forgotten how to care or how to love. But for two years, I dreamed of you. The second I heard that I had a son, I ran to you, hoping to have both of you in my life. Then I started to want you in all the ways a man wants a woman. In his bed every night, waking up beside him every morning. I wasn't going to tell you that, Essence, because it scared the hell out of me. But I do know I want you in my life."

She was moved by his words but wasn't quite ready to show it. "It sounds like your little head is talking, but what does your heart say?"

He stroked his thumb back and forth over her cheek. "I've been sitting on the bed; convinced I'd lost you forever. I believe that the woman I want to spend the rest of my life with no longer loves me."

"But Mark I'm not going—"

He clasped her face with his hands. "Woman, would you listen! I'm trying to tell you that I love you. So let me finish."

"Y-you love me?" she repeated blankly.

He nodded. "I never realized what love was until you came into my life. I think I have always loved you, and I simply chose to deny my feelings. It took my thinking I had lost you to another man to realize how stupid I have been. All I'm asking for is a chance to prove that I can be a husband and a father."

Essence's heart shuffled into her throat. He stared into her eyes and Essence finally saw it, an emotion she had never seen before. It was there...a love as strong as his handsome face. "And this isn't because of Tyler?"

"Tyler only adds to the package." He sighed. "I realize how much I hurt you, Essence. I know you're probably scared and I'm scared, too. But I promise to do my best to make you happy."

"Mark, you are a wonderful man and I'd be honored to have you as my husband."

He surveyed her with soft loving eyes. "Then you're saying—"

"Yes."

"What?" He was nearly rendered speechless.

"You heard me, silly." Essence's joy bubbled out in a laugh. "Yes, I'll marry you."

Mark brushed a gentle kiss over her lips. "Thank God. I thought you might tell me to go to hell." He stroked his thumbs back and forth over her cheeks. "I'll always be honest with you from this point forward, Essence. I swear it."

She laid her palms over his hands. "I've come to realize that in order to trust you, I have to trust myself and what I am feeling. And right now I'm feeling quite comfortable with my decision."

Mark laughed then and Essence reveled at the joyous sound.

"I still can't believe you said yes to me."

Flashing a grin, she answered, "Why wouldn't I? I love you Mark."

His hands tightened. "Would you repeat that?"

She laughed. "I love you, Mark Saunders. I've loved you for two years."

He eased her backwards on the bed until she lay beneath him and kissed her with every bit of the love he felt. She looped her arms around his neck, feeling the heat of his skin burn into hers, glorying in the thrust of his tongue and fierce pressure of his mouth.

Mark lifted his head long enough to glance over at the clock. "We've got ten minutes to midnight. How about we bring in the New Year with that bottle of champagne I spotted at the back of your refrigerator?"

"That's a wonderful idea."

"Then let's hurry. Time is of the essence."

They both scrambled into the kitchen. With the aid of a step stool, Essence reached for a pair of crystal flute glasses while Mark found the champagne. After he popped the cork they returned to his room. While he filled each glass, Essence flicked on the television just in time to hear Dick Clark and the crowd at Time Square counting down. She and

Mark joined in.

"Seven-six-five-four-three-two-one…Happy New Years!"

Mark kissed her then, a powerful kiss that left them winded by the time they parted.

They clicked their glasses together then took a drink.

Essence took another sip then said, "Here's to the start of a fabulous new year."

"I agree." Mark said. "Any New Year's resolutions?"

"Only to marry my soulmate."

"Me too, sweetheart. This year I'm getting everything I could have ever hoped for." He reached over and took the flute from her and carried both over to the nightstand. Scooping her up into his arms, he laid her at the center of the bed. "You know what they say, whatever you're doing today is what you'll be doing all year," he murmured as he lowered on top of her.

Essence's wrapped her arms around his neck and met each kiss. "And what would that be?"

"Maybe, I should show you."

He raised her gown over her head, then palmed her breasts with one skilled hand. "It's been too long."

"Mark, it hasn't even been forty-eight hours."

"Too long in my opinion." Mark's deep voice vibrated against Essence's cheek.

With enough said, he planted kisses on bare skin from her lips down to her toes. By the time he'd removed his clothes, Essence was on the verge of exploding. Mark entered her with a leisurely glide and a powerful kiss.

"You'll never regret your decision. I plan to love you like a man should love a woman," he said as he moved at a slow pace.

"I know." And she did, with every beat of her heart.

They quickly rode the storm. Mark shattered with a long shudder, adding another declaration of his love to her that she answered with one of her own. For the longest of moments, they stayed united. Even after their bodies parted, Essence knew they would never be separated again.

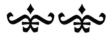

# AUTHOR BIOGRAPHY

**Angie Daniels** was born on the South side of Chicago, Illinois. At a very early age, she spent nights creating soap operas with her younger sister until the two drifted off to sleep. Never did she realize that her longtime dream to become a published author would someday become a reality.

In 1999, the corporation where she was employed as Personnel Manager went out of business. It was at that time Angie decided it was finally time to return to her love of writing. With her husband's blessings, she took a year off to write her first book Intimate Intentions, which started off as a simple romance novel and later escalated into 542 pages of romantic suspense. After two submissions, Angie was offered a four-book contract with Genesis Press and her first book was released in 2001. In September 2003, she released her second indigo novel, Hart & Soul.

Angie currently resides in Dover, Delaware where she is pursuing a Master's in Human Resources.

EXCERPT FROM

# *A WILL TO LOVE*

### BY

## *ANGIE DANIELS*

**Publication Date December 2004**

# *CHAPTER ONE*

"Why haven't you started remodeling the guest rooms?"

Pace Delaney sneered his nose down at Jesse, his eyes openly speculative. "Because I felt replacing the carpet in the living room was more important."

Jesse leaned across her desk and glared back at him. In the past week, Pace has under-minded her authority on several occasions. He obviously needed to be reminded who's boss. "You are aware that all decisions are to be approved by me?"

"Your father never seemed to mind," he drawled.

She slammed her palms on her desk then rose. "I'm not my father."

"No…you're not." Pace looked thoroughly in control of himself and of the situation. "Your father had enough confidence in my ability. Too bad you can't say the same."

Jesse groaned inwardly. He never let up. The relationship she had with her father was none of his business. Pace was a pompous ass and if she had to, she would let him go. However, there were only eight weeks left before the tourist season began and Katherine's Bed & Breakfast wasn't even close to being ready for reopening. But Jesse was not going to be intimidated. If she had to, she would hire another crew.

Although the reason why she hadn't fired them yet was because Delaney Construction was all she could afford.

Jesse glanced up at Pace's flared nose and thick lips. Despite the fact that he was barely ten years her senior, his hair had long since departed. His posture was defined and controlled. Both hands were planted in his pockets, to prevent him from biting his nails, a nervous habit he had since childhood. A parting of his windbreaker at the waist, gave her a clear view of his protruding stomach. He was poised and ready for battle, she thought.

"Maybe I haven't made myself clear. This is my house, not yours. I run things here, not you," she said rapidly. "If you have a problem with that then I suggest that you and your crew pack up and get the hell off my property."

There was a tense moment of silence and for a split second Jesse almost believed she might have gone too far, when Pace finally spoke again.

"I still can't understand why you're wasting your money trying to repair this rundown old house. Especially since in a year this establishment will belong to someone else...perhaps even me." He took one sweeping look at her then sneered with as much malice as he was capable of. "That is unless you've already found yourself a husband."

Jesse's breath caught in her throat. However, she refused to let Pace know that his comment hurt. It was bad enough her father named her after a boy, it was even worse that she looked like one.

With as much dignity as she could muster, she replied in a voice with an icy edge, "I'm here to stay, so get used to it." Lowering back in her seat, Jesse added, "I hope this is the last time we have this discussion. You may go now." She then emphasized her words with a dismissive wave of the hand. It wasn't until after the door had shut that she slumped back in her seat.

Why did I come back? Life in Chicago was so much simpler. She had been home for two months; long enough to discover that nothing was the same.

The only thing she and Pace seemed to agree on was that the B&B was rundown. She had no idea things were as bad as they were. If she had only known, she would have come home sooner.

Jesse had attended University of Illinois Chicago majoring in hotel management. She had been determined to prove to her father that she was capable of running the family business. She took a job managing a small hotel chain learning everything she could in three years. Now, after years of trying to prove herself to her father, she was finally in charge. As soon as she had gotten word that her father had been rushed to the hospital, she returned home. Only it was too late. It was not at all the way she had hoped to take over the business. She had wanted her father to ask her to come home, not because of kidney failure, but because he wanted her to take the reigns. The only reason she was now in charge was because her father had past away.

Jesse reminisced, remembering happier times, when her father was vibrant…alive. Why had God taken him away so soon, and three months before her twenty-fifth birthday? Closing her eyes, she allowed feelings of sorrow to push to the surface. His death had been too soon. She hadn't even been given enough time to prove to him that she had been ready to follow in his footsteps.

Feeling the onset of a migraine, Jesse reached into the top drawer of the large old desk for a bottle of ibuprofen. She removed the cap and slid two tablets into the palm of her hand then washed them down with a swig of bottled water. She then leaned back in her chair and closed her eyes again. Even with all her years of education and training, deep down inside she knew it still wouldn't have made a bit of difference to Jesse James, Senior.

She had tried for years to prove to her father that she was prepared to be his predecessor, but her father had never taken her serious. Nevertheless, she was confident she could have changed his mind if he had listened. Maybe then he wouldn't have tied her hands the way he had, forcing her to do something she would never have dreamed of doing.

Jesse loved her father, "Ole Man," as he was called by everyone. Jesse James, the big burly man with an ill temper and chauvinistic views, was the only family she had. Elizabeth James, who was twenty years his junior, had walked out on them when Jesse was only two years old and never looked back. As a child, Jesse had fantasized about her mother's return but as the years progressed and at her father's insistence, she finally gave up hope.

Now that her father was gone, Jesse realized she was paying for her mother's mistake. Ole Man had never gotten over his wife leaving him and as a result had turned into a cold and bitter man. He believed all women to be untrustworthy. Jesse had focused all her energy on proving him wrong and hoped to have won in the end. Instead, her father got the last word.

Under the terms of father's will, she could lose her legacy, Kathleen's, a bed & breakfast that had been in her family for generations, because she was a female.

For years, she had fought for her independence and she was not about to let some man take that away. Ole Man was an old fashion type of guy, who believed a woman's place was in the kitchen. He truly believed that if he had put his foot down with his wife, things would have been different. Jesse gave a ragged sigh. It was no wonder her mother had thrown in the towel after less than four years of marriage.

Ole Man had wanted his daughter to marry well and spend her life having babies and devoting her life to her man. When she had been offered a full scholarship to UIC, her father fought her, but in the end, Jesse had won.

It wasn't until her freshman year that she first discovered what freedom really was. She valued her independence. She hadn't known how smothering a life she had lived until she went away to school. Finally she had been allowed to think for herself. She had been able to breathe.

She loved it and never wanted to let it go.

Only now, her hands were tied.

According to Ole Man's will, she either had to be married or have given birth to a male child before her twenty-sixth birthday otherwise she would lose the B&B. Jesse loved kids, but a husband…no way. She could count the number of dates she'd had in her lifetime and it only took one hand to do so. Besides, she didn't want another man dictating her life the way her father had for years.

Jesse ran a frustrated hand through her unruly curls. She kept her red hair cut short enough for her to simply run a comb through it. It was no wonder men didn't look twice at her. She wore a man's hairstyle, she had a nervous habit of biting her nails, and cosmetics were something she knew nothing about. Fashion had never been her thing and her wardrobe proved it. She had always worn clothes two sizes too big to hide the wide hips she had inherited from her mother and the flat chest she had gotten from her father's side of the family. Rarely was she ever seen in a dress and when she had worn one, it was usually when attending a wedding or funeral. Now looking feminine was mandatory.

Just the mere thought of someone else running Katherine's made her push forward and not drag her feet. Where there's a will, there's a way. That was the motto she governed her life by.

The fortuneteller had been right. A will would change her life forever. Only it came in the form of a sheet of paper instead of a man.

Lowering her head to her hands, Jesse groaned aloud. She had paid some fancy lawyer in Wilmington to look over the papers. Apparently, her father had also hired a high priced lawyer to draw up the terms because there were no loopholes, the document was iron clad.

"Damn you, Ole Man!" she murmured.

What was she going to do? Let someone like Pace step in and steal her future or fight? Her father knew her well enough to know that she wasn't going to give up that easily. She had never been a quitter. She had inherited her determination from her father.

So, it was pretty cut and dry. She had only two choices, either marry or get pregnant. Marriage wasn't even a consideration. She could just see some man walking in and taking over, but a baby, she had given that option some real serious thought. The fortuneteller had told her that she would give birth to a son. He was all she needed.

One thing for certain, she was going to save the B&B, even if she had to lose her virginity to do it.

## *TIME IS OF THE ESSENCE*

## 2004 Publication Schedule

| | | |
|---|---|---|
| January | Cautious Heart<br>Cheris F. Hodges<br>$8.95<br>1-58571-106-3 | Bodyguard<br>Andrea Jackson<br>$8.95<br>1-58571-114-4 |
| February | Wedding Gown<br>Dyanne Davis<br>$8.95<br>1-58571-120-9 | Erotic Anthology<br>Simone Harlow & Caroline Stone<br>$14.95<br>1-58571-113-6 |
| March | Crossing Paths,<br>  Tempting Memories<br>Dorothy Elizabeth Love<br>$9.95<br>1-58571-116-0 | Office Policy<br>A.C. Arthur<br>$9.95<br>1-58571-119-5 |

*After February, the size of the titles will increase to 5 3/16 x 8 1/2, as will the price to $9.95.*

| | | |
|---|---|---|
| April-July | No Titles | |
| August | More Than a Bargain<br>Ann Clay<br>$9.95<br>1-58571-137-3 | Code Name: Diva<br>J. M. Jeffries<br>$9.95<br>1-58571-144-6 |
| September | Vows of Passion<br>Bella McFarland<br>$9.95<br>1-58571-118-7 | Time Is of the Essence<br>Angie Daniels<br>$9.95<br>1-58571-132-2 |
| | Stories to Excite You<br>Anna Forrest & Ken Divine<br>$14.95<br>1-58571-103-9 | |
| October | Hard to Love<br>Kimberley White<br>$9.95<br>1-58571-128-4 | A Happy Life<br>Charlotte Harris<br>$9.95<br>1-58571-133-0 |
| November | Caught Up in the Rapture<br>Lisa G. Riley<br>$9.95<br>1-58571-127-6 | Lace<br>Giselle Carmichael<br>$9.95<br>1-58571-134-9 |
| December | A Heart's Awakening<br>Veronica Parker<br>$9.95<br>1-58571-143-9 | Path of Thorns<br>Annetta P. Lee<br>$9.95<br>1-58571-145-4 |

## 2005 Publication Schedule

### January

Echoes of Yesterday
Beverly Clark
$9.95
1-58571-131-4

A Love of Her Own
Cheris F. Hodges
$9.95
1-58571-136-5

Higher Ground
Leah Latimer
$19.95
1-58571-157-8

### February

Timeless Devotion
Bella McFarland
$9.95
1-58571-148-9

I'll Paint the Sun
Al Garotto
$9.95
1-58571-165-9

Peace Be Still
Colette Haywood
$12.95
1-58571-129-2

### March

Intentional Mistakes
Michele Sudler
$9.95
1-58571-152-7

Conquering Dr. Wexler's Heart
Kimberley White
$9.95
1-58571-126-8

Song in the Park
Martin Brant
$15.95
1-58571-125-X

### April

The Color Line
Lizette Carter
$9.95
1-58571-163-2

Unconditional
A.C. Arthur
$9.95
1-58571-142-X

Last Train to Memphis
Elsa Cook
$12.95
1-58571-146-2

### May

Angel's Paradise
Janice Angelique
$9.95
1-58571-107-1

Suddenly You
Crystal Hubbard
$9.95
1-58571-158-6

Matters of Life and Death
Lesego Malepe, Ph.D.
$15.95
1-58571-124-1

### June

Pleasures All Mine
Belinda O. Steward
$9.95
1-58571-112-8

Wild Ravens
Altonya Washington
$9.95
1-58571-164-0

Class Reunion
Irma Jenkins/John Brown
$12.95
1-58571-123-3

### July

Falling
Natalie Dunbar
$9.95
1-58571-121-7

Misconceptions
Pamela Leigh Starr
$9.95
1-58571-117-9

Life Is Never As It Seems
June Michael
$12.95
1-58571-153-5

### August

Beyond the Rapture
Beverly Clark
$9.95
1-58571-131-4

Taken By You
Dorothy Elizabeth Love
$9.95
1-58571-162-4

Rough on Rats and Tough
on Cats
Chris Parker
$12.95
1-58571-154-3

## 2005 Publication Schedule (continued)

### September

A Will to Love
Angie Daniels
$9.95
1-58571-141-1

Blood Lust
J.M. Jeffries
$9.95
1-58571-138-1

Soul Eyes
Wayne L. Wilson
$12.95
1-58571-147-0

### October

Blaze
Barbara Keaton
$9.95

Untitled
Kimberley White
$9.95
1-58571-159-4

Red Polka Dot in a World
  of Plaid
Varian Johnson
$12.95
1-58571-140-3

### November

Hand in Glove
Andrea Jackson
$9.95
1-58571-166-7

Untitled
A.C. Arthur
$9.95

Across
Carol Payne
$12.95
1-58571-149-7

### December

Bound for Mt. Zion
Chris Parker
$12.95
1-58571-155-1

Other Genesis Press, Inc. Titles

| | | |
|---|---|---|
| Acquisitions | Kimberley White | $8.95 |
| A Dangerous Deception | J.M. Jeffries | $8.95 |
| A Dangerous Love | J.M. Jeffries | $8.95 |
| A Dangerous Obsession | J.M. Jeffries | $8.95 |
| After the Vows | Leslie Esdaile | $10.95 |
| (Summer Anthology) | T.T. Henderson | |
| | Jacqueline Thomas | |
| Again My Love | Kayla Perrin | $10.95 |
| Against the Wind | Gwynne Forster | $8.95 |
| A Lark on the Wing | Phyliss Hamilton | $8.95 |
| A Lighter Shade of Brown | Vicki Andrews | $8.95 |
| All I Ask | Barbara Keaton | $8.95 |
| A Love to Cherish | Beverly Clark | $8.95 |
| Ambrosia | T.T. Henderson | $8.95 |
| And Then Came You | Dorothy Elizabeth Love | $8.95 |
| Angel's Paradise | Janice Angelique | $8.95 |
| A Risk of Rain | Dar Tomlinson | $8.95 |
| At Last | Lisa G. Riley | $8.95 |
| Best of Friends | Natalie Dunbar | $8.95 |
| Bound by Love | Beverly Clark | $8.95 |
| Breeze | Robin Hampton Allen | $10.95 |
| Brown Sugar Diaries & | Delores Bundy & | $10.95 |
| Other Sexy Tales | Cole Riley | |
| By Design | Barbara Keaton | $8.95 |
| Cajun Heat | Charlene Berry | $8.95 |
| Careless Whispers | Rochelle Alers | $8.95 |
| Caught in a Trap | Andre Michelle | $8.95 |
| Chances | Pamela Leigh Starr | $8.95 |
| Dark Embrace | Crystal Wilson Harris | $8.95 |
| Dark Storm Rising | Chinelu Moore | $10.95 |
| Designer Passion | Dar Tomlinson | $8.95 |
| Ebony Butterfly II | Delilah Dawson | $14.95 |
| Erotic Anthology | Assorted | $8.95 |
| Eve's Prescription | Edwina Martin Arnold | $8.95 |
| Everlastin' Love | Gay G. Gunn | $8.95 |

| | | |
|---|---|---|
| Fate | Pamela Leigh Starr | $8.95 |
| Forbidden Quest | Dar Tomlinson | $10.95 |
| Fragment in the Sand | Annetta P. Lee | $8.95 |
| From the Ashes | Kathleen Suzanne | $8.95 |
| | Jeanne Sumerix | |
| Gentle Yearning | Rochelle Alers | $10.95 |
| Glory of Love | Sinclair LeBeau | $10.95 |
| Hart & Soul | Angie Daniels | $8.95 |
| Heartbeat | Stephanie Bedwell-Grime | $8.95 |
| I'll Be Your Shelter | Giselle Carmichael | $8.95 |
| Illusions | Pamela Leigh Starr | $8.95 |
| Indiscretions | Donna Hill | $8.95 |
| Interlude | Donna Hill | $8.95 |
| Intimate Intentions | Angie Daniels | $8.95 |
| Just an Affair | Eugenia O'Neal | $8.95 |
| Kiss or Keep | Debra Phillips | $8.95 |
| Love Always | Mildred E. Riley | $10.95 |
| Love Unveiled | Gloria Greene | $10.95 |
| Love's Deception | Charlene Berry | $10.95 |
| Mae's Promise | Melody Walcott | $8.95 |
| Meant to Be | Jeanne Sumerix | $8.95 |
| Midnight Clear | Leslie Esdaile | $10.95 |
| (Anthology) | Gwynne Forster | |
| | Carmen Green | |
| | Monica Jackson | |
| Midnight Magic | Gwynne Forster | $8.95 |
| Midnight Peril | Vicki Andrews | $10.95 |
| My Buffalo Soldier | Barbara B. K. Reeves | $8.95 |
| Naked Soul | Gwynne Forster | $8.95 |
| No Regrets | Mildred E. Riley | $8.95 |
| Nowhere to Run | Gay G. Gunn | $10.95 |
| Object of His Desire | A. C. Arthur | $8.95 |
| One Day at a Time | Bella McFarland | $8.95 |
| Passion | T.T. Henderson | $10.95 |
| Past Promises | Jahmel West | $8.95 |
| Path of Fire | T.T. Henderson | $8.95 |
| Picture Perfect | Reon Carter | $8.95 |

| | | |
|---|---|---|
| Pride & Joi | Gay G. Gunn | $8.95 |
| Quiet Storm | Donna Hill | $8.95 |
| Reckless Surrender | Rochelle Alers | $8.95 |
| Rendezvous with Fate | Jeanne Sumerix | $8.95 |
| Revelations | Cheris F. Hodges | $8.95 |
| Rivers of the Soul | Leslie Esdaile | $8.95 |
| Rooms of the Heart | Donna Hill | $8.95 |
| Shades of Brown | Denise Becker | $8.95 |
| Shades of Desire | Monica White | $8.95 |
| Sin | Crystal Rhodes | $8.95 |
| So Amazing | Sinclair LeBeau | $8.95 |
| Somebody's Someone | Sinclair LeBeau | $8.95 |
| Someone to Love | Alicia Wiggins | $8.95 |
| Soul to Soul | Donna Hill | $8.95 |
| Still Waters Run Deep | Leslie Esdaile | $8.95 |
| Subtle Secrets | Wanda Y. Thomas | $8.95 |
| Sweet Tomorrows | Kimberly White | $8.95 |
| The Color of Trouble | Dyanne Davis | $8.95 |
| The Price of Love | Sinclair LeBeau | $8.95 |
| The Reluctant Captive | Joyce Jackson | $8.95 |
| The Missing Link | Charlyne Dickerson | $8.95 |
| Three Wishes | Seressia Glass | $8.95 |
| Tomorrow's Promise | Leslie Esdaile | $8.95 |
| Truly Inseperable | Wanda Y. Thomas | $8.95 |
| Twist of Fate | Beverly Clark | $8.95 |
| Unbreak My Heart | Dar Tomlinson | $8.95 |
| Unconditional Love | Alicia Wiggins | $8.95 |
| When Dreams A Float | Dorothy Elizabeth Love | $8.95 |
| Whispers in the Night | Dorothy Elizabeth Love | $8.95 |
| Whispers in the Sand | LaFlorya Gauthier | $10.95 |
| Yesterday is Gone | Beverly Clark | $8.95 |
| Yesterday's Dreams, Tomorrow's Promises | Reon Laudat | $8.95 |
| Your Precious Love | Sinclair LeBeau | $8.95 |

# Valentines Sweepstakes

## Win An Expense Paid Trip to Barbados*

NAME _____

ADDRESS _____

CITY _____ STATE_____ ZIP _____

DAYTIME PHONE ( ) _____

E-MAIL_____ @ _____

## RULES & REGULATIONS

1. **ELIGIBILITY:** *Sweepstakes open only to legal U.S. residents, who are 21 years of age or older and have Internet access as of 12/17/04.* Void in CA and where prohibited by law. Employees of Genesis Press Inc. USA, and its agencies, parents, subsidiaries, affiliates, vendors, wholesalers or retailers, or members of their immediate families or households are not eligible to participate. Federal, state and local laws and regulations apply. Grand Prize Winner is required to complete and return an Affidavit of Eligibility/Publicity Release and a Travel Release. Travel companion must be 21 years of age or older and must sign a Travel Release/Publicity Release. Affidavit of Eligibility/Publicity Release and Travel Releases must be returned within 2 days of notification or the Grand Prize will be forfeited and an alternate winner will be randomly selected. Must be 18 years old or older.

2. **DRAWINGS:** *Prize Winner* will be selected in a random drawing on or about 1/10/05 from among all valid entries received. Grand Prize winner will be contacted by telephone on or about 1/10/05 at the daytime number listed. If, after two (2) attempts, contact has not been made, prize will be forfeited and an alternate winner randomly selected.Winner will be randomly selected before a panel witnesses and judge.

3. **NO PURCHASE NECESSARY. YOU MUST BE 21 YEARS OF AGE OR OLDER, A LEGAL RESIDENT OF THE CONTINENTAL UNITED STATES, AND HAVE INTERNET ACCESS AS OF 12/17/04, TO ENTER. VOID IN CALIFORNIA AND WHERE PROHIBITED.**
   To enter the Tempting Memories Sweepstakes, send above information to by postmark date 12/17/04 to P.O. Box 782, Columbus, MS 39701-0782 beginning at 12:01:01 am ET on 12/10/05 log on to www.genesis-press.com and complete an Official Entry Form. Entries must be received by 11:59:59 pm ET on 12/17/04. Proof of entry submission does not equate to proof of receipt. Limit one entry per person, per IP address per 24-hour period. All other mailed entries will be matched by name and address. If multiple entries are received, only the first entry will be entered into the Sweepstakes and all other entries will be disregarded. In case of a dispute over winner's identity, entry will be deemed to have been submitted by the IP address owner (who must meet eligibility requirements). Sponsor not responsible for entry submissions received after deadline, incomplete information, incomplete transmission defaults, computer server failure and/or delayed, garbled or corrupted data. All entries become the exclusive property of the Sponsor and will not be returned or acknowledged. Any attempts by an individual to access the site via a bot script or other brute-force attack will result in that IP address becoming ineligible. Sponsor reserves the right to suspend or terminate this Sweepstakes without notice if, in Sponsor's sole discretion, the Sweepstakes becomes infected or otherwise corrupted. By entering this Sweepstakes, entrants agree to be bound by these Official Rules and the decisions of the judges which shall be final, binding and conclusive on all matters relating to this Sweepstakes. Sweepstakes starts at 12:01:01 am ET on 1/10/05 and ends at 11:59:59 pm ET on 1/10/05.

4. Winner will be notified by certified mail.

5. Prize is non-transferable, nor redeemable for cash.

6. Once travel dates are selected by winner, they can not be modified. Any changes will forfeit the prize.

7. If winner does not respond within 30 days, prize will be forfeited.

8. One (1) Winner will receive a trip for two (2) adults to the. Trip includes round-trip coach airfare for Winner and Guest to Barbados from the major airport nearest the Winner's residence 4-days/3-night hotel stay (standard room, double occupancy accommodations/hotel to be selected by Sponsor. Prizes provided by Barbados Tourism Authority.

9. **RELEASE OF LIABILITY & PUBLICITY:** Prizewinner consents to the use of his/her name, photograph or likenesses for publicity or advertising purposes without further compensation where permitted by law. All entrants release Genesis Press USA, and each of its parents, affiliates, subsidiaries, officers, directors, shareholders, agents, employees and all others associated with the development and execution of this Sweepstakes from any and all liability with respect to, or in any way arising from, this Sweepstakes and/or acceptance or use of the prize, including liability for property damage or personal injury, damages, death or monetary loss.

10. **Genesis Press Inc.,** nor any of its subsidiaries or partners are will be held liable from any and all damages, accidents injuries, negligent actions, breach etc., that might incurred by WINNER during the acceptance of the prize pursuant to the services performed and agreed to herein.

# Order Form

**Mail to: Genesis Press, Inc.**

P.O. Box 101
Columbus, MS 39703

Name _____

Address _____

City/State _____ Zip _____

Telephone _____

*Ship to (if different from above)*

Name _____

Address _____

City/State _____ Zip _____

Telephone _____

*Credit Card Information*

Credit Card # _____ ☐ Visa ☐ Mastercard

Expiration Date (mm/yy) _____ ☐ AmEx ☐ Discover

| Qty. | Author | Title | Price | Total |
|------|--------|-------|-------|-------|
|      |        |       |       |       |
|      |        |       |       |       |
|      |        |       |       |       |
|      |        |       |       |       |
|      |        |       |       |       |
|      |        |       |       |       |
|      |        |       |       |       |
|      |        |       |       |       |
|      |        |       |       |       |
|      |        |       |       |       |

Use this order
form, or call
1-888-INDIGO-1

| | |
|---|---|
| Total for books | _____ |
| Shipping and handling: $5 first two books, $1 each additional book | _____ |
| Total S & H | _____ |
| Total amount enclosed | _____ |

*Mississippi residents add 7% sales tax*

Visit www.genesis-press.com for latest releases and excerpts.